About the Author

Joanna Mackintosh is a 32 year old mother of three from Forres, on the north east coast of Scotland. She has been creatively writing since she was a teenager and is a proud member of the forWORDS writing group based in Forres. Her favourite genre is horror and science fiction and she grew up reading Stephen King.

For the one who made sure I never gave up, with smiles and white flowers.

Joanna Mackintosh

SYMBIOSIS

A CIP catalogue record for this title is available from the British Library.

ISBN 9781784559328 (Paperback)
ISBN 9781784559335 (Hardback)
ISBN 9781784559342 (E-Book)

www.austinmacauley.com

First Published (2016)
Austin Macauley Publishers Ltd.
25 Canada Square
Canary Wharf
London
E14 5LQ

Cover illustration by David Zacardelli

Acknowledgments

With thanks to the forWORDS Writing Group for all
their guidance and support.

CONTENTS

CHAPTER ONE

Hot beads of water ran caressingly down the hollow of her back. Sighing, she placed her hands against the contrasting coldness of the evergreen tiles. Eva hated mornings, but somehow the hot shower aided in dragging her away from her waking slumber, whilst thrusting her towards mild motivation. Eva reluctantly turned off the shower, aware that she had already been under the water for too long. The early morning sunrise peaked cautiously through the half-closed blinds; its orange warmth providing a hint of consolation for the long day that lay ahead. Eva allowed her mind to wander. The white noise of the hair dryer provided a tempting distraction from rational thought. For Eva, every day began the same and every day ended the same; a challenging social cocktail of abused children, wounded gang bangers and accidental deaths; another day in the perpetual giving and taking away of life that was Mercy Hospital. Eva loved her job, but she hated it just as much. It was almost against her human instinct to distance herself from the pain and suffering of those who would walk into the treatment room. Sometimes she felt that it was her purpose to carry the weight of the world on her slender shoulders; never to falter, never to stumble, lest she should lose that which was so dear to her heart. So precious to the crying mother in the hall, the mourning husband in the relatives room, to her ability to nurture life.

The chiming of the town's clock reminded Eva again of her duty, and she began mindlessly applying her make up. She coloured in the lines of her lips with rouge too bright for the dull paleness of her skin. Her heart told her that if she could just bring the smallest pinprick of colour into a place filled with so much pale sorrow, then she would have done her job.

Eva began tightly drawing back the wispy curls of her auburn hair. She pulled sharply, expertly with the brush, her forehead becoming taut and smooth. Worry lines and fatigue ironed out with the perfection of her hairstyle. Eva became a different woman when she slipped her slender body into the smooth, ironed cotton of the nurse's uniform. The softness of her presence erased with sharp straight lines and an almost emotionless expression. The beauty of Eva's youth remained discreetly reserved for the weekends. She would let down her bouncing auburn curls from their tight prison and mellow the harshness of her make-up mask. For just now, however, her freedom would have to wait. It was Wednesday, July 9th, and today was one of the longest days that she would ever know.

An alarm broke into the silence of her preparation, and she knew that it was time to leave. Without the piercing cry of the clock, she might forever stay in this perpetual bliss, away from the world, on her side of the door. Slipping on navy blue pumps, she half trotted out of the room, wincing momentarily as her toes crushed together at the top of her shoe. Eva jangled the keys in her pocket; she liked the sound. It reminded her of the charge nurse as she wandered around the wards with that annoying air of importance that followed her like cigarette smoke. The young nurse wanted to feel what it was like to be important. She had so many ideas, so much ambition, but she was just a nurse. One step above the janitor, perhaps two above the cook.

A cold summer breeze in Blackwater's city streets made Eva shiver; she shrugged the feeling off only to be hounded again by the sensation of a thousand biting insects. A slow drizzle of blanketing cloud began to find its way into the nurse's eyes, and she blinked, conscious of her running mascara. Eva pushed up her umbrella, making her way to the sanctuary of the bus stop. The number seven was never on time, crowded by dithering old pensioners eager to collect their meagre pensions from the East End post office. Whilst Eva found herself being constantly frustrated and harassed by such time wasters, she knew that in her heart she would be wheeling at least three of them to the hospital morgue this winter. Eva hurriedly clambered onto the bus, shaking out her dripping umbrella onto the unsuspecting toes of a well-dressed business man. He glanced at her with distaste, as if she had just crawled out from underneath a stone from which he'd had the misfortune of standing on. Eva ignored his impertinence, thinking quietly to herself that if he could afford such arrogance then he could afford to take a taxi to work.

Eva rubbed a finger underneath her nose, the sweet smell of floral conditioner still lingering from her shower. It was a comforting mask with which to distract her senses from the stench of stale sweat and urine. Eva repositioned herself on the blue and red, striped seat, a plume of dry skin cells buffeted up, and she subconsciously held her breath. The nurse reached above her for the air conditioning and was not surprised to find that it did not work. Eva breathed out, biting at her lipstick; she ranted to herself every time she boarded the number seven. The thought of spending £6.80 on a bus fare to work was bad enough, but it was worse when she realised that she had to work an hour for free everyday just to sit in this moving rubbish bin; Which, whilst she was on the subject, always travelled at forty mph in a thirty limit and was still late. Eva looked gloomily out of the window at the small droplets of water running like trains down the glass. She thought as she pondered the scene that she could see all the little passengers in the carriages, their faces pressed against the glass. The nurse closed her eyes, and in her mind she could see the look of terror on their expressions as the train sped to the end of the track.

"Excuse me?"

Eva jumped from her gloomy fantasy, suddenly feeling rather confused.

"I was wondering, does this bus stop at the leisure centre?"

The nurse did not respond straight away, she was captivated by the soft emerald green eyes that gazed so hypnotically at her.

"Erm," Eva straightened up in her seat, still staring at those eyes, "No, I'm sorry. It doesn't; the last stop for this bus is the hospital."

Eva continued to stare at the young woman who stood so awkwardly in front of her. She was so beautiful, her face in perfect symmetry, her hair so blonde it was platinum. Eva began to feel her chin quivering, and she stuttered slightly as her acquaintance walked away. Eva stroked at her temples, the young woman had made her feel so strange, a sad hypnotic trance that made her want to spill her stomach. Eva sat on her hands fidgeting until it was her time to get off.

"I'll see you at half five?" the bus driver smiled at her from behind the steering wheel. He had been driving the number seven bus for as long as she could remember. They saw each other nearly every day, and yet Eva had never cared to ask him his name, nor did she feel obliged to enlighten him that tonight she would be walking home. Eva hid under her umbrella as she made her way into the accident and emergency department. She continued to carry a dark cloud that blackened her mood, and Eva couldn't help but feel that today would be a challenge.

"Nurse Gardiner!"

Eva stopped in her tracks as she heard the familiar stern voice. "Yes, sister?" The young nurse turned to see a plump older woman standing strongly in the corridor. She held a bulging clipboard in one hand and a set of keys in the other which she rotated occasionally. Eva smiled to herself as she turned to face her superior.

"What time is it, Eva?"

"Seven forty, sister." There was a momentary pause as the plump woman rotated her keys again.

"And what time does your shift start?"

"Seven thirty," Eva whispered back and then added, "It was the bus." The clipboard was thrust into Eva's hand followed by,

"It's always the bus, nurse, never you."

Eva watched the senior sister sidling off whilst still jangling her keys.

Mercy was the oldest hospital in Blackwater, and it carried this description well. From the outside, her great stone walls with archaic architecture reflected the attributes of an old asylum from a horror film. Mercy was laid out in the shape of a giant C, with its broad back containing the entrance. The East and West Wings were palliative care units for the elderly and terminally ill. Or rather, as Eva often thought, dumping grounds for relatives who couldn't be bothered giving up their precious time for their dying family. Despite the hospital's cold, unforgiving demeanour, it lay nestled among the most beautiful gardens the city had to offer. Three acres of manicured lawn, beautiful box hedging and row upon row of bright roses and snap dragons. The real treat came in the spring when the whole garden would become a bright yellow sea of blooming daffodils. The sweet smell of pollen would permeate its way through the open windows of the hospital, cleansing away the stench of death from its walls. Eva loved spring, the fresh pattering of rain on her skin and the beginning of lighter nights.

Eva retreated to the sanctuary of the tea room with the clipboard tucked firmly under her arm. Her shoes made an annoying squeak on the highly polished marble floor, and she hurried herself along. The nurse hated drawing attention to herself; she couldn't bear the thought of people watching her, talking about her. Eva was never more uncomfortable than when she was in a crowded room. She felt claustrophobic, suffocated, trapped. Eva sipped delicately at a milky cup of hot coffee, occasionally wiping her lipstick from the rim. Flicking through the clipboard the nurse was enthused to find that she would be visiting the West Wing this afternoon. She had a favourite patient there, and although the nurses were encouraged not to get emotionally involved with their charges, Eva couldn't help but grow soft spots for some. In a sense she felt it made her job more palatable, and it made the two hours she would be spending in Accident and Emergency a little more digestible. Eva gulped down the rest of her coffee, glancing quickly at the mirror on her way past. It annoyed her that the mirrors were all so coldly silver in Mercy. She much preferred the tinted glass that would give her skin a subtle, warm glow, even if it were an illusion. Eva swiftly turned the corner into the corridor, her shoes making a slight squeak on the black and white chequered floor. The pungent smell of acid alcohol made its way into her nostrils, and Eva blinked as it stung at her sinuses. Its purpose served, the nurse made her way to the sink, washing her hands with the skin-drying alcohol soap. However before she could finish drying them the familiar sound of a wailing siren infected the forecourt of the hospital, and a sudden shuffle of hurried feet signalled that work had begun.

"How many?" The sister hurried past Eva who quickly followed behind.

An attractive young doctor with hazelnut eyes and a mop of curly brown hair responded with an almost complacent attitude, "Four, and two critical."

The sister uttered a grumble almost as if she resented the workload. "What happened?" The young doctor paused as he pushed open the heavy swing doors with his hip.

"Some psychopath took out a gun on a bus and started shooting; she's arriving in a separate ambulance."

Eva moved aside to allow the first of the casualties through. The sister hovered over the middle-aged man strapped securely to the trolley, checking his pulse she mumbled, "Never would have happened in my day."

Eva skipped from one treatment room to another pushing a trolley loaded with IV drips and bags of blood for transfusion. Continuously she responded to calls for more blood, more dressings, and more equipment. Eva began to wish that she had remembered to wear her insoles, and as the patient in treatment room four was pronounced dead, the nurse couldn't help but feel that all her running around had been a waste of time. The Accident and Emergency Department remained a confused mess of harassed doctors, panicked relatives and angry walk-ins, frustrated at having been made to wait for their turn. In contrast however, Eva remained calm and efficient. She performed at her best when she was under pressure and in a way this was her saving grace. The young nurse was lackadaisical with time keeping, but her excellent standard of work prevented her from falling too deeply into the sister's little black book. Eva could little afford to worry about what other people were thinking when there were too many patients and not enough staff to tend to their needs.

Eva helped the orderly wipe up the pools of blood that had been left discarded in the treatment room. She had always felt that there was something macabre in the way that a person's life could just drain away from them. A splatter of blood left on the floor, nothing more than an ugly mess that someone would have the misfortune of dragging clean heels through. However, the nurse preferred not to dwell on such things too deeply lest she should be reminded of her own mortality. Eva consistently felt the gnarl of age on her mind, unusual for someone still in the infancy of life. She kept her birthdays quiet, preferring to celebrate by herself with a bottle of wine in her small council house on Batchen Street. Her cousin had sent her a card this year with twenty-five kisses on it, one for each year of her life. Eva appreciated the sentiment, alone but never alone. It was a small comfort when one was so far away from home.

Eva removed her blood-splattered plastic apron and exited a side door that led into the spine of the hospital. An evenly laid courtyard with benches at regular intervals provided a small haven for those in the hospital who enjoyed a cigarette or two whilst on their breaks. Eva positioned herself on a bench in the corner, away from the prying eyes of patients on the upper floors. She could almost hear the old grannies clucking at her as she sucked on her cancer stick. Still, she worked hard for her little privileges, and it wasn't as if she were smoking twenty a day. Besides, did she really care what they thought? The answer was most definitely yes, and she knew that she would be hanging her head in shame later as she did her rounds.

"Mind if I join you?"

Eva smiled and moved aside as a tubby-looking janitor dropped himself heavily on the bench. His highly polished name badge reading 'Harold' glinted brightly in the struggling sun. Eva enjoyed his company, Harold was unassuming, down to earth, and had funny little quirks that had always made her laugh.

"Bloody ventilation systems broken again; it's about time they got a qualified electrician to take a look at it," Harold paused as he helped himself to one of Eva's cigarettes. "I mean sure, I can keep patching it up, but one of these days the bloody thing will pack in for good, and not me nor the damned electrician will be able to fix it."

Eva giggled, snorting as the cigarette smoke crept up her nose.

"Hey," Harold nudged Eva, leaning over as if he were about to divulge a terrible secret, "That lunatic murderer is in the isolation room, you know the one with the gun on the bus? She's got three coppers standing guard outside her room." Eva looked up from her cigarette,

"She?"

"Yeah, if you ask me they should have let her die; she shot a twelve-year-old boy on that bus, and didn't even have the courage to do a proper job on herself!" Eva frowned in response finishing off her cigarette.

"I'll see you later, Harold; I've got a few things I need to do." Harold chuckled as Eva walked away,

"No rest for the wicked, eh?" he shouted after her.

Eva made her way quickly back to the tea room to pick up her abandoned clipboard.

"Make sure you get rid of that cigarette smoke!" a voice called out behind her and the jingle of keys told Eva she need not turn around to see who it was. The nurse flicked quickly through the crisp white pages of the patients charts, but none of them caught her interest. Finally she decided that she must look, if only for a quick glance. No one in the hospital had ever sparked her curiosity before, but the 'nutter' on the bus had stirred a grim fascination within her. She felt compelled to investigate this woman; to see the face of a killer. Eva stopped a few times on her way to the isolation unit, washing her hands the first time and re-reading her clipboard the second. She needed to find excuses to re-evaluate and rationalise her decision to seek out this woman. It was almost out of character for Eva to intrigue herself with such a thing. The nurse was expecting to find a monster lying there amongst all the wires and tubes; she found herself shaking with fear, or was it excitement, as she approached the glass doors into the unit. Two armed policemen stood on either side of the door, their faces stony like grit, as if they were guarding the gates of hell. The nurse slipped silently between them, clutching at her clipboard as if she were there for a purpose. Breathing slowly out, she stood at the bottom of the bed.

The monster's face was subtly hidden by the oxygen mask. Eva thought for a second that she would just turn around and walk out, but she couldn't, she had to know, she had to see. The nurse crept closer to the woman, shakily leaning over her pale face. Suddenly Eva stepped back, drawing in a quick sharp breath as she did. Raising a trembling hand to her mouth, Eva turned her back on the woman. It was the girl. It was the beautiful, young, hypnotic girl with the emerald green eyes from the bus this morning. Spontaneously, Eva felt sick as she remembered the girl's question and her own response. Could it be that Eva had directed her to the very bus in which she would kill those people? Eva's chin began to quiver, and she began to make her way out of the room. A sharp pain in her wrist caused Eva to spin round in alarm; the nurse let out a quiet shriek as she saw the injured woman grasping firmly at her wrist, her nails biting into Eva's skin like small scalpels. The nurse felt a wave of panic rise in her throat.

"Let go! Let go of me!" Eva shouted as she struggled to get away.

"They promised I would live forever."

Eva stopped struggling for a second as the impact of the woman's words struck her mind.

"Nurse Gardiner!" The sister burst in followed by the two protectors of hell's gate.

Eva stuttered, "She, she grabbed me."

The sister pushed Eva aside as she shone a torch into the patient's eyes.

"This woman has not regained consciousness since she was admitted." The sister shook her head as she dropped the torch back into her pocket. "She did not grab you."

The confused nurse began to make a reply, but the sister stopped her mid-sentence. "Take a break, Nurse Gardiner. Come back when you have re-discovered your wits."

Eva sheepishly backed away from the scene, cowering at the strange looks that the police slid her way. The nurse walked dazedly down the corridor, the black and white chequered floor irritating her eyes. Eva rubbed at her clammy forehead, feeling the dull pinch of a tension headache clouding her thoughts. For the first time in what seemed like an eternity, Eva began to feel a welling up in the pit of her stomach. The young nurse swung off the corridor into the ladies rest-room, sitting on the lid of the toilet seat, she locked herself in. For a second it appeared that nothing would happen. Eva sat there, motionless like a lost dog. Then, as if from the darkest chasm of her being, it began. A deep intake of air, followed by a low, heart-breaking sob, and then again and again until her tears were so hot they began to streak the melting mascara down her face. Eva couldn't stop her outburst; it was as though all her pent-up emotions were laid out on the toilet floor in front of her. Eva felt as though she were falling into a deep chasm. The fragile strings she had created to hold up her shattered emotions began to snap like toothpicks, and she wondered for a second between sobs if she had finally cracked.

"Are you all right in there?" A succession of knuckle rapping on the cubicle door snapped Eva from her woeful tears, and she jumped off the seat, wiping wet foundation from her cheeks.

"Yes, yes, I'm fine, sorry," the nurse responded loudly, almost in defence of her character. Eva sat quietly back down onto the toilet seat, holding her breath like she was an escaped convict. The sudden jolt back to reality reminded Eva of the real world, and she cursed under her breath, "Get a grip, you stupid bitch." The nurse waited for her concerned party to leave before exiting the cubicle and washing her streaked face in the sink.

Eva had not seen herself like this for nearly three years. The drawn pale face and puffy red eyes brought back a barrage of painful memories. She closed her face in her hands, hoping that when she reopened them normality would return. The young nurse patted her face down quickly and immediately began reapplying her make-up. She sponged on the foundation like it was custard, sighing with relief as her carefully manicured image began its restoration. Eva uttered a tut as her wavering hand deformed the smooth line of her eye liner, and she stopped for a second to catch her breath. Nurse Gardiner left the ladies rest-room in almost pristine condition, like a porcelain doll. Only the occasional bite of her bottom lip indicated that a finite crack had appeared in her false guise. Eva joined a couple of her colleagues in the tea room and took up her usual seat near the window. The nurse flicked through the pages of a magazine, pretending to read as she always did. All the while she wondered what the others were thinking, wondering if perhaps they were talking about her. Eva struggled to enjoy her tea break. She never truly relaxed, but could usually find a useful niche where she could at least partially switch off. It seemed that today she would struggle to even pretend.

The West Wing of Mercy denied the smooth circular curve of its outward appearance. Inside was a rabbit warren of right-angled corridors and large open rooms. Eva loved this part of the hospital. The idea that she might get lost down here and not see another living soul for ten minutes was an appealing thought. Many of the other members of staff preferred to stay at the newer, front end of the Mercy, where solace was nowhere to be found. Eva consistently swapped shifts with other nurses so that she might spend more time down there. The sister didn't seem to mind as long as the work was done. The East and West Wings were the only parts of the building that remained consistent with the hospital's Victorian architecture. Gone were the bright contrasting floors and Peach Melba walls of the newer revamped sections. Instead a calmer, neutral solid wood floor and an unassuming shade of forest green graced the old plaster walls. Only the fluorescent strip lights and modern medical equipment gave the game away. Eva often imagined herself in a long, grey, heavy dress with the white bonnet of days gone by. Life and death was simpler then; life expectancy wasn't measured in percentages.

Eva poked her head around door number five, wearing the cheekiest grin she could muster.

"Hello, Mrs Stephen, how are you this afternoon?" An incredibly thin old woman with a purple rinse and thin silver-rimmed glasses glanced up from her book.

"Eva! Am I glad to see you, get me out of here will you, that bloody television is blaring my ear drums out!" The old woman put down her book before gesturing at the nurse with her arm. "And it's Edna, girl, Edna!" Eva giggled, half trotting to her favourite patient's side. "God I wish this cancer would get on with its job and finish me off so I don't have to suffer those infernal deaf busy bodies!"

The nurse stifled a laugh. Edna Stephen could make Eva laugh no matter what was going on with her life. Edna had been on the ward nearly two years. She had already been in remission from breast cancer and bowel cancer. The nurses had affectionately begun to call her the iron lady, but the cancer had made its way to her liver and it looked as though her great battle was coming to an end. Eva had a great respect for Mrs Stephen and the feeling was mutual. Whilst the rest of the nursing staff scorned her wishes for a quick death, Eva chose to understand. She held a great fondness for Edna, but also recognised that she had had her time. Tiredness was creeping upon her, and it seemed almost cruel to prolong a life that had no meaning for its keeper. Besides, Mrs Stephen was adamant that the next life would be better than this one, and Eva clung to that sentiment.

Edna had a large family, but in the past eighteen months, they had only bothered to visit her twice. Mostly for the purposes of making funeral arrangements and of course her will. Eva couldn't help but feel bitterly angry that people could care so little for their relatives. Mrs Stephen didn't seem to care either way, and as she repeatedly reminded Eva, "None of those miserable buggers are going to get a penny out of me; I've left it all to Macmillan." The young nurse couldn't help but feel secretly pleased every time she heard her say it, and she wished reverently that she could be there at the reading of the will.

Edna and Eva enjoyed each other's company in the hospital gardens. For brief periods of time the nurse managed to forget about the bus and the woman with green eyes. In the back of her mind however, there was a constant irritation. For brief periods Eva couldn't remember what it was that troubled her. She knew something was wrong, and it felt as if she were slightly off balance, with no-where to fall. Then all at once she would remember, and it made her breathe in sharply as if she had jumped into a cold bath. Eva hated the feeling. It reminded her of when she was a small child and her mother would chastise her for doing something wrong. Eva would be reminded of her naughtiness for days after, and it lingered with her like a bad tea stain. However, as Eva kept reminding herself, she was no longer a child and could little afford such trivial emotions.

"Brrrr, it's getting a bit nippy I think." Edna looked up at Eva from her wheelchair, rubbing at the small goose pimples that stood up on her papery skin. Mrs Stephen was right. Large grey cumulus clouds had covered up what little summer sun there was on offer, and the air began to smell distinctly of rain.

"Time to get on those dancing shoes and rush us in before we both get a good soaking!" Eva did immediately as Edna suggested. The pair made it to the sanctuary of the Mercy roof just as the first few droplets of rain began to fall. After making sure Edna was back in her room and comfortable, Eva began to say her goodbyes. Catching her by surprise, Edna grabbed the nurse's arm.

"I'm sure whatever is troubling that pretty head of yours will come right, it always does." Eva smiled at Mrs Stephens perceptiveness, bending down to give her a quick hug, "Eva, I want to give you this, you know how I feel about my family, but I don't always get things right, I want you to read it after, ok? Maybe you could use it to help others like me." Eva took a small white envelope from Edna with curiosity, before returning to the main building.

The rest of Eva's shift remained dull and uneventful; a yanked-out catheter being the only warrant for her attention. Normally the nurse would welcome such quite; peaceful times. Not today, the last few hours of her unusually long eleven-hour shift seemed as if they would be her last. Eva had always felt so comfortable within the sanitised walls of the Mercy. She knew exactly what her purpose was and why she was there. Sometimes her workplace reminded her of the familiar classroom setting of childhood. Simple rules; easy to follow, easy to understand. Eva flicked at the small silver watch that hung purposefully from her blouse. Five past, ten past, quarter past. The nurse bit nervously at her carefully manicured nails. She had begun to feel out of her depth, and the source of her anxiety evaded her. Muddling her way through the last remaining minutes of her shift, she collected her coat from the tea room. Thank God tomorrow would be her day off.

The hard droplets of heavy summer rain had turned into nothing more than a persistent drizzle. Eva welcomed its cool fresh presence on her face. Now that her shift was over, the young woman was happy to let the make-up slip subtly with the blanketing moisture. The evening had begun its plight to turn day into night, and Eva knew that she would be under less scrutiny. The dim fluorescence would make passing eyes strain to see her pale features in the fading light. Eva loved the sanctuary of darkness. It was comforting to think that everyone else was sleeping whilst she was busying herself with simple chores and the quite reading of Stephen King by candlelight. The evenings belonged to her. Eva answered to no one in these small hours, and occasionally, she would shut her eyes for as little as two hours before rising again to start a new day. The nurse was well aware that this was the primary cause of her poor time keeping. However, whilst her job at the Mercy remained safe, she would continue her late night escapades.

Blackwater, whilst booming with busy commerce and crowded streets during the day, was altogether more subdued at night. The weekends however encouraged a barrage of young club goers to drag themselves from bar to bar. They stopped only to throw up on the corner of the street before going on feeling mildly rejuvenated. Eva avoided the streets during the weekend, lest she should be engaged in conversation that she neither cared for nor wanted. During the week, however, she chose to walk home rather than catch her customary bus. Nurse Gardiner lowered her head to avoid the bright lights of a passing car and turned quickly into Balsen Street. The glowing orange street lights tinged her hair a fiery red. And it helped to mask her identity.

Eva walked briskly down the street before stopping to re-trace her steps back to an off licence. She grinned to herself as she stepped inside the brightly lit shop. A bottle of wine would go well with her book tonight, and it was worth showing a little running make-up for. Eva gazed naïvely at the rows of perfectly aligned wine bottles. Reds on the right, whites on the left, and rose in the middle. The nurse knew nothing about wine, only what she liked and what she didn't. After staring blankly for some time at the wine regions of Versailles and Chile, she picked up an old favourite.

"Jacobs Creek, a perfect choice." A tiny petite young girl beamed up at Eva as she spoke from across the counter, and the nurse wondered if she was even old enough to drink. Eva nodded in appreciation.

"Thought I'd relax with a glass of wine and a good book," Eva whispered.

Sarah, as her name tag read, sighed in pretend jealousy, "Make sure you have a second glass for me."

Eva nodded her head, laughing as she left the shop. It was strange how just one person could lighten the mood of another, and Eva left the off licence feeling just that little bit brighter.

A sudden pitter patter on her carrier bag signalled the arrival of more rain. Eva pushed up her umbrella in readiness of its onslaught, staring blankly ahead as she wandered aimlessly down the street. Eva was so consumed by the thoughts inside her head that she was completely oblivious to her surroundings. Despite this, she expertly dodged the potholes and uneven pavements in the street like she had put them there herself. Occasionally, Eva would feel a pang of homesickness as she felt the cold hard slabs of concrete underfoot. There were times when she would have given anything to return home to the springy green grass of the country. Eva's heart remained where she had grown up, but like most young people, she had moved to the city to study and find work.

The nurse shuddered slightly as the cold slimy feel of wet leaves crept inside her court shoes. Despite the sudden chill, Eva welcomed the cooling sensation on her tired feet. The presence of decaying leaves also signalled her arrival at the park. The small green, tree-surrounded square was one of the few beauty spots in a city so full of smog and pollution. Eva tugged at the heavy black iron gates and whispered a "hello" in response to its high-pitched squeal. In reality it was quicker for Eva to continue further on down the street to get home, but the park provided a convenient route to the graveyard, and she had an appointment she could not miss. The path through the cemetery dipped sharply for a few seconds, and the auburn-haired woman disappeared from view, almost as if she had never existed. Tall oak trees arched over the path, elements of their youth lay crisp and dying underfoot. The graveyard was silent and dark, and Eva remembered the first time she had walked through it with Adam. She had been so scared. He had squeezed her hand, and the nurse had felt safe again. Now, she walked through the graveyard every week and felt nothing.

The wind and rain had torn at her jacket and hair, and the woman looked as if she had been out in a storm for hours. Despite this, Eva felt a hollow silence as she stepped quietly onto the consecrated ground. It was a cold, dark place. Sometimes, above everything else, the nurse could smell the pungent odour of rotting vegetation. Although it made her feel like death was resting on her shoulders, she would lower her head and carry on walking. Eva had quickly recognised that she could not afford to take her emotions with her to the cemetery. In case she should fall back into that dark pit that had already taken so many of her young years.

Eva made her usual stop at the water tap, borrowing one of the many watering cans that littered the grounds. She hurriedly ferried fresh water to Adam's grave; it didn't matter that the flowers didn't require the water. It was part of her routine. The graveyard was vast, and the newest part of it was at the farthest point from the park. It was almost a punishment that those with the freshest wounds had to walk the farthest to pay their respects. Everywhere that Eva turned stood silvery black headstones. The newest ones had careful even spacing between them, and sometimes in the light of the breaking dawn, it would appear as if a great grey sea had engulfed the grounds. Eva wondered if it could ever be possible to feel alone in a place so full of souls. As she approached Adam's grave, she understood all over again what loneliness meant. Allowing her knees to sink into the wet grass, she shakily poured her water over the vibrant red carnations. A single tear made its way down her cheek, and she wiped it away with embarrassment before whispering.

"I had the strangest day today, Adam. I really don't know how to explain it."

Eva swallowed away her pain before continuing to tell Adam about the strange events at the Mercy. Time was irrelevant in a place such as this and passed without warning. Occasionally three or four hours would pass before the nurse finally made it back through her front door. Eva's life consisted of three things and had so for several years. Work, Adam, and, when her mind would permit it, sleep.

Adam never responded to Eva's continuous ramblings about her work. The young nurse felt his silence a heart breaking reminder of the truth. Instead she imagined his response. Inside her head she would hear the soft dulcet tones of his voice, and just for a while, she could pretend that he was there with her; offering the same calm comforting words that he had always whispered. Eva stood up, brushing away the leaf litter from her knees. She kissed her finger, placing it lightly upon the letter A of his headstone. She slowly walked away promising to visit again in a few days. The young nurse clutched at her bottle of wine, waiting until she was outside the cemetery before putting her umbrella back up again. Eva left Adam every week with a wry feeling of hope. She almost regretted the glimmer of light that would seep into the dark recesses of her mind. Sometimes she wondered if she were betraying his memory. She had failed him once, and she knew that. She would never do that again. No, she would always come here, once a week, to water his flowers and subdue her guilt.

The relentless falling of summer rain had yet again changed in pattern. Eva pulled her umbrella down closer as large heavy droplets bounced off the fabric like rubber balls. It was quite deafening. The young woman did not hear the anguished cries for help until the young man screaming them was almost upon her. Eva jumped, dropping her umbrella in alarm. An untidily dressed man bounded about in front of her.

"Please, you've gotta help me. It's my brother; he's having a fit or something!"

The young man pointed to a soft spot off the path about eight feet from Eva's position. The nurse ran a hand past her soaking wet face and peered into the darkness. Through blurry eyes, she could just make out the faint outline of a body on the grass.

"Here, take this and phone for an ambulance." Eva thrust her mobile phone into the young man's hand and ran towards the outline. Behind her, the untidy boy scrutinized the phone in his hand before deftly slipping it into his pocket. Eva crouched down next to the victim and began feeling for a pulse. Suddenly the seemingly unresponsive man responded by thrashing her hand away. Eva jumped back in alarm as the young man's brother suddenly sat up. Bearing an awkward smile, he glanced up at his sibling towering above Eva.

"We do need your help; we need your purse."

Eva slid backwards on her bottom along the sopping grass. She clutched vainly at the handbag draped across her shoulder.

"No," she blurted out amongst the falling rain drops, before scrambling to her feet. Sliding as though she were on ice, she ran. Eva had never felt as alive as she tried desperately to get away. The noise of the falling rain and the pounding of her own thundering heartbeat drowned out the noises behind her. She knew they were there, less than two steps behind her. The nurse let out a scream which was stifled by wet grass and mud as her face hit the ground. Flipping herself onto her back she stared into the faces of the two young men who tugged wildly at the bag on her shoulder. Eva was pulled about like a rag doll for a few seconds before the pain in her twisted shoulder forced her to retaliate. Lashing out, she kicked wildly with her legs. Her assailant fell backwards. A howl rang out in the dark, and Eva knew in that second that she had made a mistake.

"You bitch! You fucking bitch!"

The nurse stopped struggling. Paralysed with fear, she sat back. The young man rose to his feet. The expression on his face was one only the devil would recognise. Reaching inside his pocket, he lashed out at Eva.

"No! Mark! Oh Jesus! What have you done?"

Suddenly Eva took a shallow breath. The noise was like that of a punctured tyre. Eva spluttered for a second as a familiar metallic taste spread across the back of her throat.

"Come on! We need to go! Now!" "Fucking idiot!" The noise of the two men shouting was a distant echo in Eva's mind.

The younger of the two, leaned over her whispering, "I'm sorry, this wasn't supposed to happen."

Eva felt her mobile phone being pushed into her hand its brightly lit screen displaying 999, she managed to hit the call button before a pattern of soft dull thuds signalled her attacker's departure. As Eva lay crippled in the wet park, she felt a sudden aura of peace. Her senses dulled, and her mind tired. She closed her eyes.

In the distance of the city an ambulance tore through the streets, its blue flashing lights brightening the black sky like a strobe. It pulled up sharply at the entrance of Mercy hospital, and Eva would find herself, yet again, back at work.

"What have we got?" a familiar voice rang into the cloudy silence.

"Caucasian female, single stab wound to the chest, BP eighty over fifty and falling. Pulse one hundred and ten." A concerned voice responded over her shoulder.

Eva rolled her eyes in her head. The familiarity of the voice awoke her to consciousness.

"It's okay, dear, you're safe now." There was a momentary pause as a face leaned in. "Oh my god, it's Eva!" The young nurse tried to smile as the shrillness of the sister's voice amused her ears. The ordinarily intimidating hand of her superior became somewhat of a comfort as it enveloped her own.

"I want to know what happened! And alert theatre!" The sister's voice began to drift again, and Eva's struggle for consciousness was lost.

THE CAVERN

A large oval table sat in the centre of an empty room. The shine on its highly polished surface was so brilliant that it shone awkwardly like a drunken pageant queen. Seven men sat evenly spaced around its edges, the thick noxious smell of cigar smoke hovered over them like a bad omen.

"What's the story on this Turnbull killing, Andrew?" The only man not smoking clasped his hands together on the table.

"The chief of police is regarding this as a murder suicide; there have been no leaks"

Sitting to the left of Andrew was an older man sporting a greying moustache, his hair had obviously departed him a good few years before, and his bald scalp was the only thing to rival the brilliance of the table. He snorted slightly as he spoke.

"Any chance of questioning the girl?" The balding man sighed.

Andrew shrugged his shoulders, "She's in a coma at the moment, but I've got a couple of my boys at the door to her room. If she wakes up, I'll be the first to know."

"This is the third incident in Blackwater in the past three months, and that's not counting all the rumoured incidents in other towns and cities that we don't have information about," said a man in his early sixties. He took a breather to inhale on his cigar before continuing. "It's obvious now that this problem is increasing; it's becoming difficult not only to

33

monitor, but to contain. There is going to come a point soon when we will have to act."

There was an odd silence in the room, as though every man had something to say but couldn't articulate. A squeak from Andrew's chair startled everyone from the moment.

"That's all good and well, professor, but we haven't even begun to formulate a plan of containment, let alone preventing them from manipulating us," Andrew spoke confidently, asserting his familiarity with the issue and his obvious first-hand knowledge.

"We need more information; it's vital we get to this Turnbull girl before they come back to finish the job. Without her insight, all we are left with is dated accounts and second-hand information," the professor snapped unduly at Andrew as the difficulty of their situation became clear.

"I'll see what I can do," Andrew murmured. His chair creaked noisily as he slid it away from the table, his frustration voiced only by its strained fixtures as he quickly exited the room.

"If you will excuse me, gentlemen, I think it's time I called the ministry of defence; I think we could use a little more backup on this one." The professor rose from his seat as he spoke, there was an air of reluctance in his body language.

As the professor left the room, the bald man lit up another cigar, coughing mildly, he announced to the rest of the room,

"We are going to need more than a bunch of bureaucratic diplomats," his comment went unregistered as the rest of the table packed up their paperwork.

CHAPTER TWO

"You couldn't pick up a packet of fags on your way home could you, babe?" Eva looked up from pulling on her tights.

"Adam, you really need to try and leave the flat today." Eva frowned as she finished her sentence. A sudden spark of adrenalin leapt into her chest, and she stood paralysed.

"I don't feel like going out today," replied Adam. Eva watched with terrified silence as he left the room.

"You're dead," she whispered silently under her breath. Eva's hand shook uncontrollably as she finished rolling up her tights. Cautiously, she glanced around the room. Adam's guitars hung gracefully from the walls, as though they were a shrine to music; a long cabinet packed full of CDs and endless copies of *Kerrang!* stood neatly in the corner. Eva could smell the familiar sweetness of freshly burned marijuana, and she breathed in as the smell triggered a barrage of long-forgotten memories and feelings she wasn't expecting. This wasn't her flat, but everything looked oddly familiar. Eva began to panic as she realised she knew exactly where she was. This was her and Adam's flat, from nearly four years ago.

The bathroom door banged angrily in the corridor, and Eva jumped with alarm. Retreating quietly to the sanctuary of the kitchen, she paused for thought.

"This can't be happening, this can't be happening," she repeated to herself hysterically before glancing into the mirror. "Oh my god." Her chin quivered as she recognised the face of her younger, less-troubled self. "I don't understand."

"Understand what?"

Eva spun round to see Adam standing in front of her. She breathed in sharply, attempting to stifle her urge to cry. He was so beautiful. She had almost forgotten just how attractive his emerald green eyes and bleach blonde features were. He was so real standing there. His eyes glistened with moisture and his lips held a warm rosy glow. Eva turned away with painful anguish as she remembered the day she found him. His expression was blank. His eyes glazed over like firm jelly and his lips, his lips were white. "Are you going to pick up those fags or not?" Eva nodded her head in acknowledgement.

"Adam?" she took a step forward, placing her hand on his face. "Twenty or forty?" Eva bit her lip as Adam walked away.

"Twenty will be fine."

Eva had forgotten just how troubled their relationship had become. Adam was complicated. He'd always been this way, but it wasn't until he had started drinking that things really deteriorated. Eva had loved him so much. She had promised that she would stand by him – even when his mental illness was at its worst. It didn't matter what he said or did, underneath it all, he was a kind, loving, generous man. Eva would hang on for as long as it took. Retreating to the living room, she rested her head in her hands. She wasn't sure she wanted to relive such painful memories. It made no sense. This was the past, she shouldn't be here. Unexpectedly, a voice broke into Eva's thoughts.

"Not all is lost." A whisper, smooth like pure liquid. The subtle sound glided around the room, bouncing from every wall like an echo. Eva lifted her head from her hands and blinked with confusion. Luminous light filled the space like a cascading waterfall. It was as if she had been enveloped in a blanket of snow. Eva peered around. The objects that had surrounded her became nothing more than faint grey outlines, their matter appearing to phase out into the translucent glow surrounding them.

"There is a way."

Eva deftly turned towards the source of the echo. Her mouth dropped crudely open as she stared at what she recognised to be.... an angel. In those few seconds, Eva could say nothing. Her eyes were captivated by the purity of the entity that stood before her. It was as though she had fallen into a pit of pure energy. Her companion stared back with an almost infinite understanding. Eva let out a stifled laugh as a tear fell down her cheek.

"I'm so confused," she blurted out between her sodden lips.

"So are all who face this moment." The entity stretched out a hand towards her, and Eva wondered how she could ever touch it. It was as though the being had no form, and yet it was here. It was everywhere. Eva felt as if she had been drugged with something euphoric. She no longer felt the terrifying burden of confusion eat at her mind. Instead, everything had become clear, like a frozen lake in winter. She was exactly where she was supposed to be. The one place where she could begin all over again. Eva had been given a second chance in death, and now she could save him. The price was small. All she had to do was let go. Let go and she would finally be rid of the guilt that had infested her soul. Suddenly without fear, Eva reached towards the outstretched hand. Her mind fixed securely on the man sleeping in the bedroom. The man she loved, and would do anything for. Now they would be together again, and this time they would get it right.

Without warning a sudden deep wrenching impact exploded from inside Eva's chest. She gasped as the air was torn from her lungs. Desperately the nurse reached out again towards her angel. Again, a burning, tugging sensation. Eva began to scream with frustration, and suddenly everything around began to alter. The luminescent glow that had soothed her so effectively became warped and distorted. Eva watched with horror as the air around her became tinged with static. Blackness began to creep its way around her.

"No!" Eva screamed out into the air before stopping with shock as she caught sight of her glowing deity. The purity of its form had faded. Instead, a charged blue bolt replaced the softness of its previous outline. It spat and sparked like an angry power line. Eva pulled away her outstretched hand, suddenly feeling under threat.

"You are mine," a piercing sound ravished at her eardrums.

Eva turned her face away as a sudden shard of electricity made its way towards her. She could smell it. That metallic, burning, acrid smell of raw power. Another deeper sharper shock struck at her chest. Eva cried with confusion as she found herself hurtling backwards. The blue shard becoming nothing more than a jagged line in the distance.

FOUR DAYS LATER...

An irritating scratch niggled at the back of Eva's throat like a cushion of needles, and she coughed with the discomfort.

"Sister! She's awake!"

Eva wheezed a high-pitched whistle as the tube was guided gently from her mouth. The wounded nurse spluttered as loose saliva gathered around her airways.

"Take it easy, Eva. You're okay." The rosy red cheeks of the sister hovered over her. Eva blinked as her superior wiped away moisture from her eyes with a tissue. "It's good to have you back, girl," she whispered. "I wouldn't want you to miss your next shift." Eva managed a wry smile and then grimaced as she realised that breathing was painful. "I'll go and fetch the doctor to check you over." The sister patted her hand. "You've got some fight in you, girl."

Eva lay in shock and bewilderment as the doctor rattled through her list of injuries. A punctured lung, severed artery, loss of blood. It all meant nothing. The nurse's mind continued to wander to images of angels, Adam, the blue shard. Eva shuddered as a sudden feeling of dread washed over her. That blue shard was no angel. No, it was something else. Eva could almost sense its presence still lingering around her, like a virus in her blood. The young woman pinched herself to ensure that she was indeed alive.

"Anyway, you're going to be here for a little while longer yet."

Eva looked up at the surgeon as she realised he was talking to her.

"We can take the drain out of your lung tomorrow I should think." The nurse looked down at her side. A clear plastic tube carried small amounts of a blood-stained liquid away from her chest. Eva hadn't realised the tube was even there.

"Yes, thank you," she replied.

The surgeon acknowledged her response with a nod. He left the room with the same surgical arrogance he was renowned for. The sister slipped back into the room carrying a jug of water and some sponges.

"I haven't been able to contact any of your family, Eva. Is there anyone you can think of?" Eva shook her head to answer 'no'.

"I have some cousins in Newbury. But we're not that close." The young nurse moistened her mouth with the sponges and water before abruptly announcing, "I saw something. I'm not sure what it was." The sister straightened the covers at the bottom of Eva's bed before pulling up a chair beside her.

"What kind of something?"

Eva licked at her lips. "I don't know, I thought it was an angel at first, but I was wrong, it was dark, malevolent." The sister smiled back at Eva and patted her hand.

"Your body has been through a lot, perhaps it's just your mind dealing with the trauma." Eva nodded and smiled back, feeling slightly unconvinced. "Perhaps you're right."

Eva huddled underneath the covers of her bed as she watched the sun set from her hospital window. The Mercy was stiflingly hot as it always was, but the nurse felt safer under the protection of the heavily starched white linen. Eva desperately wanted to sleep. She could feel her face becoming numb with the exhaustion, her mind clouding over like a winter day, and yet she fought to stay awake. The nurse was not afraid of seeing the faces of the men who had attacked her, but rather the acrid, electric blue of the false angel. Even as she sat awake, she thought that she could feel its presence around her, almost as though it were waiting for her to fall into an exhausted unconscious.

"Hello again, Eva, sorry I forgot to mark your chart." The nurse jumped, suddenly startled by the arrival of the sister.

"Yeah, that's no problem." Eva breathed hurriedly as the awkward skipping of her heart made responding difficult.

"You're looking pretty pale, girl, you need to get some sleep." Eva nodded her head reluctantly as the sister felt her pulse. "Incidentally, there's going to be a couple of police officers outside your door, don't worry about it." She patted Eva's arm, "I think it's just a precaution, I don't believe they have caught who attacked you yet."

Eva peered around the sister's shoulder as she left the room. Eva frowned, sitting quickly back into her uncomfortable pillows. She recognised the two men at the door. The nurse bit at her lip, wishing reverently that she could escape the bed to get a better look, the numerous wires and tubes still attached to her body kept her trapped like a hostage.

The two police officers, dressed in black suits, looked as though they were getting ready to go to a funeral. Eva distinctly remembered the same oddly dressed officers outside Louise Turnbull's room. The only indication that they were anything other than funeral directors was the loosely dangling ear pieces that hung unceremoniously from their left ears. Occasionally one of the men would raise a finger to his ear and nod his head as though a secret command had been whispered into his eardrum. Eva watched them suspiciously; despite her agonising tiredness, she was wary of falling asleep. The thought that they were there to protect her didn't wash; Eva couldn't believe that police dressed out of uniform were present just to protect a lowly nurse who had happened to get mugged. As the hours wore on and the men continued to stand like figurines outside her door, the nurse began to let go of her fears, sleep was so inviting, inviting enough for not to care what the men were up to anyway.

RECUPERATION...

The days to follow were as long as they were dull. The Mercy continued on in its usual fashion, and Eva wished fervently that she were working, not lying in a harshly starched bed on wheels. Regardless of the rational explanation provided by her superior, Eva continued to feel uneasy. Rest was no longer a therapeutic break from reality. Each time she closed her eyes she saw it – the thing that had tricked her so cleverly into believing its false guise. The more she thought about it the more Eva began to feel sickened. It was cruel to have deceived her in such a manner. To make her believe that she could be with Adam again. Perhaps that's all that death was; a deception, a ruse to steal us from life.

Not content with her own explanations, Eva spent the rest of her long hospital stay writing and drawing about her experience. She noted every single aspect of her encounter, even the most personal of feelings. She even attempted to draw what she described as the "false angel." No technique she utilized could fully capture its hideous beauty. The complex inter-connecting of its crystallised matrix was almost too much for her hand to imitate. Eva was glad to finally see the back of her black-suited protectorates, after a few days they had disappeared, and Eva's persistent questioning of the sister as to their real agenda went unanswered. The sister watched Eva's activities with concern, suggesting once or twice that she should seek counselling. Eva ignored what she regarded as unfounded ramblings, until she found herself cornered, agreeing with her superior's stern suggestions only when it appeared she would not be allowed to return to work until she had completed at least six sessions.

Eva attended these sessions with mild reluctance. They were a means of getting back to work, but that was all. She talked about her assault in a way that felt appropriate, and elaborated only when forced to. Richard, her psychiatrist, was dull at the best of times. He was completely consumed by his work. She could sense that his entire social life outside of his office was spent living and breathing psychology. The absence of a wedding ring appeared to confirm as much. Despite her misgivings about Dr Richard Wellar, Eva felt a strange attraction towards his dull personality. He was oddly soothing, almost like a warm tonic on a cold winter's day. Often she would spend as much time analysing him, as he would her.

Eva played with the watch on her wrist. Richard had already kept her waiting twenty minutes, and now he was fiddling with his paperwork.

"Sorry to keep you waiting Miss Gardiner; there have been some unexpected pop-ups this morning."

Eva smiled in response, attempting to hide her obvious agitation. It wasn't until their session was nearly over that Eva spotted something that made her heart pound. Amongst the untidily strewn paperwork on his desk was a file. It was obvious to Eva that this patient must be a recent development, perhaps even a last-minute, unexpected one. After all, it was incredibly unethical to leave someone's personal medical information on view for just anyone to see. Eva discreetly shuffled in her chair, cautiously leaning forward.

"Are you alright?" Dr Wellar looked in puzzlement at Eva as he caught her awkward movements.

"Yes, sorry, just a little cramp," Eva blushed with embarrassment whilst consciously making a mental note of the exact position of the file.

Eva stood outside the psychology department of the Mercy Hospital. It was a separate building from the main building and altogether modern in appearance. It stood out rather crudely from the rest of the hospital, rather like an afterthought, hurriedly implemented and poorly designed. Eva considered it astigmatism. It stood out shockingly, like a single daffodil in a field of crocus. If anyone saw you enter this building, then it was clear you either worked in the field of clinical psychology or you had a screw loose. Eva found neither particularly appealing. The nurse fidgeted as she smoked her cigarette. Never before had she contemplated committing a criminal act. Eva was always so straight-laced, proper. Her mother would be turning in her grave if she knew what her daughter was thinking.

Eva closed her eyes as she lit up a second cigarette. She needed more time. The thought of breaking into the doctor's office made her want to cry with fear. At the same time she felt a strange pang of excitement. It was so confusing, like having butterflies in your stomach and not being sure whether you enjoyed the sensation. Eva desperately wanted that file. Every string of common sense she had, screamed at her to stop. Dangerous nonsense. She could lose her job. Eva swallowed, ignoring the nagging sting as she re-entered the building. She approached the psychologist's door with in trepidation, biting at her fingernails. Suddenly, as if from thin air, Dr Wellar opened his office door and stepped out in front of her. Eva jumped, her cheeks beginning to flush scarlet rouge.

"Is everything okay, Miss Gardiner?"

Eva stuttered. "Erm, yes, yes, it's just that I forgot my next appointment time." The psychologist looked at her with wry amusement.

"It's 2 p.m. every Tuesday, Eva."

Eva stifled a laugh.

"Yes! Of course it is, sorry."

The nurse chastised herself under her breath as the doctor walked away. "Stupid cow."

Eva left herself no time for more cautious thinking and darted into the office. Wildly she grabbed at the file on the desk, stuffing it underneath her coat. Eva stood paralysed in the hall for a few seconds. Her heart was beating so fast that she had broken into a sweat. Fearing that she would bump into her nemesis psychologist again, she made her way out of the rear entrance. Walking into the gardens, she finally breathed. Eva steadied herself. Suddenly she felt quite dizzy. Eva had no idea that simply borrowing a file could make her feel so ill. Perhaps it was the realisation that "borrowing" was perhaps the incorrect term. "Stealing" appeared more appropriate. With this terrifying thought in mind, Eva began to make her way out of the gardens.

"Eva!"

The nurse spun round, thinking for one terrifying minute that she had been caught. Instead Eva's fear was transmuted to relief.

"Edna!" Eva shouted back and ran almost like an excited child to see her friend. Edna had changed so much in the seven weeks of Eva's absence. The nurse felt a surge of griping sadness as she looked upon her friend's sudden deterioration. Edna had become so thin and frail. The wind buffeted around her wheelchair like a menacing demon, and Eva wondered if Edna might blow over. Eva's friend was as sharp as she was intuitive.

"Don't worry, pet," she whispered as she patted at the nurse's arm. "We all have to go some time." Eva bent down and hugged her frail patient; carefully she wiped away a tear from her eye. She did not want Edna to see how upset she was. The two friends chatted away for almost half an hour before a nurse came back to fetch Edna to the warmth of her hospital room. Eva stared thoughtfully into Edna's eyes and almost like an impulse she whispered into her ear.

"There is a better place, I've seen it, and it's beautiful." Edna sat in her chair with a smile that could brighten any storm, and as Eva walked away, she prayed that she was right.

Eva hastily latched the door behind her as she returned to her flat. Biting at her fingernails, she closed all the blinds, taking in a deep breath as she felt her heart skip a beat. Ignoring her landlord's rules, Eva lit up a cigarette in the hallway. Now was not the time to get pissy over a few building regulations when she had just committed theft. Sitting with a cup of tea at her coffee table, Eva held the file in her hand. She fingered the edges of its crisp white pages with anticipation, and still she hesitated. The nagging consequences of a criminal record worried her.

"Shit, it's too late now," Eva spoke aloud as she finally flipped over the first page. What met her eyes did not disappoint. Eva smiled as she instantly recognised the name on the file. Louise Turnbull, the girl from the bus. Eva wasn't entirely sure why she was so interested in a woman who had deliberately killed several people. Perhaps it was because she had spoken with the woman before she had pulled the trigger, Perhaps it was because since Eva had met this girl, she had been to hell and back. Or was it those words she had whispered so intensely to Eva in the hospital, when she was supposed to be in a coma. When she was supposed to be unconscious. Regardless, Eva felt she had to investigate. Her curiosity had been ignited so much in these past few weeks. In a way, Eva thought that she had become a different person. Her brush with death had reminded her that life was for the living, especially now that she was convinced that there was something out there other than an afterlife; something hidden amongst the false guise of angels, an entity, a predator.

Eva's living room became a smog of cigarette smoke and confused thoughts. Miss Turnbull was hardly your average homicidal killer. In fact, she was quite unremarkable. A biology student at Blackwater University, she lived with her parents. No criminal record, no driving offences, not so much as a parking ticket. And then, murder. Eva shook her head, it didn't make any sense. This was a twenty-two-year old girl with average grades and a pet cat called Jerry. This was not a murderer. Eva continued to read through Louise's file. The more she read, the more she became convinced that there had to be something else. Something she'd missed, perhaps something not in this file. Eva came across a report, which at least in part, began to answer some of her questions. On February 24th, nearly five months ago, Louise was involved in a road traffic accident. Her injuries were so severe that she was not expected to survive. Miss Turnbull had spent the following three months recovering in hospital. Her quick rehabilitation was described as remarkable by surgeons. Eva raised a hand to her mouth as a sudden thought struck her. She and Miss Turnbull appeared to have something in common. Both were unfortunate enough to find themselves at the brink of death, and yet had survived.

"Maybe you saw the false angel. What did it tell you?" Eva continued to flick through the pages of the file, skipping through Dr Wellar's scrawled notes, she came across something intriguing. A note, handwritten by Louise, the date suggested that it was only three weeks old. Eva was stunned by the beauty of the handwriting. Every turn of the pen had created a meticulously formed letter. Care had been taken to dot every i and cross every t. It was conscientious, thoughtful. Eva read....

"Such dark things dwell when the light has no room to bless the shadows. Sometimes when I'm on my own, I can feel this void of empty sorrow swallow me up into a dark pit. There's no ladder, no light, no way out. I feel as though I ought to run. I'm not exactly sure where, anywhere. Somewhere where there's no pain, no memories, nothing to care for or care about. Here I am, standing locked up like a wild animal. I wonder to myself what people are thinking. Inside my head are visions of people joking. Making fun, looking at me as if I were scum. I have this terrible coldness inside of me, I know that something awful is happening, but I don't know how to stop it. It's almost like one of those silly

films. When the character discovers his daughter has been killed by the bad guy and sets out to exact his revenge.

I'm not sure if I can do this. All I wanted was to die, but I am denied even this simplest of requests. All the safe places in the world are gone. Even the sanctity of one's own coffin is no longer safe, and I wonder if there's an escape. I search inside my head for happy places and all I find are reminders. Reminders of what I have been forced to become. So much time has passed, so little is left. What do I tell my mother? My father? Do I tell them about the pit of pain the demon drags us all into? Do I tell them that when we die heaven awaits with its big pearly gates? All I have seen is hell, governed by soul-hungry beasts that will stop at nothing to shred us all. I'm in hell already, even when the sun is at its brightest, I am cold. It's like my soul is shivering, and I cannot control the sadness. It infests my being, changes my mood. Someone help me. Take me away. Save me from the demons that chase me even in death."

Eva shuddered. A cold spike of freezing recognition trickled down her back like an icicle. Eva had found what she was looking for. Now there were no options, she couldn't just walk away. The nurse breathed in deeply as though it was the last breath she was ever going to take. Eva knew that she wasn't herself, her pristine image had faded to a dull shadow, and inside she felt polluted. Something had forced its way into her mind and soul, she could feel its presence burning behind her eyes, it made her angry, deceitful, vengeful. The nurse rubbed anxiously at her palms as though she were summoning a magical genie to solve her problems. In the back of her mind she could hear them calling, whispering in the shadows like poltergeists.

CHAPTER THREE

Eva chewed deliberately at the end of her pencil; she swung it from one side of her mouth to the other as though she were trying to extract lead that did not exist. Her mind buzzed with frightening possibilities, possibilities that any rational mind would dismiss as childish fantasy. A long line of ash hung from the end of her cigarette. Eva barely noticed it fall to the floor as she threw the end into the ashtray. A thought passed her mind, and she stood up suddenly. Grabbing her jacket, she left the smouldering cigarette and made her way to the door. There was only one place that she could think of going to research her theory, and it was the one place she knew would be safe.

Eva boarded the number three bus with some trepidation. She had used public transport all her life, and yet she fidgeted with anxiety. It was almost as though the bus had become a vessel for harbouring bad memories. The nurse watched intensely as each new passenger boarded, she couldn't help but judge them. An old lady with a tartan shopping bag passed Eva's scrutiny with ease, whilst a young man wearing a hooded jacket was not so fortunate. Eva eyed him warily as he sat down, moving a little closer to the window to increase the distance parting them. She knew that she was perhaps being a little paranoid, yet she felt fragile and intimidated. Her closed behaviour did not go unnoticed, and she winced as she caught the odd glance from fellow passengers. Her curled-up, withdrawn posture was catching attention, and Eva attempted to straighten herself in the seat. She shuffled uncomfortably, finally making the decision to stand up and walk to the front of the bus. Her stop was not for another mile, but she just couldn't stay on this wheeled hell trap any longer. The bus driver reminded her that she had paid too much to get off at this stop. Eva shrugged her shoulders, a nervous smile crept across her face, and she shook her head.

"That's okay, I need some fresh air."

The driver shrugged his shoulders in an almost dismissive manner, and Eva breathed in deeply as her feet touched the cold stone slabs of the road. At least she could breathe out here; the lack of air in those buses was intolerable. Eva shook out her hair, running her fingers through the loose curls as though she were ridding them of lice. Shivering away the last of her anxiety, she began her twenty-minute walk to the library. Although the air was chilly, she decided that next time she would just walk. Failing that, she would get a taxi.

The library in Blackwater was surprisingly modern. The town itself had been around for hundreds of years, and the town square was littered with boards giving away interesting little snippets of Blackwater's history. Eva especially liked the notice board pinpointing the exact position of the last witch burning in the town. She could almost imagine people hopping off the spot with horror as they realised what they were standing on. Despite this, the library stood out like a testament to modern times in a town so embroiled with the past. Rummaging around in her bag, Eva finally found her library card. She need not have used it, however, as before her attack she would regularly hire out books. Eva smiled warmly at a red-haired woman as she entered the library.

"Eva! God, we haven't seen you in ages! Are you better? We heard about the incident," a large woman beamed at Eva from across the counter, the giant dimples in her cheeks indicated her glowing personality. Eva relaxed in her company.

"I'm fine, Shana, just took a little time to recuperate." Eva sat down on one of the library computer desks and laughed as Shana brought over a cup of coffee and a slice of banana cake.

"You still have a book out, Eva, but I just kept renewing it for you, just bring it in when you have the chance."

Eva put a hand to her mouth, "Oh no, I forgot about that, you know, I haven't even read it? I've been so caught up with other things lately."

Shana put a gentle hand on her shoulder whispering, "Don't worry about it, hun, us librarians have plenty of time to renew a few books. If there's anything you need, just give me a shout."

Eva smiled back, she was always welcome here, and in a strange way, it was almost as though the library had been with her through all the tough times in her life. Eva was sure to spend time here when she was troubled, it was so quiet and safe, and her thoughts could get lost in any fantasy she wanted. All she had to do was turn the pages and she could leave her life behind, if only for a few hours.

The nurse sat for a few minutes wondering where on earth to begin. If she were being honest, she didn't exactly know what it was she was searching for. Finally after a few false starts with the search engine, Eva finally typed in "Near-death experiences." Her computer screen jumped into life with streams of accounts, forums, and websites all dedicated to the subject. Eva hadn't realised just how popular the topic appeared to be, the problem now, was finding exactly what she was looking for. The volume of white light encounters and out-of-body experiences was exponential, but it wasn't what she was looking for, and after three hours she was about ready to give up. Eva shook her head; her eyes were beginning to lose their focus as the screen blared out its annoying fake light at her. Sighing heavily, Eva stood up; she paced back and forth across the library floor, holding her empty coffee cup like it was the chalice of God.

"Having trouble?" Shana popped her head around the corner like she was a beacon for Eva's problems.

"I can't find what I'm looking for." Eva shook her head in disappointment. "I just don't know what to research."

Shana folded her arms under her bosoms pushing them up until they were nearly touching her chin. "Have you tried describing it? I mean, sometimes if you just describe what it is you're looking for, the search engine finds something similar, and then you can take it from there."

Eva smirked, rolling her eyes, "If I had your brains, Shana, I'd be dangerous." The librarian laughed as she walked away – only Eva could be so complimentary.

Half-heartedly smoking her cigarette, Eva pondered over Shana's words. It was an almost impossible thing to describe without sounding ludicrous. Suddenly the nurse realised that she had forgotten something – It wasn't just about the image of the false angel that had appeared when she was at the very brink of life. When she was drifting, unconscious, it was the events that occurred in the real world that were the most worrying. It was that girl on the bus, her words, the fact that she had killed innocent people, children even that were what she needed to investigate. Returning to her chair, Eva began a new search. This time she was looking for something solid, concrete, something that was very real in this world. Murder. Eva began trawling through the search engine results on killings. Specifically murders where there seemed to be no reason for the perpetrator to commit such an act. More often than not the suspect would commit suicide before being caught, but there were a few cases where the individual was caught before he could commit his final act. It was in those newspaper reports that Eva wondered if perhaps she was beginning to find what she had been looking for. Eva printed off the cases that she felt were most relevant. Reading through them, the nurse began to wonder if she could dare believe her suspicions.

NEW YORK COURIER

August 24th, 1967

"The small backwater town of Cleveland was rocked yesterday by the shocking murder of a mother and her twin daughters. Mr David Sim attacked his wife and two daughters without provocation. The seemingly quite hard-working family man shot his wife in the back after murdering his twin daughters as they slept, before finally attempting to turn the gun on himself. Neighbours awoke to hear the first gunshots, and Mr Sim was interrupted before he could take his own life. Mr Reginald Burke, first man on the scene and neighbour to the Sim family, stated that he was in utter shock at the incident. He stated that Mr Sim was waving the gun around like a mad man shouting, 'They made me do it! We have to die, we all have to die.' Mr Sim is awaiting psychiatric treatment before being put to trial."

SILVERTON COMMUNITY PRESS
17th May 1973

'Five people were killed and two were seriously injured after an unwarranted attack from the top of the state building in Oakstown. Miss Leslie Charmichael, mother of three, took pot shots at passers-by as they shopped in the busy high street. Using a three-calibre rifle the shooter instantly killed five people, one of which a city doctor, and an off duty police officer, whilst lying in plain view on the roof of the building. Miss Charmichael apparently left her children with her estranged mother before climbing to the top of the building and commencing her crime. Police arrived to see the woman fall to her death, after apparently jumping from the roof. Onlookers state that Miss Charmichael threw flyers from the roof detailing the end of the world, and the coming of Satan's minions. Although not confirmed yet, early indications point to Miss Carmichael's belief that demons from beyond the grave had possessed her soul, coercing her to commit the crime.'

Eva shuddered as she scrambled up the rest of her printed articles, she had no need to read the rest, they all had the same thing in common. Eva prepared to leave the library, but before she could reach the door, she stopped. Something felt wrong. Eva shook slightly as she stood, her face began to drain of colour and she suddenly felt too terrified to stop the small dribble of saliva that crept its way down her chin. A cold had entered the walls of the library, an empty cold like the dormant voids of space. Eva blinked as her senses suddenly became aware of a sharpness. It was like burning sulphur, she broke free of her paralysis as her throat gagged against the acrid taste smothering her tonsils. Eva moved her eyes to the left, suddenly in front of her stood an old lady. It was the lady from the bus, she had an empty expressionless face, but underneath her skin, Eva could sense something stirring.

"You belong to us, you cannot escape," the old woman hissed at Eva, small droplets of spit spurted from the gaps between her brown, crumbling teeth. Eva shook her head, terrified. She dared not turn to look at the woman; the sulphuric atmosphere made Eva's eyes water, yet the knot in her stomach prevented her from blinking.

"You cannot escape us."

Eva struggled momentarily with the old woman, who appeared to have the strength of three adult men. Eva's eyes locked with the wrinkled, half-shut eyes of her aggressor; there was no light in the fading blue of the old woman's irises, just the cold stale wane of death. Eva wriggled for a moment attempting to break free from the confrontation. Over the head of the stooped old woman, Eva realised that they had attracted some attention. Several other library attendants whispered among themselves as they watched, and Eva noticed from the corner of her eye a black suited man hovering near the fiction section. The nurse looked away and then quickly back as she realised that he was again the same dark-suited man that hovered outside her hospital room and outside the room of the comatose Louise Turnbull.

"Eva? You okay? What's going on?" Shana appeared from behind the woman and broke the confrontation. The old woman edged away from Eva, using her walking stick like it was the only thing keeping her up straight.

"I've gotta go," Eva whispered back between tremors.

"Eva?" Shana questioned the nurse again, this time with a little more panic in her tone.

"Be careful, Shana, something's not right, but I'm working on it. I'll stop it I promise," Eva blurted out at her librarian friend, quickly sliding a glance back towards the fiction section of the library, but the man in the black suit had gone. Eva quickly made a break for the doors, carrying her news clippings haphazardly under her armpit. Shana looked on after her; rubbing her arms, she suddenly felt a chill and began closing the windows of the library.

Returning to the sanctity of her flat, Eva collapsed onto her bed. Her clothes and hair were soaked with the persistent drizzle from outside, but she cared little about it. Exhausted from the three-mile walk and emotionally broken, she gave in to her body's demands and closed her eyes. Sleep came without effort, and so did a barrage of twisted imagery. Eva twitched uneasily on the bed as her mind spewed a vomit of disturbing dreams. The nightmares came quickly, thickly polluting the safe environment of her unconscious mind. She was back in the park; the rain was coming down so heavily that she could barely lift her eyelids to watch where she was going. She was running, her heels were sinking into the wet mud, and she could hear them behind her, relentlessly chasing. Suddenly, she stopped, like all hope of escape had vanished from her soul; she turned to face her pursuer. As the rain fell down between her eyes and his, she slumped onto her knees. Adam stood before her, his face wore a smile she did not recognise, and Eva suddenly lost herself in the pit of sorrow she had become so familiar with.

"Why?!" Eva blurted out into the night.

"This is what you want, isn't it? To be with me again?" Eva took a sharp intake of breath as Adam forced her chin up to look at him.

"We can be together again, you know how."

Eva shook her head weakly in a vain attempt at defiance.

Adam dropped her chin roughly. "It's your fault, Eva. It's your fault I'm here. I asked you to stay but you left, and now look at me!" Eva howled out her sobs as she watched Adam's eyes turn black; sinking back into his skull, they became glazed and lifeless. Eva watched in horror as the skin covering his body began to flake and fall at her feet. Scrambling up, the nurse attempted to run. Instead she was falling, falling so fast that she could not catch her breath, suddenly she hit the bottom.

Waking with a start, Eva sat up. She was on the floor in her bedroom, her newspaper clippings spread all around her like cheap confetti. Eva rubbed at her face with the back of her hand. Her skin was wet with the tears that were still streaming down her face. Using the edges of her bedspread, she pulled herself up onto her knees. Eva left her face buried in the softness of the duvet, it was as though this was the only comfort that she would experience. Finally she negotiated her way into the bathroom, her chest felt tight and she struggled for a second to catch her breath. Looking into the mirror, she hung her head. A woman stared back at her, her hair, dishevelled and matted; it clung to her head in damp clumps. There was no make-up on this pale face, just a white canvas of misery. Filling the sink with water, the nurse began washing her face. She winced for a second as her finger caught the underside of her chin. Lifting her head, Eva frowned to see the familiar red swelling of burned flesh.

"Damn you, Adam!" she shouted out as she slammed her fists onto the porcelain sink. "It was not my fault! It was yours," she whispered into the bowl, before retiring to the living room for a cigarette.

Outside, Blackwater's streets were filled with the noise of sirens. Two miles away a bus lay on its side, the crippled bonnet lying unceremoniously on the roof of a blue car. On the pavement lay the passengers, side by side, like skittles in the bowling alley. Faint sobs filled the air as dazed and injured people made their way towards those in uniform. From the side of the bus an old woman climbed out. Using her walking stick as a lever she clambered over the body of another passenger before slowly resuming her walk down the pavement.

CHAPTER FOUR

Eva lifted her head from the side of the arm chair as she heard what sounded like knocking. It was light and only consisted of three raps for a start, but gradually became heavy and more persistent the longer she ignored it. Rubbing at the stiffness in her neck, she made her way to the front door. The nurse was in no hurry as she slowly meandered along the hallway. Eva began unlatching the door then stopped as she took a peak through the spy glass instead. She closed her eyes in annoyance, cursing as she continued to unlatch the door.

"Hi, Dr Wellar, how are you?" Eva smiled sweetly between her grated teeth.

"Hi, Eva. I just thought I'd pop round to pick up that file you took from my office, and of course to remind you that your next session is tomorrow."

Eva stood speechless for a second; she couldn't decide whether to deny knowledge of the stolen file or to just hand it over.

"Fancy a cuppa?" Eva smirked at herself as she realised her feeble attempt to change the subject was futile. Dr Wellar looked around suspiciously as Eva removed the newspaper clippings from the chair so that he could sit down. Before Eva had had the chance to return with the cup of tea, Dr Wellar had found the stolen file and was sitting with it on his knee. Eva said nothing as she tentatively sipped at her brew.

"I don't suppose you can tell me why you wanted this file."

Eva looked up and shrugged her shoulders. The nurse had not prepared herself for this moment, and had not had the chance to think of a suitable explanation.

"It's something personal that I'm working on." Eva's response was quick and lacked further elaboration. The psychiatrist laughed as he ran a hand through his hair.

"You do know that what you did was theft? And that you could very well be prosecuted for this?"

Eva looked at the floor before continuing. "I was just borrowing it; I would have put it back."

Dr Wellar bit at his lip in disbelief. "Eva, this is someone's personal file, you above all others must recognise the importance of patient confidentiality."

Eva nodded her head and lit a cigarette. "Yes, yes, I do, but this was important, there were some things I had to know."

"Why this file?"

Eva sat back trying to work out how she was going to explain herself, carefully she continued. "I was working on the night this woman killed those people, it was the same night I was attacked. I saw her and she spoke to me, I just wanted to know a little bit more about her." Eva shrugged her shoulders as though she had said the most normal thing in the world. The psychiatrist nodded his head.

"I didn't know you had met Louise before."

Eva rolled the cigarette around between her fingers. "She grabbed my arm and said something … strange; anyway, after I was attacked, I saw something that I think she might have been warning me about." Eva waved her arms around, almost to dismiss her own comments as childish gibberish.

"What kind of thing?"

Eva rolled her eyes aware that it was at this point that she really would be labelled as crazy. "I don't know, some kind of entity, I think." Eva shook her head. "Look, you're probably going to think this is all the ridiculous ramblings of a troubled mind anyway, so take the file back and tell the police if you want to. I'm probably safer in jail anyway."

Dr Wellar raised his eyebrows, "You know, that's what Louise said, too, that she would be safer in jail?" Eva looked up and bit her lip. "Besides," the doctor continued, "You're not the only one who would be in trouble, I would be in the shit for losing it, so let's leave it at that, shall we?"

Eva breathed out aware that she had been lucky this time. It seemed apparent to Eva that Dr Wellar was showing a flicker of leniency that she had not expected from him. Whilst he was correct that it was probable he would receive a reprimand for losing the file, he was a smart guy, and she felt sure he could cover his own ass.

"What are all these newspaper clippings?" Dr Wellar loudly broke into Eva's thoughts. The nurse looked about her suddenly aware that her home looked as though she were gathering newspaper to pack up her belongings with.

"Louise said that she had seen some kind of demon," Eva whispered. "I think I saw something similar, and when I did a bit of research, I discovered that so did these people."

The doctor flicked through some of the clippings. "Eva, these people were murderers, you're not a killer."

Eva nodded her head quickly. "I know, but I don't think these people were either, look at Louise, does she match your typical killer? I think these people were forced into it by something … I just haven't worked out what yet." There was a curious period of silence where Dr Wellar' raised eyebrow met Eva's odd commentary. The nurse breathed in, holding her breath for a second as she realised how ridiculous she was beginning to sound.

"Maybe we can talk about it at your session tomorrow," said Dr Wellar.

Eva sighed realising that she was back to being the patient again.

"If I could talk to Louise, maybe –"

"Absolutely out of the question," Dr Wellar broke in before she could finish her sentence. "Louise is locked up at the psychiatric hospital, and believe me she is in no condition for accepting visits, especially from other patients." Eva rolled her tongue over her teeth; she couldn't help but feel angry about being labelled as another 'nut case'.

Dr Wellar put down his cup and stood up, "Thank you for the tea, Eva, I will see you tomorrow." Eva managed a wry smile as he left her flat, which quickly turned into a grimace as soon as the door was closed behind him. There was no way that she would be attending her session tomorrow.

Eva sat down heavily on the chair, her pride was bruised, and she hated the fact that someone might think of her as crazy. The nurse had always been careful to maintain her credibility. She was proud to be as educated as she was, and the fact that someone more educated than her was questioning her reasoning was almost unbearable. The nurse banged her heel off the bottom of the couch as though she were releasing her pent up frustration. Dr Wellar was her colleague; in fact she had been present at several of his ward consultations with other patients, including her dear friend Mrs Stephen. His awkward authoritarian attitude angered her; he could at least give her the respect she deserved as a professional, if nothing else.

Eva knew that she had to get away. Dr Wellar would surely start hounding her if she failed to turn up, and despite the fact that she would probably be putting her career at risk, she decided to leave Blackwater. Eva's decision was impulsive and lacked the privilege of proper thought. The nurse had always had this tendency, although she tried to keep it reserved for weekends only. However, now that everyday had become a weekend since her absence from work, she allowed her impulsiveness to take over. Eva began to pack a small suitcase, she wasn't planning on spending more than two weeks away, any more than that and someone might report her as missing, but it would give her the time she needed to sort things out, or at least to make an attempt to research this thing a little bit further, without the prying eyes and listening ears. Eva racked her brain on where she could go, her parents were dead, and the few cousins she did have didn't really bother to keep in touch. Using up the last of her savings, Eva booked two weeks in a small bed and breakfast in County Main. It was over one hundred miles away, far enough to avoid attention but not to far as to disappear completely. Eva had never visited County Main before, but the picture on the internet portrayed a quiet country town nestled in a tranquil valley. Perfect for a quiet retreat, and the possibility of some social seclusion.

Like everything in Eva's life, her flat was oddly neat and square in appearance. Her clothes were tightly pressed and folded into neat packages in her wardrobes and dresser drawers. She had a place for everything and everything had its place, the chaotic fashion in which she tossed these clothes into her suitcase suggested a dramatic change in her pristine character. Eva's packing was rushed, haphazard, and strangely careless. The tight lines in her shirts and trousers became violated and crushed as she crammed as much as she could into the case. The nurse had always been oddly regimented in the way that she kept her personal belongings, she liked everything to be clean, neat, and in an order that suited her lifestyle. Since her attack nearly three months ago now, she had begun to let things slip. A thin layer of dust on her mantelpiece and cupboard handles suggested that they had not seen a cloth for a long time; instead other things had infested her flat and life. Newspaper clippings, drawings, ashtrays, and piles of dirty unwashed clothes. Eva cursed aggressively as the zip struggled to close with the weight of the clothes inside. Neglecting her rancid bins, she grabbed her keys and case, closing the door heavily behind her as though she were saying goodbye to an old lover.

The nurse couldn't help but feel an odd sense of relief as she quickly made her way towards the train station. Her case with its small plastic wheels rattled noisily as she dragged it over the badly paved streets, but Eva didn't care. She felt as though it didn't matter who saw her. She was leaving, and it was as though a great iron block had been lifted from her chest. Blackwater had begun to feel exactly that, black, murky, somewhat dangerous veiled in its mask of homeliness.

Home, the nurse wasn't sure what that was now, but the sensation of being somewhere fresh and new was enough to spur her into forward action. As Eva approached the station, she was surprised at how busy it was. The gathering of people in the ticket office and on the platforms made her wary. It was one thing for someone to pass a glance at you on the street, but another one entirely if a person had the chance to actually stand and watch you.

Eva stood uneasily on the platform, occasionally hopping from one foot to another as though she had hot bunions on her toes. The nurse was desperate to avoid too much attention; every newspaper stand in the town carried the news of yesterday's bus crash, an accident that Eva had strangely managed to avoid. The nurse shivered, the overpowering feeling that she was carrying death around in her pocket prevented her from feeling anything other than dread. Eva wondered quite suddenly whether it was herself that was the demon. She shrugged the sensation off as the train crept up to the platform; she didn't want to find an excuse not to board it, although she knew there were plenty.

Eva cringed as she sat gingerly on the dusty fabric of the orange and grey seats. She purposefully positioned herself on the last seat of the carriage, as close to the doors as was humanly possible. Thankfully (in her opinion) there were only four other passengers in the compartment she had chosen. A young couple sat opposite her three seats back, and to the right and behind them a gentleman in a rather coarse-looking tweed suit sat, squinting awkwardly at his newspaper. Eva allowed herself to relax a little; slumping into the seat, she stared at the drizzle coated windows. It had been raining like this for three days now. Eva wondered if a black cloud were to permanently follow her around, but that was nothing new, not for her.

The clicking of the trains wheels on its tracks was oddly soothing, and Eva felt that she could quite comfortably close her eyes and forget the world for a while. The nurse felt as though she were in a constant state of turmoil. It was as if everything she knew about herself had been thrown into a tumble dryer, and she was left to sift through the remnants of her character, attempting to piece back together the parts of herself that she recognised whilst adopting those that she did not. There was a burning sense of frustration that welled in her stomach, recent events had confused her logical sense of reality, and her highly educated mind struggled to understand events which were so disjointed from scientific reasoning.

Eva rubbed away the thoughts from her mind with the back of her hand. As she stared out the window, the nurse noticed that she was being scrutinized, a face peered back at her in the glass; despite the rain's distortion, the nurse could tell that it was not her own. Turning round, Eva looked into the face of a beautiful tanned woman. She was sat next to a young man who appeared embarrassed by their eye contact. Eva looked away herself, aware of how uncomfortable the situation was. Despite Eva's attempts to fix her attention upon something else, she couldn't help but feel that she was being stared at. She could feel the young woman's eyes burning holes into the back of head, and although Eva tried her hardest to ignore the woman, she ended up looking straight back at her.

The nurse was almost jealous of the woman's beauty. She was definitely of Greek or Italian descent. Her olive skin and large brown eyes were testament to her ancestry. Eva eyed the beautifully straightened, chocolate brown hair and wondered why she could not have been graced with such features. Still, the girl had nothing on top, and Eva felt that that was one thing she had nothing to complain about.

Eva shuffled around in her seat. The girl's constant staring was becoming a bit of a nuisance. It also didn't help with Eva's continuing paranoia about anybody who dared to come within two feet of her. Eva was relieved when another couple of people entered the carriage at the next stop, even if it was two young men of apparent forces background. They came armed with a pack of cards and a carry case of six beers. Eva rolled her eyes, thinking about how much she fancied a bottle of Jacob's Creek. Maybe she could relax tonight with one in her hotel room. The idea was appealing and served to distract her thoughts for a second from the persistent staring of the woman in the window glass. The young nurse was beginning to feel enraged and was about to ask the beautiful woman with the chocolate hair if she could help her with something, when the man in the tweed suit plunked himself down beside her. Eva jumped with a start, lifting her arms as if to defend herself from this unknown intruder of her space. He leaned in towards Eva's face, and the nurse backed away as an odour of peppermint filled her nostrils.

"I implore you to get off this train at the next stop. It's not safe; you must do as I tell you,"

Eva frowned at him. "What?"

"Please trust me!"

Eva continued her frown as the man exited her seat and returned to his own behind the young couple. Suddenly Eva felt intense fear. She had been found again by someone or something, and now she felt certain that everything would go wrong.

Eva desperately looked around her, the two young armed forces recruits continued to play cards and drink beer. They were too far away for Eva to contact them without raising attention. Eva then turned to the obvious answer, discreetly beckoning; she attempted to raise the attention of her silent watcher. The young woman stared at Eva with such open-eyed wideness that the nurse was sure she must have understood her beckons. Eva frowned as she received nothing from the woman but the same cold, hard stare. Eva tried again and then stopped as the young woman's male counterpart shot a warning glance in her direction.

Eva could take no more. Standing up abruptly, she hurried to the doors of the train. From behind the closed doors of the carriage she saw the tweed suit rise from his seat. Eva hopped about from one foot to another as she desperately willed the train to arrive at its next destination. She knew that it would not be the correct stop, but she couldn't give a shit if it arrived in Iraq, as long as it arrived quickly. Before the train had even stopped at Oakwood Station, Eva was busy trying to prise the doors open. In her haste to exit the carriage, she fell through them, landing heavily onto the platform, skinning her knees.

"Shit," she cursed under her breath before quickly scrambling to her feet. The nurse looked vainly for the exit to the station, but before she could find a route out, the man in the tweed suit approached her. Eva stood back defensively. The man raised his hands in a submissive manner before reaching into his pocket for ID. Eva continued to step backward until the man threw his identification at her forcing Eva to catch it.

"I'm sorry if I frightened you; that was not my intention. I was just trying to warn you," the man explained.

Eva looked suspiciously at the small plastic card he had thrust at her. She instantly recognised the medical symbol and handed it sheepishly back to the doctor.

"No, I'm sorry," she whispered back, "I got a little spooked." The doctor nodded his head before replacing the card back into his pocket.

"I was sitting behind that young couple on the train when I realised that something wasn't quite right. I mean that woman didn't move a muscle the entire journey."

Eva nodded her head in response recognising her own communication difficulties.

"I think she may have been dead. I think the man that was with her may have been responsible for it, too."

Eva put a hand to her mouth in shock.

"I've already called the police," the doctor continued, "They are going to stop the train at the next station. I saw you were on your own and wanted to warn you." Eva nodded her head in appreciation, "Thank you." The nurse let out a sarcastic laugh. "You know, I'm a nurse, you would have thought I would have recognised it myself."

The doctor shook his head, "It's not so easy to spot when you're not looking for it. We all die, don't we? But it's not often you find yourself looking at a corpse, although I expect you've seen a few."

Eva nodded a reply and watched in silence as the doctor made his way to the reception at the station. The nurse stood dumbfounded on the platform as other passengers pushed past her. She was reminded of how isolated and alone she was and fought the temptation to rush up to the doctor and blurt out everything that had happened. Swallowing hard against the temptation, she bent down to pick up her case.

Eva waited for the doctor to leave before entering the ticket station to get a number for a taxi. She'd had just about enough of public transport in recent days, and couldn't be bothered waiting for another train. The nurse fidgeted as she waited in the ticket office for her ride to arrive. The man behind the desk continued to read his newspaper as though she wasn't there, and Eva began to feel the annoying palpitations of her heart irritating her chest. Eva's anxiety got the better of her from time to time, and she suffered with secondary stress symptoms as commonly as she caught a cold. She rubbed at her forehead as she attempted to take slow deep breaths unnoticed. She wasn't worried about herself, but the man behind the desk troubled her, however irrational, the nurse began to worry who would be next on her death list. As the bright white glow from the roof of a car arrived in the car park, Eva felt she could begin to breathe again. The nurse was careful not to engage herself in too much conversation with the cab driver simply stating her destination with a polite "thank you." Eva began to consider the possibility that those around her were safer the less contact she had with them.

The drive to Eva's destination was uneventful, and she was glad of it. The driver seemed the quiet type, and Eva relaxed in the knowledge that not only would she be left to her own thoughts but that she wouldn't appear rude ignoring him. Eva smiled briefly as she realised just how much the driver valued his cab. It was almost like a family home in the front. He had pictures of his family on the dashboard and an adamant no-smoking sign nestled perfectly around a picture of a little girl. Clearly a man who loved his family enough to protect them even at work. Eva looked away from his pictures, suddenly realising that she had no one to protect or love; in fact, she wasn't even sure if there was anyone out there that would give a damn about her. If she were to be honest, Mercy Hospital was her love; it was the one thing she climbed out of bed for every morning. Now, she was leaving that behind too. The nurse was becoming deeply troubled by recent events. It was as though wherever she went this thing, or what-ever it was, followed. The problem was that it didn't just bring fear for Eva, it brought death. The bus, the train, Eva wondered what would be next, and whether she should be near anyone at all. Eva reflected back upon Dr Wellar's' words about Louise and the other people in her newspaper clippings. They had all physically killed or been responsible for deaths. Eva wasn't like them, she hadn't killed anyone and neither did she intend to. Eva stared out of the taxi window, wondering what made her so different. True, she had not physically injured anyone, and yet it appeared that wherever she went death followed. People were dying when she was around, and it didn't seem to matter where it was she met them. At that moment, Eva decided that she must distance herself from those whom she may inadvertently hurt, keeping to herself wasn't a problem; in fact, she preferred it that way.

The nurse marvelled as the high-rise, tightly cramped streets of the city dissolved away into the distance. The taxi driver seemed to know exactly where he was going, and the nurse soon found herself travelling on quieter, less-assuming roads. The cold metal street lights were gone, replaced by the tall wooden trunks of trees. The nurse breathed in deeply as the faint smell of forest and wet grass crept through the car's ventilation system. She sucked up the air through her nostrils as though it were a balloon of pure oxygen. She closed her eyes as she sat back into her seat, the sudden temptation to stay out here in the wilderness was appealing, forgetting the troubles she had encountered in the city; maybe it would all go away if she just kept to herself, maybe she would be okay on her own. Eva sighed as her daydream floated away with her moment of tranquillity. The nurse knew that if they could find her in her dreams they could find her anywhere.

County Main was exactly as she had imagined it would be. Giant rolling hills with stone-crested peaks lined the road through to the village. It was as though she were entering another world from another time, a place only to be found between the pages of a book. Eva was delighted by the single-track road and the absence of traffic and streets. The population couldn't be more than fifty, and that meant less risk to all involved. There was a sense of calm about the old-fashioned picked and pointed stone walls of the cottages, their gardens immaculate and proudly maintained. Eva wondered if perhaps County Main was like a retirement village for all those who had made their living and now had time to do the simple things in life, such as gardening. The nurse stared with admiration at the straight rows of red and yellow rose beds. They were nearly as pristine as her mother had kept hers. Eva remembered spending long hours in the garden with her mother as a child; they would take away all the dead heads from the rose bushes and sometimes Eva's mum would let her spray them with the insecticide she used to keep the green fly away. The nurse was warmed by the memories that this village had triggered; it was almost as though she was meant to come here, if only to escape her torment for a short while.

Eva's bed and breakfast was on the main road through the town. A simple B & B sign swung from a small wooden stake, and as Eva paid the taxi driver his extortionate fee, she knew that here she would be safe. It was almost six o'clock by the time she had arrived, and Eva was left ringing the door-bell for ten minutes before someone finally opened the door. Eva blushed slightly as the middle-aged owner turned up at the door in his pyjamas and slippers.

"I'm so sorry I'm late," Eva whispered, "I'm afraid I boarded the wrong train."

"Not to worry, lass, you're the only resident we have just now anyway."

Eva breathed a sigh of relief at the welcome she received and gladly followed her host to the room she had booked.

"Having a little break are we?"

Eva nodded her head in sincere agreement.

"A break from the world," she responded with a smile, and the man winked as though he knew exactly where she was coming from.

"Breakfast at nine," he shouted behind him as he closed the door.

Eva fell backwards onto the bed and then grimaced slightly at the hardness of the mattress. Still, what could she expect for twenty eight pounds a night? Eva turned on the television and slipped off her shoes. She wished now that she had bought that bottle of wine, but settled for a cup of coffee instead. Aware that she would be here for some time, Eva took out her newspaper clippings and arranged them neatly on the table. Grabbing a pen, she wrote down names and dates and towns, starting with the earliest and working up to the most modern. She became aware that she needed to know more about the background of these people and wondered if County Main had a library. It seemed unlikely that she would find an internet café here, especially considering the only available channels were on Freeview, and they were sketchy at best.

Eva had only managed to collect ten articles from the library in Blackwater, but she had the feeling that there were hundreds if not thousands more cases. She needed to find something that brought them all together, some kind of similarity that went past the fact that they were all murder cases. The nurse was already aware that she and Miss Turnbull had both had near-death experiences prior to the happenings. She wondered if the same could be said about these people, too. Eva rolled a pencil around in her mouth, chewing with her right molars and then her left. Surely every human being has the capability of being a killer? Not everyone has to have a near-death experience to become a murderer. Eva knew that her research would have to be carefully implemented. She was looking for a majority, not just the odd one or two, and to do this, she was going to need to look at hundreds of cases.

Eva sat in the chair of her hotel room. She clasped her hands on her knees and slowly rocked back and forth. Her mind seemed settled at one point on the green and blue patterned carpet, and her thoughts and feelings had slowly ebbed away like the retreating tide. There were so many questions, such undeniable proof that there was something else pushing her, driving her, forcing her, and yet she was lost, lost in a schizophrenic swirl of confusion and madness. It was them, she knew it was them. The false angels. She longed to be near them, to feel their soft waves of electricity around her fingers, the smell of their presence in her nose.

As Eva allowed herself to drown in the fantasy of their presence, she felt that she was almost there with them, wallowing in the atmosphere of Adam, nurturing and comforting her thoughts. Reality was far away now; they were not whimsical ghosts of her imagination. They were real, and always with her. Eva nestled her head deep into the palms of her hands. She couldn't help the tears; they burned like fire as they dripped between the gaps of her fingers. There was something hollow and empty in her stomach. God, she knew that she could never really be there; she couldn't just reach out and touch him. It hurt so much, like she had been dragged away from him in some horrific car wreck, and she knew he would never see or talk to him again, unless of course she joined him, unless she let the false angels take her body, her life. Eva wallowed deeply in her own misery. It suffocated her, drowning her like wraps of wet cotton wool, invading her ears, nose, and mouth. Eva felt that she could just give in, why should she fight when it was so much easier just to drown?

The nurse suddenly stood up, pacing around aimlessly back and forth. She caught sight of the phone sitting innocently on the bedside table. It was like a sudden ray of sunshine, perhaps offering some kind of medicated plaster for her bruised and bleeding emotions. Eva searched in her notebook for the extension number of the psychiatrist, at least hearing his voice would bring reality back, if only for a moment. The young woman felt so worked up that by the time she had found his name, her fingers were shaking so much she could barely key in the numbers. Eva drummed her fingers rhythmically and impatiently on the wooden table as she waited for what seemed to be an eternity for someone to answer her.

"Hello? Hello?" Eva pressed for an answer, a tired-sounding voice responded, but Eva did not care to register it. "I'd like to speak to Dr Wellar please; it's urgent." There was a subtle cough from down the telephone as the receptionist for the psychiatric ward made clear her annoyance at Eva's demands.

"I'm afraid he's left the office; I can take a message if you'd like." The secretary on the other end of the phone paused for a response, and Eva suddenly realised that she had made a mistake, dropping the receiver quickly back onto its pedestal she sat back down on the bed. The nurse cursed at herself; she couldn't believe after all that she had been through that one moment of fear had made her nearly blow her entire get away. Eva rubbed at her face; she felt so alone, so vulnerable that she just wanted someone to talk to, someone to listen to her fears, someone to help her rationalise her own mad ramblings. Eva shook her head.

"No harm done," she whispered to herself as she paced the floor of her room. Her constant re-tracing of her steps began to slowly clear her head, and in this clarity she began to wonder if her decision to come here had not been a rash one; the town may not support the resources required for her research. Eva sighed; curling up onto the bed, she was too tired to think. Tomorrow she would scout around the town and see exactly what County Main had to offer.

Back in the city of Blackwater, Dr Wellar picked at the skin surrounding his cuticles. He winced slightly as a small spot of blood trickled onto his thumb nail. He wiped it onto the back pocket of his trousers before continuing to stare hard at the two drawings placed before him; shaking his head, he brushed them aside before taking a second look.

"This is ridiculous," he chastised himself, but struggled to get past the creeping feeling that slithered up his spine. Taking a drink of scotch, he brushed a hand through his thinning hair. The two pictures were almost identical; despite the obvious artistic licence that both drawers had, the form and colour were the same. Richard slipped one drawing back into Louise Turnbull's file, and the other he stuffed back into Eva's. Every bone in his logical body told him that there must be another explanation for the similarity – maybe Eva and Louise had discussed it in the hospital and Eva had recreated it herself. The psychiatrist recalled Eva's words at the flat and realised that she had mentioned seeing something during her period of unconsciousness, she had drawn it, and so had Louise. Dr Wellar instantly picked up the telephone, dialling the number like he knew it was burned into his memory. He tapped his fingers on the desk impatiently until someone answered.

"Chief Inspector Hollands, Blackwater police station." The voice was droll but distinctive.

"Hey, Andrew. It's Richard; listen, I need a favour."

CHAPTER FIVE

Eva's chosen place for seclusion was exactly that. Other than a small post office selling cigarettes and sweets, and a red phone box, there was little else to be found in County Main. The locals were friendly, although it appeared that they did not get much in the way of visitors, as her sudden appearance had attracted more attention than she had wanted. The village was curious in the way that it was laid out. The houses were dotted randomly across the countryside; the roads appeared to suit the homes, meandering like tiny grey snakes up and down the small foothills. Occasionally one would just stop, as though it were a forgotten path to a forgotten home. Eva preferred this natural look, inner-city streets were so stiff, so regimented. Straight and wide like a simple crossword.

Following the small street down to the end of the village, Eva came across a large stream meandering its way down into the valley. It was almost like the scene from a film, and as Eva slipped off her shoes and allowed the water to trickle over her feet, she imagined that she were a character in such a film. The pace of life was so slow in County Main. It was as though everything had stopped, and nobody cared whether tomorrow came or not. Eva wished that she could stay and forget about everything. Perhaps one day she could return, when she was old and grey, with the cares of the world little more than a distant memory on a mantel piece. Such happy, safe thoughts were uncommon to Eva's troubled mind, and it was seldom now since her attack that she could just engage herself in flights of fancy.

County Main reminded her of her youth, Eva had been happy as a child. Her life had been simple then, just Eva and her mum in a little cottage not unlike the ones in here; A warm coal fire in the hearth to ward off the windy October nights in the countryside. As a teenager she was curious of the city, eager to discover the wonders of suburban life. Now, as a woman, she would give anything to be back there. Back next to the fire and the innocence of her childhood.

The wind blew softly in the nurse's face, gently washing away loose strands of hair from her chin. She closed her eyes to dwell in the freedom of the moment. Her strict routine of tightly pulled hair and angled corners of make-up and clothing seemed so senseless and dull. She missed the freedom of the great outdoors once so familiar to her. Eva felt herself yearning once again to be that child running barefooted through the tall grasses of the meadow outside her house. Eva had sworn that she would never leave there, but with time brought age, and age brought the necessity of a career and money. The nurse wondered for a second whether the stone-built cottage and its white picket fence were still there. After her mother's death, the cottage was sold and the leftover money had funded Eva's university degree and bought the first flat herself and Adam had lived in. There had been many times since then that she had wished that she had kept her childhood home.

Eva discovered quite suddenly that she had achieved nothing by coming here. She had no means of doing research, and without those means, she couldn't possibly hope to figure out what was going on. Eva had always been clear, oddly translucent in her thinking. Problems and barriers were worked through in a progressive, methodically logical manner. Never before had the nurse found herself drifting amongst confused decisions with little or no clear path to guide her way. Even in the most traumatic periods of her life she had had focus. A check-list neatly organised in her mind: 1) Call the funeral director, 2) Register the death, 3) Call the insurance company, 4) Let the relatives and friends know, 4) Arrange the flowers, 5) Cry. Now, there was no check-list forming in her mind, just a cloud of blue electric mist and an overbearing urgency to be sick. Snapping herself out of her daydream, she slipped her shoes back on. The nurse grimaced slightly as she made her way along the loosely gravelled path. The wetness of her feet made her court shoes slip uncomfortably on her heel, and Eva could already feel the beginnings of a blister forming. It quickly became apparent to the nurse that her plan to escape was flawed not only in its bad planning, but in its poor execution as well. It appeared Eva's already-stretched budget would have to suffer the blow of a new pair of trainers, too. Returning to the post office, Eva hoped to find out where the nearest town with a library was.

"You young people don't do very well without technology, do you?" said the post master, as he smirked at Eva, who grinned back in near embarrassment. "Twenty miles is the nearest town with populace enough to require a library, Granville, that's right, you can phone for a taxi if you like." Eva accepted the man's generous offer then bought another packet of cigarettes from him in an attempt to buy his thanks.

Eva grimaced as she exited the taxi for the second time in two days. She was fast spending her cash, and would soon have to use her credit cards to boost her funds. She knew it meant sure financial disaster, but nothing else seemed to matter much anymore, nothing was as important as chasing down her false angel. Eva exited the taxi in Granville town centre. There was no library to be found, and she ended up having to ask a passer-by for directions. The library was situated on a side street at the far east of town. There were the usual shops to be found along the high street, including a Victoria Wine that Eva made a mental note of as she passed. The streets were nicely cobbled with multi-coloured stones, and every few feet sat a beautifully arranged barrel, graced with flowers of the season. Eva had never seen such a carefully manicured town before, and she looked around with interest as she walked. A large stone clock tower sat in the square and underneath it stood tarpaulin-covered stalls selling fruit and various trinkets. Eva stopped for a quick look; she felt relaxed and thought that perhaps she might find something of interest. In the very last stall a woman sat, she weaved expertly at some coloured wool, and Eva watched with interest. The woman did not acknowledge Eva's presence by lifting her head; instead she spoke directly to her as if she already knew that she was there.

"See anything you fancy?"

Eva jumped slightly not aware herself that the woman had noticed her.

"Oh, I'm just browsing, they're very beautiful," said Eva, as she lifted some croquet from the table.

"You can take that one if you like, maybe it will bring you luck." The woman continued her weaving, still not lifting her head. Eva put the table cloth down, quickly shaking her head.

"No, no, I couldn't."

Suddenly the weaver got up off her seat and approached the nurse. It was at that point that Eva realised she was blind.

"Please take it. I want you to have it." The woman handed the cloth back to Eva before continuing, "Some life is meant to be here, child; we cannot stop it just because we don't understand it." Eva swallowed hard, her words appeared to mean nothing, and yet they reverberated around in her head like a bouncing ball. "The library is just around the corner." The woman pointed with a long delicate finger. Eva thanked the woman and continued her walk to the library; she was nearly at the front doors before she realised that she had not told her where she was going.

Eva walked in as though she had to hand in her dissertation the next day. Granville Library was exactly like the town it resided in. Sweeping lines of precisely organised book shelves formed a double row of arcs in the large oval room. A copious bouquet of flowers mimicking those of the town centre sat on the front desk. Eva smiled at the disregard for the "books and water" rule so often found in city libraries. The floors were heavily carpeted with a rich red pile, and Eva was glad of the silence as she walked upon it, her court shoes were deft at signalling her presence as she walked with a 'clip-clop' on the more common solid wooden floors. Eva was delighted to see that the technology suite of the library was in a room to the far left. The old-fashioned ideology of "pick up a book and read it" was not tainted by modern technological advances, and the peacefulness of the room had been carefully preserved.

It was incredibly easy to find what she was looking for here; the library seemed to have a penchant for old newspapers and articles, which was exactly what she needed. Unable to leave the library with the original copies, Eva spent her time hovering around the printer, aware that she was blocking its use for other library visitors. She smiled sweetly as the occasional glance of annoyance made its way from the computer chairs in the technology suite. Eva's phone suddenly rang out in the silence of the room, and the librarian offered Eva a quick glance to suggest that she should silence it quickly. The nurse obliged and quickly left the room in order to answer it; normally she would just ignore the call, but the number was from the hospital and she sensed that it was important. Eva stared blankly ahead of her as the sister spoke softly down the receiver. Eva bit her lip as she thanked her former superior, dropping the phone into her pocket as though it were worthless. Eva knew that one day she would hear this news, and that she would finally pay for a friendship that she wasn't supposed to have encouraged. Professional distance, that's what it's all about. For Eva, however, it was just too cold to implement. Quickly gathering her papers, Eva telephoned for yet another taxi to take her back home to Blackwater. She wasn't going to stay; in fact, she didn't even think that she could handle the funeral, but she owed it to Edna to at least return and pay her respects. The librarian eyed Eva with a sense of sympathy as she gave the nurse her change from the printouts. Eva's eyes, although dry, portrayed a sense of grief that only someone who had lost a friend would recognise, and the librarian smiled with understanding as Eva quickly made her exit.

Eva sat quietly on the bench at the Mercy Hospital. Her thoughts were so heavy that she could almost feel them dragging on her heart. This had once been such a place of comfort, a small secluded spot where the nurse could watch the summer flowers and dream her lunch hour away. Now, even the autumn blooms of the roses failed to raise Eva's chin from her knees. Eva felt so angry, angry that she should find herself yet again in a pit of despair that she had done nothing to warrant. She had lost so much, everyone that she had loved, and now those she cared for too. It was as though the world had designed a plan that she did not fit into, like a jigsaw with a piece that just didn't quite match. Eva suddenly remembered the white envelope that Edna had given her, and she rummaged in the pockets of her handbag to find it. Slipping her fingers underneath the tightly sealed flap of the envelope, she pulled out a written note. Squinting against the dull light of the grey day, she read:

'A DAY TO CHANGE ALL OTHERS'

My dearest mum,

I am writing you because I do not know how to convey my feelings to you in person, a flaw of mine, but one that I know you will forgive. I have never believed in God, as well you know, but lately I'm wondering if I might try, maybe then I can buy myself a seat next to you in heaven. I have struggled so much with this and I feel I have betrayed you in some way; things have never really been the same since February. I can remember it like it was yesterday, and I imagine that it will be a day I will never forget. Your words were so plain, so straightforward, and yet in those few seconds, it was as if an atomic bomb had exploded in the living room and we were stuck in the vacuum of its aftermath. Silence. Nothing to say and everything to feel. In those first few moments, everything had stopped. Only the noise of the television in the background reminded me that the world was still turning. It's strange how the world can suddenly change. Life continues on as normal, and then one day it's over, and you know that it will never be the same again. And it never has been. You and I have what could only be described as an interesting relationship, and it has never been any different, even when I was a child. We are both strong opinionated women and, as such, spend a great deal of our time either arguing or having heated discussions on anything that we could possibly have differing opinions on. As much as it sounds odd, I miss those arguments. You were never the same after that day, and as each month has worn on and as each treatment has taken its toll, you have been transformed from my strong overpowering mum to a mere child. I realised that my mother had already gone. It's not the case that you are dying, and I am going to lose you, that has already happened.

I'm so sorry that I have not been there as often as I know you would like, the problem is that you have spent so much time in the hospital that for me it has become almost routine. For you, however, I know that each day is a struggle, and you will never get used to it. It suddenly became clear to me as I sat with you in Mercy during my last visit, we discussed the events of the day and I remember you suddenly broke into my sentence. You asked me for a teddy bear; I remember looking at you with a strange feeling of confusion. It was then as I looked around, that I realised that all the other patients had cards and gifts and flowers, and you had nothing. I spent the drive home that night wiping tears from my cheeks. So much time is spent organising medications, patient transfers, and hospital appointments that you have almost become an object, a task. Sometimes it's not the big problem that makes you cry, but the little things that are carried along with it.

My dearest mum, I will live every day with a full heart and a bright smile. I will make the most of everything, and I feel sure, that everything good will come my way in your memory.

All my love

A fine mist of drizzle began to find its way into the grounds of the hospital, but Eva stayed on her bench as others made their way back inside. Eva frowned as she watched the small droplets of water run down the neatly handwritten note;

suddenly she realised how misunderstood things could be, how twisted an unnoticed fear might manifest itself as an object of hatred. Her hatred, the hatred of all those who could not understand. Looking up at the sky, Eva closed her eyes, the nurse had always found the rain to be a refreshing retreat, but today it seemed to mirror her mood. Eva couldn't help but regret her last words to Edna. She knew that her words had been of comfort, and yet she also knew them to be a lie. There was no heaven, no continuation into an everlasting peace; just false truths and fear. Something that she knew nothing about yet preyed on the living like fungus on wood. It was her fear of not knowing that terrified her. The world thought that it had all the answers, and yet life and death were still enigmas; explained only by the hopeful writings of religious leaders. None of whom made any sense any more.

"You all right, lass?" Eva looked up from her knees with surprise as Harold sat himself beside her on the bench. "I saw you from the window, thought you might appreciate this."

Eva smiled as her former colleague and friend put up an umbrella. Eva sighed, "I was just thinking about how big the world is when you're all alone in it." Harold patted Eva on the knee in a way that Edna once had.

"You're not alone, but it's surprising how loss can make you feel that way, lass."

Eva snorted under her breath. "I doubt if anyone has lost the number of people I have, my mum and dad, my fiancé, my friend." Eva shook her head in disbelief, as though actually saying it made it unbelievable. The hospital janitor rubbed his hands together in appreciation of the cold.

"You'd be surprised; loss doesn't just mean death."

Eva looked up at Harold, whose expression revealed a glimmer of his own life. "I'd better get back to fixing that damned air conditioning." Harold smiled at Eva as he stood up, "It'll all come right, lass, in the end." The nurse smiled a response before leaving the bench to make her way towards the Blackwater cemetery.

Eva grimaced as she walked with the slow-moving procession past the familiar black gates of the graveyard. This time she had no need to answer its familiar low groan as the gates already stood open. A strangely cold welcome to its most recent resident.

Despite Adam's death having been only three years previous, Eva found herself walking past several dozen more headstones before reaching the hole in the ground that marked Edna's plot. It served as a stark reminder that life was merely a stepping stone to a deep hole in the ground. Eva kept her distance from the other mourners as she watched Edna's coffin being slowly lowered into the earth. She felt oddly out of place amongst the snivelling friends and relatives who had known Edna for years. Eva had only had the pleasure of knowing her patient for a couple of months, but in that short precious time, they had built a friendship that would last forever. Eva managed a wry smile to herself as she thought that Edna probably had a greater fondness for her than she did half her own relatives.

Eva felt silent tears run smoothly and quickly down her cheeks. They graced the pain of the moment that she felt so keenly, and the nurse did nothing to hinder their progress. As the pale white roses Edna had loved so much were placed carefully on her rested coffin, Eva wondered if her friend had seen the false angels in her last moments. The nurse closed her eyes, hoping that Edna had not seen the truth behind their mask. Eva knew frighteningly well that on first impressions they were angels, beautiful and serene gliding with flawless perfection, only those who dared to argue with death saw the falseness in their motives.

Eva slowly wiped the tears from her eyes; as her vision began to clear, she saw something that made her step backwards in alarm. Amongst the darkly suited mourners were black suits of a different kind. The nurse grimaced slightly as she realised that she had seen these men before. At the hospital, in Blackwater. Eva breathed in, holding the air for a moment. When she noticed one of the black suits turn to look at her, he quickly turned away again as though he had been caught as a peeping tom. The nurse felt her fear rising in her throat; she couldn't help but feel under attack, like she were being followed, monitored in some way. Eva slowly began to back off from the funeral, her steps quickening as she saw the black gates ahead of her.

"Miss Gardiner?"

Eva screamed slightly, jumping in alarm as a heavy hand rested on her shoulder. Her follower immediately removed his grasp at the response.

"Hi, sorry, didn't mean to startle you. I'm Detective Andrew Hollands with the Blackwater police station."

Eva eyed him suspiciously maintaining her distance. Gesturing with her hand, the nurse glanced back at the two black-suited men.

"Are they yours?" The detective raised his eyebrows at the abruptness of her reply.

"Yes." He paused for a second. "They are for your protection."

Eva laughed nonchalantly. "Protection from what? Are you seriously telling me that I've got armed guards against a couple of muggers who probably aren't even in this city?" Andrew said nothing to her angry shout, and Eva shook her head. "You know what? If that's the case, then you guys need to find some real work to do!" Eva began to walk away from the detective, who scratched at his chin before going after her.

"Miss Gardiner, wait."

Eva stopped walking, but did not turn around as Andrew caught up with her.

"You need to watch your back," he nodded as he spoke. "There are more dangers out there than just muggers and thieves." Eva frowned in silence as she watched the detective walk back to the funeral.

RICHARD

Dr Wellar twisted the gold cross between his fingers like he was about to deal a poker chip. The marquis cut on its shiny surface glinted like a warming beacon, yet the psychologist failed to see its lustre. In his youth, he had been a devout Roman Catholic, his faith nurtured by persistent church-going parents, and a family lineage of free masonry. It was not until his graduation as a psychologist, and his following role in the police department at Blackwater, that his faith began to dwindle.

Richard dropped the cross unceremoniously onto the table. Standing up, he turned a deaf ear to its jingle jangle as it revolved on the glass. He couldn't help but feel a deep pang of regret that he could no longer believe in the ideology that had comforted him for so long. This comfort had begun to fade as the dark images of homicide victims and killers spurred on by religious conviction clouded his mind. The psychologist couldn't get past the notion that God had failed them, failed them in such a way that forced him to question his very existence.

As a child, his father had carved a wooden plaque that had hung above his bed. It was Psalm 9:10:

"Those who know your name will trust in you, for you LORD, have never forsaken those who seek you."

Richard had always believed that when the day came when he truly needed the help of his Lord, he would be able to reach out with his faith and brush away the evils that stifled him. Instead, he found no trust, no enlightened guidance, and nothing more than an empty void in which to seek. Just like thousands before him, Richard had found his faith waning and the symbol he had worn so lovingly around his neck became nothing more than a shiny trinket, with which to flash an unwarranted allegiance. Despite this, Richard continued to keep the cross in his drawer, not in the hopes of religious favour, but because it reminded him of what was once the happiest days in his life. His progress into adulthood had become a bitter disappointment, full of failed endeavours and broken relationships. Whilst his career had been successful and fruitful in its rewards, it had also shown him some of the blackest inherent characteristics of human consciousness. Realisations that even the sickest of dreams could become a twisted reality, a reality that was his job to explain and explore.

Richard paced around the floor of his office; having cancelled all his appointments, he now waited impatiently for the phone to ring. Something told him that he was losing his mind, and yet for the first time in countless years, he chose to ignore his common sense. He found it quite refreshing; life had become such a routine in recent months that he had begun to grow weary of it. He had even contemplated giving up his job and starting afresh. Nothing was around to tie him down now, now that Judith had left him and taken the kids with her. Still, he was expected to pay child support despite the fact that her new lover was on a wage three times the annual salary of his own. The psychologist reached into the drawer of his desk. A small bottle of cheap scotch whiskey lay nestled discreetly amongst his papers, and he grabbed it enthusiastically. Forgetting the etiquette of a glass, he took a quick gulp from the bottle, anxiously wiping his mouth as he replaced the cap. Everyone had to have their weakness, including the normally pristine Dr Richard Wellar. The phone rang with its familiar office sound, and Richard almost threw the whiskey back into the drawer before grabbing at the receiver.

"Hello?" he attempted to answer, as though he were not expecting the call.

"Hi, it's Andrew. Listen, I found your girl, she was at a funeral in Blackwater but I traced her credit card to a hotel booking in County Main. When you approach her please don't implicate me will you? You know, as much as I like you, Richard, I like my job just as much."

Richard nodded his head on the other side of the receiver, "Yeah, sure. Thanks, mate." Dr Wellar put the phone down abruptly, as though he had no more time to idly chat.

The psychologist's colleagues eyed him with curiosity as he quickly exited his offices. He carefully concealed several files under his jacket as he left the building. Normally he wouldn't think twice about them, but for some reason, he felt that he should not let his colleagues see what he was leaving with. Quickly starting up his Mercedes, Richard shook his head. "Bloody paranoid idiot!" he berated himself as he smoothly took off in first gear.

Leaving the normality of his world behind him, Richard set out onto the motorway. He still couldn't believe what he was doing, but told himself that he was just looking out for the best interests of his patient. Pulling back on his professional demeanour, Richard smartened himself up in the mirror. He pulled forward his thinning brown hair in an attempt to cover his recessing hair line, whilst chewing noisily on a stick of gum he hoped would mask the smell of whiskey on his breath. He was aware that his drinking had become a problem since Judith had left, but he had been careful not to allow it to interfere with his work. Still, he knew perfectly well that it would only end up escalating, but he would deal with that later, or so he kept telling himself. Richard was a complicated man; he was so crystal clear on the surface. Professional beyond professional, yet underneath stirred a bubbling pot of turmoil. He had worked hard; nothing had come easy for him. Even at university he had to study twice as long as everyone else to get the same results. He wasn't an individual who had difficulties learning, it was just that he had to do things in a slow and methodical manner, otherwise it didn't enter his head. Only meeting and marrying Judith had been easy. Perhaps he should have known that it wasn't meant to be, but it was exciting to fall in love so quickly, so easily. He knew that his marriage hadn't been a dead loss; he had his two sons, when he was able to see them. Judith and her new lover had moved to Scotland only three months after they had met. Richard didn't get a chance to have a say in the matter. He only had a one-bed apartment, and there was just not enough time to find a bigger one before the boys had to move with their mother. Still Judith had told him he could have them for Christmas, and God, he was looking forward to that. He thought he missed his wife, but nothing burned him more than not being able to see his sons.

Richard increased the pressure on the gas pedal; he urged himself to keep going even though every now and then an intense knot would rise in his throat. He knew that knot well; it was the reminder to him that he was starting to lose the plot. This feeling had kept him in check so many times in the past when things were beginning to get a little rough. It kept him sane, on the right side of his brain where everything was normal and safe. Choosing to ignore it now could have a devastating result, yet he felt that perhaps he had played it too safe for too long. He was human, and humanity deserved a chance to air its voice. He deserved a chance to step outside that plastic-lined safety box inside of which he had lived for so long.

"In two hundred metres take first right, then second left," the familiar sharp sarcasm of the sat nav broke into the silence of the car, and Richard fidgeted uncomfortably in his bucket seats. Checking his mirror, he suddenly realised that he could hardly remember the last hour of his journey. He glanced briefly at the passing faces of other drivers, and realised they all looked the same - blank and expressionless like the driving dead.

The psychiatrist pulled over at the side of the road to check his sat nav. The sign said County Main, but the road suddenly narrowed to a single track, and as Richard looked over into the distance, all that met his eyes were roaming fields and forests of emerald green. Richard shuddered suddenly; he preferred the busy lights and bustle of city life. The secluded lonely road that lay before his eyes chilled him, and he turned the heating up in the car as if to compensate for his unwarranted fears. Turning on the lights of his Mercedes, he gingerly followed the road towards County Main; the overhanging branches of great firs darkened his path creating an arch of eerie silence and solitude. Richard wondered why anyone would want to live out here. The road was quiet, as if the only life to be found was the hidden in the forest, and he was sure that he would not want to go looking for it. Increasing his speed, Richard accelerated to a comfortable fifty, anything above that and he felt he might encourage a nasty negotiation with one of those strangely off-cambered bends he had come across. Richard tried to relax; according to his navigation system, he should arrive within the next twenty minutes. Amen to that.

The psychiatrist was surprised by the cosy appearance of the little village B & B that stood before him as he rolled into the parking bay. It was oddly homely, not jazzed up by overly ornate hanging baskets and badly painted advertising boards. Just a simple black and white sticker graced the front door advertising rooms to let. Richard rubbed at the stubble on his face, aware that perhaps a shave would have been appropriate before he presented himself to Eva; still, he didn't want her thinking that he had gone out of his way, although his one hundred and twenty mile drive said otherwise. Straightening his crumpled and creased suit jacket, he approached the front of the B & B. Before he had had the chance to ring the bell, a pale face peered around the door. Richard stumbled slightly as he asked the man if there was a room for the night. The owner looked as though he wasn't feeling his best. Richard noted the man's persistent attempts to massage his sweaty palms, and small beads of sweat had begun to form lingeringly on his forehead, the psychiatrist eyed him cautiously.

"Erm, yeah, sure, any room you like, just take a key from the wall," said the owner, who gestured half-heartedly at the keys hanging behind the front desk, and Richard couldn't help but feel uncomfortable as he stretched well beyond his reach to grab one.

"Is there a Miss Eva Gardiner staying here?" Richard asked quickly, suddenly feeling that the man wanted to get away as quickly as possible.

"Yeah, yeah, I think she went into town; she'll be back later." The fidgety man half whispered his response to Richard as he walked away. Richard eyed him with some concern as he walked into what was obviously a private room of his own house. The psychiatrist couldn't be sure, but he thought that he heard him mumbling to himself as he closed the door behind him.

Richard looked at the number on his key. Thirteen.

"Unlucky for some," he whispered as he attempted to find the room the key belonged to. Although Eva wasn't here at the moment, he knew that it wouldn't be too difficult to spot her, since it appeared that the only two keys missing from the owner's plaque were the numbers ten and now of course thirteen. Richard entered his room and wrinkled his nose at the slight musty smell that lingered. Most of the surfaces appeared to be covered in a thick layer of dust, and it was apparent that he was the first occupant to grace the room in quite a while. Opening the windows to let in some fresh air, Richard organised the table with the files he had taken with him from the office. He was aware that following Eva here made him look a little suspicious himself, and he wanted to appear as professional as possible. The last thing he wanted was for Eva to think that he was stalking her, especially given her recent history. He could not deny, however, that his reasons for following her were not entirely professional. The questions that had been raised and the odd similarity between Eva's account and Louise's were remarkable to say the least. Anybody would want to know more; there was something oddly unbelievable about it all, something that warranted further investigation, even if it was just to debunk any fanciful ideas that might have arisen out of the coincidence.

Richard glanced at his wrist watch; it was nearly four o'clock. Eva certainly hadn't appeared yet, and as the manager had removed the sign saying there were rooms to let and replaced with one stating that the B & B was full, he knew that the only person coming in would be Eva. Richard allowed himself to stretch out on top of the bed. His drive had knocked the wind out of him, and he realised that all he really wanted was a whiskey and some sleep. Since the whiskey was not an option, he closed his eyes and drifted off into a somewhat uneasy sleep. The disturbing random images of his sons and flashbacks from his own childhood were not enough to wake him, but the constant dull thud from somewhere in the B & B made him sit up suddenly. Glancing back at his watch, he realised that he had only been sleeping for about half an hour. Another thud made him slide off the bed. Creeping carefully to his door, he stopped and listened intently. Thud, and then again another thud, this time louder than the last one. Richard screwed up his face, wondering what on earth could be making such a noise. He stayed standing at his door for almost a further half an hour listening to the intermittent, yet persistent, thudding from the walls. One such thud made the wall next to his door shake with a small tremor, and the psychiatrist decided that such a force could only come from a hammer or similar implement. It appeared that the owner of the B & B had decided to do some DIY, which would explain why he had closed the inn to other travellers. Still, it would have been nice if he had told Richard those were his plans before he had checked in. By about five o'clock, the thudding had stopped, and Richard decided that he would take a small walk around the grounds. Mostly out of nosiness, but also because he was starting to get a little bored. As Richard left to walk around to what was nicely named "the walled beer garden," a black taxi pulled up opposite his own car; Eva emerged from the front passenger seat, carefully grappling with mixed paper and her purse. She didn't notice Richard until she had nearly walked into him.

"Hi," Richard mumbled, standing in front of her, trying to look as casual as he could. Eva looked at him with horror, and began fumbling with the paperwork in her hand. "What do you want? Did you follow me?" Eva began to get nervously angry, and Richard realised that he had achieved exactly what he was trying to avoid.

"No, well yes, but listen, I have to talk to you, I found some correlating evidence." Eva shook her head in frustrated anger, "Look, just leave me alone, OK? I haven't done anything wrong. I'm just doing a bit of my own research, and I got these legitimately, alright?" Eva shoved the papers under Richard's nose before sliding past him and entering the B & B. Richard stood outside for a second wondering what he should do, before deciding to follow her.

"Miss Gardiner!" The psychiatrist paused for a second, and then altered his call, "Eva!" The nurse stopped in the hallway, reluctantly turning to face her flustered psychiatrist.

"I'm not trying to stop you from doing anything," said Richard. "In fact, I've found some intriguing things myself; they might help you find what you're looking for."

Eva glanced at him suspiciously. "What things?"

Richard let out a small sigh of reluctant relief, "I've got some paperwork in my room; if you've got a minute, I'll show you." Eva didn't move, still feeling in trepidation at his sudden appearance.

"Look, I've driven a long way, broken God-knows-how-many rules, are you going to give me those few minutes?"

Eva smirked at his unprofessional response before finally deciding to follow him to his room.

CHAPTER SIX

"I still can't believe that you followed me all the way out here," Eva mumbled to Richard as she sat herself on his dishevelled bed covers. Despite Eva's annoyance at having been followed, the loneliness of the past few days had taken its toll, and in a way, she was glad to have some company, regardless of its unexpectedness. Richard half laughed his response, almost as if to remark that he couldn't believe he had followed her either.

"This is the picture you drew, in the hospital, of what you claimed you saw whilst you were unconscious,"

Eva took the picture from him, studying it carefully. It was a little rough, she thought, since that time she had managed to draw a much more accurate representations of the false angel.

"Now look at this drawing," Richard handed her another crumpled piece of paper. Flattening it out with her palms, Eva instantly recognised the same jagged lines, blue sharp edges, and twisted metal appearance of her own drawing.

"Who drew this?" Eva handed it back as though she did not want it to be in contact with her skin.

"Louise Turnbull." Richard placed the drawing next to Eva's on the table to scrutinise them again, like he had been doing for the past two days. Eva nodded her head in a response that suggested she was not surprised by the revelation.

"You can think what you like Dr, but the fact remains that me and that girl saw the same thing, and we're not the only ones." Eva tossed him the newspaper clippings she had collected from the libraries in County Main and Blackwater. "There are some striking similarities, don't you think? Look at this one." Eva rummaged about on the pile of papers on the bed before pulling out a small copy of a newspaper clipping from the early 1900s "This is what an inmate of the county insane asylum drew of the demon that made him murder three passers-by in the street." Eva showed Richard the roughly drawn picture with some sarcasm. "Still think I'm crazy?" The psychiatrist slowly took the picture and placed it next to the others on the table, taking a trembling hand, he rubbed his brow.

"This is insane; I mean, what are we talking about here? A demon? A supernatural entity?"

Eva stood up to join him at the table; shaking her head she uttered a thoughtful response. "No, I don't think so. I don't think this has anything to do with the supernatural; I believe these things exist. They are real; a part of our existence."

Richard took a step back, his logical mind fighting to process what was ordinarily a fanciful pile of crap. "Well I prefer the idea that this is grounded in some sort of scientific methodology," he retorted defensively "I have to say the idea of ghouls and demons doesn't ring much truth with me."

"No, me neither, I might be a little screwy at times, but I'm still a nurse. I know the difference between fact and fiction, doctor."

Richard shrugged his shoulders in wry appreciation of her comment. "Well, what to do now then? And you can call me Richard, Eva. It's not like we are in a professional relationship anymore."

Eva smiled shyly for a second lowering her head in an odd sense of embarrassment. The nurse was aware that she could be very persuasive, and as she sneaked a peek into his dark chocolate eyes, she couldn't help but feel pleased that it was him she had managed to persuade.

"There's something else," said Eva. She frowned as she realised that she had forgotten all about them. "I think I'm being followed, men wearing black suits. They were at the hospital, and they also followed me to a friend's funeral."

Richard sighed, rubbing his head as he recognised the situation had become a little more precarious. "Did they follow you here?"

Eva shook her head and said, "No, no, I don't think so. There was a detective; I think he said his name was Andrew. He was trying to warn me about something, but it was pretty vague." Eva shook her head again in her own confusion.

Richard bit the inside of his cheek, carefully trying to mask the flicker of recognition that had spread across his face. The psychiatrist began to wonder if perhaps he had placed his trust in the wrong man.

"Well, I'd really like the opportunity to talk to Louise. I don't think I'm going to get very far staying here," Eva mentioned her name hopefully.

Richard screwed his face up broken from his frightening thought. "We might as well spend at least one night here, Besides, I'm going to have to think up some way of getting you in to speak to Miss Turnbull; in my professional capacity I shouldn't have too much bother, but they are going to wonder what you are doing with me."

Eva shook her head. "No, I've got my nurse's identification with me; you can just say that I'm doing some kind of training course in psychiatry."

Richard laughed and said, "I still can't believe I'm doing this." Eva shrugged her shoulder. "In that case, no one is going to be thinking anything suspicious, are they?" Eva walked back towards Richard's door and said, "I'm hungry; let's see if we can find the owner and order a pizza or something, if pizzas even exist here."

Richard and Eva took a stroll around the B & B in the hope of finding the owner. The building itself looked like any other house; aside from the welcome desk at the front door, there was nothing to suggest that this was anything other than someone's home. Although welcoming and homely in feel,

Eva and Richard felt rather uncomfortable as they continued their search; it was almost as if they had invaded the man's house. It appeared that there were only five rooms in the whole building that were used for guests; the rest appeared to be private.

"Maybe he's still doing DIY?" said Richard.

Eva looked up at Richard with a confused expression on her face.

"What?"

"Those thudding noises that have been going on for more than an hour, bloody annoying, too," Richard grumbled, "I could barely think for it, although I haven't heard them for a while now."

"He never said anything to me about doing DIY, really nice man, though,"

Richard made no comment to Eva's last remark. Nice perhaps, but there was clearly something odd about him.

"I'll have a look behind the desk; he didn't seem to mind me getting my own key, so maybe I can find a telephone number for a takeaway or something." He scrambled around behind the desk for some advertising slips. "Looks like we are the first guests he's had in a while; there's hardly anything in his sign-in book." Richard dragged out a large red leather bound book, its edges were tatty and it appeared that he had kept the same book since the very first day his doors had opened to the public. Richard had not exaggerated when he had commented on the number of guests. In the past six months, Eva had counted only ten names.

"Perhaps he just runs this as a hobby,"

The psychiatrist mumbled a response. After a few minutes, Richard dragged out a rather old and weather-beaten menu slip for the Indian Curry Palace.

"Looks like Indian it is then," Eva took the menu and reached for her mobile phone, carefully scrutinising the worn numbers before she dialled. Richard left Eva with a quick request for Chicken Tikka before having another scout around for the home owner. The psychiatrist listened carefully as he walked around the corridors of the house; he was hoping to hear some kind of noise, a thud like last time, or any sign that the man might be doing some DIY somewhere. He was tempted to enter some of the rooms that were marked private, and he placed his ear against the door he had seen the owner enter earlier. He didn't just want to walk in, but if he could hear some kind of activity, then he could at least knock. Silence was all that met him, and as Eva walked up Richard couldn't help but feel uneasy.

"Maybe he's gone for a nap or something?" Eva shrugged her shoulders.

Richard nodded in response, still feeling slightly unusual. "Well, they won't deliver this far out, but if we order a taxi, then they will give it to the driver, the man said it would be about fifteen minutes for our food"

Richard nodded with a distinct lack of enthusiasm. The psychiatrist had a keen intuition and the absence of the B & B owner made him twitch with anxiety. Richard continued to hover for a few moments outside the door. He struggled with the temptation to open it, but the sudden smell of leaking battery acid made him gag and he turned to follow Eva to the front door.

The fifteen minutes they had expected to wait had turned into a stomach-grumbling twenty five. Still, the wait had been worth it and despite the absence of plates and cutlery, Richard and Eva managed to scoop up their meals with chunks of naan bread and a degree of intrepidity.

"So," Eva mumbled, whilst wiping away drops of Korma sauce from her chin, "isn't your wife going to wonder why you're all the way out here?" Eva asked with a hint of nosiness. She had already spotted the absence of a wedding ring and the tell-tale white mark left on his tanned skin where one used to reside.

"I'm not married; well, I am but I'm separated," Richard said quickly, as though this was not a topic he was entirely comfortable with.

"I see." Eva paused briefly before continuing, "So, have you any kids?"

Richard looked up from his naan bread and continued, "Two boys. They are with their mum." The psychiatrist looked back down at his meal, and Eva sensed that this was painful ground. Eva could not think of a response that would not deepen the conversation and was grateful when the phone rang at the front desk, breaking the awkward silence. Eva and Richard sat, expectantly waiting for the B & B owner to make his appearance, but after a few minutes, the phone stopped ringing and no one appeared.

"Maybe he's not even here," said Richard, shrugging his shoulders as he wrapped up the remainder of his meal. "A bit odd, though, I don't think most people would leave their hotel unattended with guests."

Eva nodded in agreement, "Maybe we should check on him? Or at least try to find him?" Eva's question was more of a demand but Richard was wary about entering the part of the house marked as private, but considering the man hadn't looked too good the last time he had seen him, it was the only out of concern that they would.

Eva and Richard hovered outside the door of the room once more. Then, realising how childish they both looked, Richard finally knocked. The phone rang again in the foyer, and the guests stood back in case the owner would finally emerge to answer it. As the phone rang off again, Richard finally took a deep breath and opened the door. Eva peeked around Richard's shoulder as she watched his arm grip tightly to the door frame. Richard stood like a frozen stone pillar, blocking her path; squeezing past him, the nurse entered the room. Eva quickly turned round and pushed past Richard to get back through the door. Violently she vomited her chicken korma onto the cheaply carpeted floor. Richard took a few stumbling steps backwards, allowing his back to collide with the corridor wall. He breathed as though he just finished the London Marathon; his skin was pale and reflected the light like luminescent chalk.

"What the fuck is that?" Eva swore, whilst wiping loose strands of saliva from her chin and blouse. The two companions stood outside like unwanted guests at a party before finally gathering themselves and entering what appeared to be the man's living room. Eva put a hand to her mouth as the rank smell of bloodied meat crept up her nostrils. It was mingled with an odd sweetness, like burnt dog hair on a barbecue. The humidity of the room reminded Eva of the atmosphere inside a slaughterhouse.

Inside, the room appeared as though he had been burgled, yet it was beautifully decorated and not at all like the cheap but clean decoration in the public part of the house. A corner lamp lay smashed on the fireplace, its bulb shattered all over the pretty flowered rug. The curtains looked as though someone had been swinging from them; several of the silver hooks adorning the pelmet had been torn from the fabric. Richard shook; swallowing hard, he stepped over the body and caved in head of the B & B owner. There was a curious crispness of charred skin around his eyes, as though he had been trying to burn his own eyelids. "It wasn't DIY he was doing" the psychiatrist whispered dully. Eva tried to control her quivering chin as a single tear left her cheek to become lost in the pool of blood on the floor. Richard closed his eyes as the thudding noise from a flashback suddenly made brutal sense. He had listened to a man smashing his own head off a wall.

"I've seen suicide before, but never like this." Richard looked concerned at Eva as he spoke. Even in his professional capacity, he had never been witness to such carnage. He had counselled police officers in the past that had seen images so horrific that it had mentally scarred them, but that was as close as he had ever come to the reality of it.

"It's happened again. It's wherever I go; this is all my fault,"

"What?" Richard stepped back over the crumpled body to join Eva on the far side of the room.

"Look at this, now do you understand? It's me they want; it's me," Eva shouted.

Richard said nothing as he examined the craters in the plaster where the victim's head had impacted. Scrawled like some kind of sick eulogy, blood-inked words and partially formed sentences created a hell's wallpaper adorning the room. Richard reached for the camera phone in his pocket and began taking random pictures of the now-ruined magnolia wallpaper.

Eva turned away, making her way to the door; she whispered behind her, "We've got to go." Richard took a few last snaps with his phone, and then chased after Eva, who was already in her room, hurriedly stuffing her clothes into a bag.

"What are you doing? We can't just leave; we have to call the police,"

Eva stopped what she was doing in disbelief and turned to face her former psychiatrist.

"And what do you think they will think?" Eva snapped.

Richard shook his head in puzzled bewilderment, "Eva, this is just a suicide; it has nothing to do with us."

Eva rolled her eyes with frustration. "For you maybe," she ran an angry hand over her face. "Look, wherever I've been, someone has either died or been killed." She paused for a moment, hoping a sudden light of dawning would descend upon Richard and spare her the explanation. "I met Louise Turnbull on the bus, right before she killed those people; in fact, I even told her what bus to get on! That road traffic accident a couple of days ago in Blackwater? I was on that bus; I got off for no reason just a couple of minutes before an old woman caused the crash that killed five people." Eva paused quickly to take a breath. "And you know what? She left that bus without a scratch on her body, like nothing had happened, and now this, how much more of an explanation do you need? Because I've really got to leave now!"

"Eva," Richard pleaded with his hands, as if he could correct all wrongs with one fell swoop. "You've had a really tough time lately, but you can't go around thinking that you're responsible for other people's misfortunes." Eva smiled sarcastically pursing her lips.

"Really? Maybe you should take a look at those pictures you took." Brushing past her companion, Eva made her way to the front door of the B & B. Richard stood dumbfounded in the hallway. The open door of the hotelier's room was like a gateway to hell, and he quickly closed it, moving away as though he might catch some deadly disease. Richard reached into his pocket for his phone; examining the photographs he had taken, the psychiatrist rubbed at the sweat on his forehead. The blood-scrawled sentences were disjointed, broken, faded as each lethal blow to the man's head had made him more and more incoherent, but there was enough to ascertain a meaning.

"You belong to us," Richard whispered the words, shuddering as he failed to see why a suicide victim would write such a thing. He glanced up in the direction that Eva had been walking. Her absence made him nervous, and he quickly made his way to his own room.

Richard stood for a minute before gathering his things up. Looking out of his window, he spotted the tell-tale spiral of cigarette smoke, indicating that Eva was waiting for him outside. He shivered as a cold wave of emptiness crept around his shoulders. Suddenly, the atmosphere felt stale, devoid of feeling or thought. The lifeless body of the man three doors down prayed on his mind, and he hurriedly stuffed his paperwork back into the brown leather briefcase.

With a degree of urgency, Richard took out his mobile and sent an SMS to Andrew. Richard was in two minds as to whether he could trust him, but the reality of the situation was too much for the psychiatrist to ignore. He couldn't just leave without letting someone know; he felt sure his police friend would take care of it without creating too much fuss. After all, he did owe Richard a few favours, and now seemed like a good time to cash in on them.

Praying he was doing the right thing, he bundled himself and Eva into the car; smoothly he exited the car park, as though nothing untoward had happened. Richard felt like a criminal, and it broke every moral sense of his being to leave the scene of what could only be described as the most brutal suicide he had ever witnessed. He also couldn't help but feel that the girl sitting next to him might be responsible for more than just being at the wrong place at the wrong time. Eva was right when she had said that she had been at every incident in the past couple of days, and Richard couldn't be exactly sure where she really was when the B & B owner committed his apparent suicide. Richard tried to steady his leg, which was trembling on the gas pedal with nervous distraction.

"Where are we going?" Eva clicked the window down of the car whilst lighting a cigarette. Richard said nothing, despite being aggravated at the putrid smell of burning tobacco infesting his car. Eva sucked purposefully on her cigarette as though she were hoping to harvest some kind of salvation. "I want to see Louise; I think she can help us."

Richard snorted a response, "I don't think so Eva, not now; there's going to be enough suspicion as it is without harassing the authorities at the mental hospital."

Eva threw the remainder of the cigarette out the window with annoyance. "Well what else are we going to do? Did you come all the way out here to help me or hinder me?"

Richard shook his head as he tried to think of a suitable response. It was true that he had come all this way, and had already done things that were completely out of his character. Biting his lip and wondering what on earth he was thinking, Richard indicated to turn back towards Blackwater.

Eva cursed as her finger slipped on the shiny thin paper of Richard's patient portfolio. A thin smear of blood trickled down the corner of the page, and she sighed as her vain attempt to remove it only acted to smudge it further. The nurse found herself lost in the story of Louise's life; it was so ordinary, so unassuming and in a way so perfect. Miss Turnbull's life had been full of uneventful normality; two hard-working parents had brought her up with loving care. She had progressed smoothly and neatly through primary, secondary and had been lucky enough to secure a university placement at Blackwater. Blackwater University, as Eva was well aware, was held in the highest regard by fellow educational institutions.

"Quite a bright girl, isn't she?" said Eva.

Richard nodded his head slowly in response to Eva's remark.

"Seems a little strange that a girl so ordinary would pull out a gun on a public bus and randomly shoot its passengers."

Dr Wellar licked his lips as he changed gears. "Psychiatry isn't a perfect science, Eva; to be honest, there are a lot of strange things that people do that are completely out of character."

Eva frowned, raising her eyebrows to show her disdain at Richard's comment.

The psychiatrist recognised her disagreement and raised a finger to silence her comment so that he could continue. "You for instance, a young nurse, hard-working, not so much as a library fine and yet you found it acceptable to steal a patient's file from my office."

Eva bit at her lip; she felt a well of anger rise in her throat and a sudden desire to defend herself, and yet she found herself sitting in silence. Partly because she had indeed committed the crime, and partly because Richard was right, it was out of character.

The cockpit of the Mercedes had become uncomfortably hot; Eva twitched in her seat, loosening the top button of her blouse.

"Yeah, you're right." The psychiatrist responded to Eva's body movements and began fiddling with the electronic temperature controls of his car. "According to this, the climate control is set at fifteen degrees; it's not going to get any cooler than that."

Eva looked with disbelief at the console. "Really? I'm sure those vents are blowing warm air."

Richard nodded, waving his hands at them as though they might respond to his concerns. "I'll turn the air conditioning on; maybe there's something wrong with the console,"

Eva laughed under her breath. "How much did this thing cost you?"

Richard smirked "Too much."

Despite it being uncomfortably warm in the car, the incident served to distract Eva from her embarrassment and resulting silence. "Maybe you're right, maybe it's the out of character behaviour that is the correlation between me, Louise, and the others in the newspaper clippings."

Richard squirmed in his seat, attempting to remove his jacket whilst driving. "I agree, that does makes sense, but surely someone else would have noticed such a correlation by now. I mean, are we just talking about Blackwater here?"

Eva sucked at the paper cut on her finger as she thought. "Maybe they do. I mean, those guys in suits aren't following me around for the good of my health." A long period of calm silence followed Eva's last comment. It was not the uncomfortable silence that Eva had become accustomed too, but a silence enriched with the tick tock of reasoned thought.

"Jesus Christ!" Richard broke into the thought like a jack-hammer. "I'm sweating like a stuck pig in this car; the bloody air conditioning is blowing hot air." The psychiatrist punched at the air conditioning button with frustration. "This car isn't even two years old yet!"

Eva nodded her head in confused agreement. "Well, I'll open my window, and whilst it's open, I'll have a cigarette."

Richard didn't show any objection at Eva's smoking. In fact, he was relieved at the cool autumn breeze that rushed into the cabin, even if it was tainted by the smell of cigarette smoke. Eva finished her cigarette quickly, throwing the butt out of the window.

"You know, I'm beginning to think I'm cursed. It doesn't matter what vehicle I'm in, a car, a bus, even a bloody train something always goes wrong. Maybe it's me, maybe I'm the one consciously or not that's causing all this mayhem."

Richard began shaking his head at her comment, but Eva was insistent on her reasoning.

"No, seriously, what were the chances of that man committing suicide when I happened to be there? And in such a weird and violent manner? Would that really have happened if I had not checked in?" Eva answered her own question before the psychiatrist could comment. "No, I don't think it would have." Eva's remarks were loud and to the point, and the nurse was so adamant of her own convictions that Richard found himself speechless to comment; instead, he drummed his fingers with tense anxiety on the steering wheel.

"My phone," Richard announced quietly to Eva. He gestured to the pocket of his partially removed jacket. "My phone. I took some pictures of the walls in the B & B; maybe we can decipher some more of that scrawl on the walls. The nurse searched through Richard's phone for the pictures with a degree of reluctance. Eva was not entirely confident that she wanted to see that scrawl again, let alone try and decipher what the rest of it had said. If Eva was right, and this was wrapped around her in some way, then she knew for certain that she would not like what she found.

"It looks like the guy ripped his own fingernails out, scratching this on the wall," Eva muttered, her mouth, watering in anticipation of sickness.

Richard screwed his face up as the image of detached nails and torn cuticles made him shudder. "Is there anything on there that we didn't see earlier?"

Eva shook her head as she squinted to read the blurred images on the small screen. "No, just some jumbled words that don't make sense, 'Punarbhava' and 'Palingenesis.'" Eva spelled the words as though they formed part of a foreign language. Richard began drumming his fingers off the steering wheel again.

"I think that means something; I just can't remember what,"

Eva bit her lip as she responded. "We need access to a computer."

CHAPTER SEVEN

LOUISE

"37," Louise whispered as she counted yet another rain drop finding its way down the glass to fall carelessly from the pane. Louise stood dejectedly, watching the black clouds form solemnly outside of her window. She would give anything to feel that rain on her face, to feel the realness of her surroundings instead of the false life she was now forced to live. Just a pane of glass away was a feeling, tactile world, a world she had once lived in and yet had never appreciated. Behind her stood a 9ft square grey room, an iron bed with a thin mattress, and one chest of drawers containing several replicas of the outfit she was currently wearing. Even the air smelt stale, just constant recycled, air-conditioned oxygen, no life, no sweet smell of passing flowers in bloom, nor the fresh aroma of mown grass. Louise would have settled for a passing hint of dog shit if it would have brought some change.

Closing her eyes, she floated back to the promising young life she was all set to lead. A university placement and good friends, every day was an adventure, and she was ready to live it to the fullest. Louise closed her eyes and wandered blindly back to her bed in the corner of the room; All that was gone, nothing more than a fairy-tale with a sad ending. Louise wiggled her toes as she sat in the darkness. Sometimes she could feel the tendons in her feet and ankles twitch with the movement; it reminded her that she was alive. Most of her sensations were dulled with the medication that she was forced to take. Nothing of herself was truly left, just watered-down memories of another life. Occasionally she would think of her parents in the darkness, her thoughts for them were as strong as they ever were. Sometimes they were the only thing that kept her going in the silence of the night. Perhaps she would see them tomorrow. They had promised to visit her, and Louise's doctors had said that this would be good for her. They hadn't arrived yet, and Louise couldn't really remember how long she had been here. Perhaps they will come tomorrow. A familiar sentence spoken over and over again in her mind, it was something to cling onto when everything else was lost.

Louise rubbed at her running nose, a strange copper like sting nipped at the top of her sinuses. She had grown quite used it now; it was an early warning that they were close. They always caused this sensation when they were near. After her accident, the doctors told her it was just a side effect of the medication she was being given to treat her injuries. Louise knew better than that now, and in a way, she welcomed their presence, hoping that they would finally take her with them and stop the life that she was so desperate to end. Reaching under her mattress, she pulled a piece of paper and a blunt pencil. She had been writing a letter to her parents, she had been writing it for weeks now, but she struggled to tell them exactly what she wanted, so she just kept writing. She was on page twenty-two maybe she would finish it tonight, if the right words would come. There was so much to be sorry for and no proper reason she could give as to why. No reason that anyone would believe anyway. Still, she was proud that her writing was neat, her mother always praised the way she perfectly formed her letters, never forgetting to dot an 'i' or stroke a 't.' If they couldn't understand her words, at least they would recognise her handwriting.

The clouds clung over the outskirts of Blackwater like hungry vultures waiting for death. Eva shuddered slightly as the gloomy blackness reminded her of the night in the park. She had avoided the park since, only breaking her own rule to attend Edna's funeral, but a sickening feeling of betrayal punished her every-day. Her regimented visits to Adam had become nothing more than a torn promise on a calling card. She had sworn to visit him regularly, but her own fear had defeated her loyalty. As the heavy drops of wet rain splashed relentlessly onto the windscreen, Eva wondered if she would ever be the same again.

Richard pulled into the long, single track road leading to the high security mental institution. Tall bushes lined the way, their exact spacing and perfectly cut lollipop tops suggested a rigid perfection, reflecting the reality of the correctional facility.

"Are you sure you want to do this?" Richard questioned, slowing the car as he approached the large courtyard at the front of the building. Eva nodded her head whilst nervously biting her lip. "I didn't realise what an ominous building it was." Richard smirked. "Yeah, I don't think this place has changed in over a hundred years, if it makes you feel any better, it gives me the creeps, too."

Mercy Hospital was of the same old-fashioned, stone-walled appearance, and yet it seemed kinder to the eyes than what befell them now. The stone that formed its structure was grey and as the rain ran from the roof and walls it shined like black granite. The building was laid out into one giant square. Dimensionally perfect, small square windows graced every room, and they, too, were exactly the same width apart, exactly the same height, exactly regimented. A white metal sign with black lettering stood at the back of the loosely beige chipped courtyard. It read simply "Elizabeth Hope Mental Hospital."

Richard stopped the car; gathering up his briefcase, he turned to Eva and said, "Listen, we have to be professional, make sure you have your nurse identification pinned to your jacket." Eva nodded her head, quickly rummaging in her bag for the plastic card. As she pinned it to the front of her black leather jacket, she realised that this was the first time she had worn it in nearly three months.

The oldness of the building was denied by the electric doors that swung open automatically as Richard and Eva approached. The interior of the building remained as cold and stale as that of any maximum security prison. The walls were plain white, not the warm magnolia to be found in the more inviting of institutions, but the white that reflected back your glance like snow on a winter's day. Eva looked around cautiously, electronic devices were dotted intermittently along the walls, some for door lock combinations, others appeared to be serving no purpose, but the strong presence of security cameras suggested otherwise. The floors were that of any hospital, forest green linoleum, not a hint of shading or pattern to break up the plainness of the colour, just simple, unassuming green. A small halogen heater sitting on the front desk offered the only hint of glowing warmth in an otherwise cold building. The orange glow looked out of place in the foyer, a small ray of sunshine on a planet with no sun.

The psychiatrist straightened his tie as he walked with confidence to the front desk. A balding older man sat uncomfortably on a swivel chair, flicking at a magazine without interest.

"Dr Wellar, I thought it was your car I saw pulling in. I haven't got you on my schedule for this evening, in fact," said the receptionist, glancing briefly at his watch. "It's a bit late for house visits."

Richard nodded his head, giving the balding man an exasperated look. "I know, Grant. But, listen, I've got this student I was supposed to be taking her for a training session last week, but with all the work, I haven't had the chance. The guys at Mercy are on my back about it."

Grant nodded his head from behind the desk, rolling his eyes he moaned. "Yeah, everyone seems to think you have all the time in the world, eh? What patient was it you wanted to see?"

Richard flicked through his notes as if he had forgotten. "Louise Turnbull, I think. Yes, Louise."

Grant licked his lips. "Ok, I'll let you through, but I think they are delivering the meds soon. And that girl's on plenty, try not to be too long, eh?"

Richard slapped the receptionist on the back as he led them through the security-coded doors and onto the wing. "Thanks, mate, I appreciate it,"

Eva smiled at the receptionist as he eyed her, although it seemed to Eva that he was more interested in her appearance than the identification card pinned to her jacket.

Grant opened the heavy metal door into Louise's room. "Dr Wellar is here to see you," he mumbled, as he shuffled back out the door allowing Richard and Eva in. "Fifteen minutes, OK?" He winked at the psychiatrist as he left.

"Hi, Louise, It's Richard. How are you feeling today?" The psychiatrist pulled out the blue plastic chair from under the side table and seated himself to the right of her bed. Eva stood cautiously in the background, unsure of where to stand.

"Louise, this is Eva; she's a student nurse," Richard attempted to sound confident. Eva took the opportunity to approach the bed. A young woman sat in the corner of the room. Her back was against the wall, and she hugged her knees with her arms, as though she were cold. Eva noticed how she continuously wiggled her toes, which poked their way over the edge of the bed. There was an awkward few seconds where Louise did not acknowledge their presence; Eva began to wonder if her coming here would prove to be useless.

"You know they will catch up with you eventually," Louise whispered. Eva breathed in as a pale, startlingly normal face emerged from behind her knees. She looked so harmless, the soft lines of her features portraying a kind serenity. This girl was not the monster Eva had encountered at the hospital all those months ago.

"What do you mean?" Richard stepped into the conversation before Eva had had the chance to respond. Louise sat forward in a cross-legged position on the bed.

"She's not supposed to be here, neither am I, we were chosen, and because we came back, the balance is wrong." Louise shrugged her shoulders as though her comment was inevitable. "There's no such thing as a second chance, not for us anyway." Eva moved forward, losing her feeling of trepidation; she quickly sat herself on Louise's bed.

"You mean the false angels?" Eva questioned. Louise laughed as though Eva's comment was naïve.

"If that's what you want to call them,"

Richard shook his head, "Wait a minute, you're telling me that both you and Eva have seen the same thing?" Louise smiled at Richard as though it was ironical that a person such as herself would have knowledge that he did not possess.

"Everyone sees them, only not many of us come back to talk about them. I died, and I was supposed to die," Eva pulled her head backwards suddenly as Louise pointed a finger aggressively at her face. "You're supposed to be dead, too!" Eva nodded her head with shock, blinking her eyes as the realisation brought a hot redness to them.

"What do they want? Can I stop this?" Eva pleaded, leaning towards Louise with desperation, the girl responded with a sense of sympathy.

"No, no, you can't, because you lived, one of them has been denied its right to life."

Eva shook her head in confusion "I don't understand."

Louise recoiled suddenly into the back of the wall and said, "Can't you smell them? You have to go. They're here; they've found you."

Eva got off the bed; grabbing Richard by the shoulder, she began to walk backwards towards the door.

"Professor Stanton, Blackwater University, he knows." Louise uttered, nodding her head like it were on a loose spring. Richard said nothing; standing up, he followed Eva quickly, unbarring the door.

"Eva, they won't stop, they won't stop until you're dead, and everyone you're with, too."

Eva looked behind her as she left Louise's cell, the young girl was once again sitting with her back against the wall, wiggling her toes. Richard and Eva made their way hurriedly back towards the reception desk.

Grant was quick to meet them, holding a flashlight. "You two wouldn't mind seeing yourselves out would you? There's been some sort of brown out with the electricity on C block." Eva opened her mouth, looking at Richard with concern; the psychiatrist shook his head in response and ushered her out of the building. The psychiatrist wasted no time, quickly turning the key in the ignition, leaving the flickering lights of The Elizabeth Hope Mental Institution behind them.

Richard drove the silver Mercedes around the outskirts of Blackwater like he was a seventeen-year-old boy driving a circuit. He drove without purpose, taking the same route time and time again, wasting away the minutes like they were an endless commodity. The atmosphere inside the car was that of a coffin; a stale stillness, full of nothing but decaying thoughts and empty ponderings. Eva said nothing as she sat rigid in the passenger seat. To comment on their meeting with Louise was to face the facts of her words. Eva wasn't ready to discuss or even try to comprehend their meaning. As for Richard, his constant driving of Blackwater's city limits was buying him the precious time he required so desperately to think. The glow of an orange warning light on Richard's dashboard reminded him that he needed to fuel, and he swerved the car across the road, pulling neatly into a brightly lit BP station.

"Do you want anything?" Eva met Richard's words with a brief shake of her head; worried that she may empty the contents of her stomach should she open her mouth to talk. The psychiatrist filled the Mercedes to its limit. He wasn't sure exactly where they were going to end up, and a full tank seemed preferable to a half-empty one. Searching through his wallet for his over-used credit card, Richard walked over to the small shop to pay.

"Just fuel is it?" A middle-aged woman with glasses, looked up briefly from her copy of Dan Brown's "Angels and Demons."

"Yes, thank you." Richard handed over his card poised to enter his pin. The glare of a television screen behind the woman caught Richard's attention, and he recognised the familiar silver outline of his Mercedes in the forecourt.

"Must be getting foggy out there tonight." The woman jabbed her thumb towards the close circuit television as she handed him the chip and pin machine. Richard peered awkwardly over her shoulder, and his finger began to shake uncontrollably as he entered the last two digits of his pin. Richard watched with confusion as a fine mist hovered over the roof of his car. It appeared to be nothing more than a patch of freezing fog, yet it moved with a strange sense of purpose. Hovering not more than two inches above the roof, it glided down towards Eva's open window. Richard quickly removed his card from the chip and pin meter. Not stopping to collect his receipt, he ran out onto the forecourt and towards the car.

"Eva!" Richard shouted at his ignorant passenger. The nurse jumped, startled from her absent-minded doodles on her notepad. Richard reached for the door handle of the car yelping in pain as an electric blue static charge pricked at his fingertips.

"Oh my God!" Eva shouted out as she suddenly became aware of the static blue cloud surrounding herself and the car. The terrifying familiar smell of caustic metal filled the cabin and Eva's heart leapt in her chest. Scrambling across Richard's seat, she opened the door from the inside, allowing the injured psychiatrist to dart into the car.

"Fuck, fuck," Richard mumbled as he struggled to force the keys into the ignition. "Come on, come on!" Richard shouted with frustration as the Mercedes struggled to burst into life. The car limped from the courtyard as the engine management flashed like a lighthouse beacon.

"Has it gone?" Richard looked with horror at Eva as her hair stood up from her head like she had spent the last half hour rubbing a balloon across it.

"I … I don't know. I can't see it," Eva squirmed around in her chair as she peered through the wing mirrors. "Oh God, look at your fingers!"

Richard's attention was drawn to the hand he had clamped around the gear stick. Suddenly he became acutely aware of the pain surging from his fingertips, and he re-coiled his hand in shock.

"You'll need to let me have a look at that," Eva whispered to Richard. Her injured companion, nodding his agreement, turned the failing Mercedes in the direction of his own flat.

A black Audi Estate cautiously followed Richard's speeding car from the garage. Andrew peered nervously from underneath his baseball cap as he slipped the Audi into fifth gear.

"Those things are desperate to get to Miss Gardiner. I've never seen an attack like that before," Andrew spoke over his shoulder to a hidden occupant on the back seat.

"I'm surprised she's survived on the run for this long. If that psychologist friend of yours is not careful, he's going to end up on the list as well." The professor commented from the back seat.

Andrew smirked shaking his head in response. "I wouldn't worry about Richard, professor. He knows what he's doing." A grunt came from the back as a curly, grey-haired fifty-something leaned into the cockpit.

"You'd better make sure you get those security tapes from the garage. How are things with your captain?" The professor leaned forward as he spoke. Andrew rubbed his face as he eased off the accelerator, aware he was catching the Mercedes in front.

"He's desperate to arrest Miss Gardiner and Richard now as well. I think he believes they are on some kind of mass killing spree." Andrew mumbled his response as though it was a conversation he was hoping to avoid. The green tweed-suited man stroked his moustache before replying,

"I suppose they are. As long as they are hunting her, she will end up indirectly killing those around her until they catch her … Just try to keep that captain of yours from doing anything rash; if he makes an arrest attempt, let me know and we will get our boys to step in." The professor said sternly. Andrew nodded a response, slowing the Audi down to twenty miles an hour as he watched Richard's car approach his flat. "If these two have been to see Louise Turnbull, then you can expect a call from the sanatorium in the morning. Turn around; we can't follow them any farther tonight." The professor ordered with authority and the Audi performed a skilful three-point turn in the road, its bright lights momentary highlighting the huddled shadows of Richard and Eva.

CHAPTER EIGHT

Richard's flat was not entirely as Eva had expected it would be. It was a handsome flat to be sure, a large, open-plan kitchen and living room with the latest wide screen television and audio equipment. Yet, his rooms were cluttered, untidy. Richard seemed to have a passion for leaving his loose paper strewn all over the place, and Eva now realised why it had been so easy for her to steal the file. His flat was endowed with rich furnishings, but lacked character and comfort. The floors were entirely laminated, no carpets and the curtains a plain cream. Eva recognised Richard's home as not a place for relaxing and passing time, but a place of work. A large desk with a black leather swivel chair was the main object of furniture in the room; it imposed onto the living space like a large moon blocking the sun. It was the one place in the flat that looked remotely tidy. It appeared that Richard organised his paperwork on top of other items of furniture, and left them there until he needed them.

Eva watched with a degree of amusement as Richard attempted to quickly tidy with his one good hand. Eva removed her jacket, placing it on a clear patch of kitchen surface next to the drinks cabinet. Richard's liquor cabinet was one of the largest items of furniture in the house, aside from a bottle of Bacardi and perhaps two bottles of red wine, the cabinet was comprised nearly entirely of whiskey. Eva could tell that it wasn't just that he enjoyed drinking whiskey it was also a passion. Richard had vintage bottles that not only looked old, but looked as though they cost him a fortune. Eva tried not to peer too closely so as to look nosey, but his liking for alcohol was something that she had not been expecting. He was so straight-laced and proper; alcohol suggested a hint of exuberance of mindlessness. The nurse smiled as she suddenly realised that he might not entirely be the man that she thought he was. He was complicated, and she could sense that. It appeared ironic to her that she should find herself in the company of a man who appeared to have as many vices as her last tragic lover. Eva wondered if she had a penchant for choosing men with troubled minds. He was interesting, though; he had a cool calmness that soothed the hot-headedness of her own fiery personality. Deep down, Eva could sense that he was a good man, caring when no one else would bother, trying when there was nothing left to try for.

Eva peered closely at the few photographs that Richard had adorning his pale walls. They broke up the staleness of the room, and since they were the only ones on display, Eva recognised that they were of importance. The first was a family picture of what appeared to be a skiing trip. Eva smiled as she saw Richard warmly hugging his two boys in the cold appearance of the background. The woman standing behind him must have been his wife. Eva pulled a face discreetly; she was no Angelina Jolie that was for sure. Perhaps not such a great loss, but that was her opinion.

Eva grimaced as she gingerly peeled the loose flaps of charred skin from the tops of Richard's fingertips. "Sorry," she whispered sympathetically as the psychiatrist winced into his large glass of whiskey. Smothering Richard's fingers in Sudocreme, she dressed his wounds. "It's not burn cream, but it will have to do." Her companion offered a wry smile in response, and Eva walked to the large window in the open-plan kitchen to smoke a cigarette.

"I think your car alarm is going off again," Eva said.

The psychiatrist leaned past her to cancel the alarm with his keys. "Yeah, I think all that static has knackered the computer."

Eva bit her lip and said, "I'm sorry I got you into all of this. I still can't explain what's happening, but I know I've got to keep searching." Richard topped up his whiskey glass and joined her in the kitchen. "If I don't figure this out then I think I'm going to die." Eva spoke, looking at Richard with a twisted confidence, and the psychiatrist felt a sudden pang of guilt, as though he were responsible for the position that she now found herself in. Richard could no longer deny that the things that haunted Eva were real. It was no longer a simple delusion brought on by a troubled past, but an "object" a "thing" that could cause pain and injury just the same as any other living being. Richard considered his strict outlook on life for a second and wondered if perhaps it was because of people like him, people, so consumed by their own academic ignorance, that people like her were forgotten and unheard. For the first time in his twenty-year career, Richard felt that perhaps this time there was nothing he could do. Maybe she was right, maybe he would lose her, and the notion terrified him.

Richard moved towards Eva, pushing his whiskey glass to the far back of the kitchen counter. He carefully stroked a strand of hair away from her cheek; he did so with nervous gentleness, lest his advances be met with recoil. There was a moment of soft nothingness, where Eva stopped breathing and found herself falling into the moment. Eva closed her eyes as she felt the subtle brush of his skin on her face. A familiar twinge from her abdomen signalled that she desired his touch, his comfort. A sudden knot of fear crept upon her, and she swallowed as if she could just make it disappear with a simple motion. She was not afraid of him, but afraid of the consequences that her heart would have to bear if their encounter lead to nothing more than a forbidden mistake.

Turning to face him with moist eyes, she kissed his parted lips. Allowing herself to slide into the passion of his embrace, she lifted her body onto the kitchen top. As Richard removed her blouse with an urgent intensity, the whiskey glass crashed to the floor, its broken presence unregistered in the thick atmosphere of the room. Despite her fear, she did not stop the heavy-handed fumbling of his hands upon her body. She did not want to, it had been so long, and this time it felt as though it were the first time, exciting, fresh, new. As Eva and Richard moved with rhythmic perfection, the only disruption to the harmony came from the awkward chiming of Richard's car alarm.

Eva twitched uneasily in her sleep, the silk bed covers clinging uncomfortably to her sweat-soaked skin. She twisted like a snake in the grass, her arms thrashing out like she was attempting to escape the trap of a hunter's net. Her movements made her aware of the sleeping Richard lying silently beside her, yet she could not rouse from her slumber-like state. Eva frowned as she attempted to break a seemingly medication-induced coma. She knew that she was awake, she could feel and hear the soft whirring of a breeze passing through the open window, the reality of the coldness on her skin allowed her to visualise her surroundings. Feeling suddenly exhausted, Eva stopped her semi-conscious battle. In the motionless grey cavity of her own thoughts, Eva waited. Calming herself, she invited the presence that lurked in the shadows. She could smell its burnt energy; taste the acrid metallic flavour on her throat. Her invitation accepted, the presence emerged from the shadows of her mind, and she was once again the audience for her false angel. Eva did not react to its appearance; it was though she had become used to the abnormality of its being.

"Why? Why do you follow me like this?" Eva mentally whispered to her companion who responded before her sentence was even finished.

"We are what you leave behind." Eva's false angel softened in the greyness of her mind to reveal a crystal structure of delicate beauty. Eva had seen this image before, and she was almost tricked by the freshness of its light. This time she saw beneath the masquerade. "Our life begins when yours is at an end. The energy you discard is the core of our being; we depend upon your death to survive."

Eva frowned from within her thoughts and said, "But we all die, why now?" The entity moved like a floating cloud across the sky. The grey wallpaper of Eva's thoughts became illuminated like frozen glass as the being glided through her thoughts.

"Your life is predetermined before you are even born, as is ours. We live in balance, as one dies another begins; the being intended for your life has already been born, without your energy it will die."

Eva breathed in heavily with a sense of sadness that evoked a deep guilt within her soul. It was not her intention to deny life. But hers had been returned, and she desperately wanted a chance to live it.

"But I don't want to die," Eva whispered with desperation into her mind. The crystal beauty of her thoughts returned quickly to the electric blue she had become so familiar with. Eva struggled to focus as her surroundings became whirled as though she were standing in the eye of a tornado.

"The choice is not yours to make."

Eva jumped as the loud sharpness of the words reverberated in her eardrums; wincing, she quickly awoke. Sitting up in bed, she placed a hand to her ear, the warm sensation of blood moistening her fingertips.

The early morning sun glided onto the sleeping bodies of Richard and Eva; the nurse welled in its presence, welcoming the warmth on her skin.

"Fancy some breakfast?" Richard suddenly rolled towards her, catching her by surprise. Eva nodded her head, the idea of a bacon sandwich was appealing, and the rumbling in her stomach agreed. The nurse watched with amusement as Richard wandered around his kitchen in nothing but his underpants. "I was thinking we could take a walk down to the park today. It's the Blackwater Fete,"

Eva said nothing for a second as she thought. "Don't you think that would be a little dangerous? I mean, the police are bound to be looking for us by now."

Richard nodded his head, smearing butter thickly onto the bread. "Yeah, but it's going to be pretty busy, and I doubt whether they'd think we'd be stupid enough to be there,"

Eva laughed as she took the sandwich from Richard. "Are we?" The psychiatrist laughed and said, "I would just like to have one normal day with you, if that's OK." Eva smiled, despite the obvious risks, one normal day sounded like the best thing since her bacon sandwich.

Richard and Eva walked hand-in-hand into Blackwater's vast park. The nurse was uneasy about their visit at first; in her mind, she could almost see the blood-stained grass where her punctured body had lay three months ago. Eva hid her fears, and the tight grip of Richard's hand upon hers was enough to remind her that she was safe.

Blackwater Fete occurred at the same time every year; it was an elaborate affair that the council could ill afford and yet spared no expense organising. In all the years the Eva had lived in the city, she had only attended the fete once, not because it was dull, but because the enormous crowds of people milling around stalls and attractions gave her an odd feeling of claustrophobia. With the bright early morning sunshine already soaking down, Eva knew that today would be busier than ever.

"I wish they would make one of those for adults," Richard said, pointing at a large bouncy castle, its edges spilling over with the excessive amount of children jumping on its air-filled walls.

Eva laughed and replied, "A psychiatrist on a children's bouncy castle, now that would make a good article for the hospital magazine."

Richard shook his head in dismay, pulling Eva towards the direction of the penny arcades. "I love these. My parents didn't approve of gambling, but my grandfather would always slip me a couple of pennies to play when my parents weren't watching." Eva laughed. "I've never tried one."

Richard looked around sharply at her as if she had just committed the crime of the century. "What? Are you kidding?

Well, I'm sorry Miss Gardiner, but that's something that your psychiatrist is going to have to put to rights." Eva giggled like a school girl as Richard reached into his pocket and pulled out a handful of loose change. "There you see, I've got five two pennies, try your luck." Eva smiled. Biting her lip sheepishly, she took the brass and began sliding them into the machine. "No, no. Look, you've got to aim them for the side that has the biggest outcrop near the edge," said Richard. Eva peered into the machine as Richard guided her hand and timed the drop of the penny perfectly.

"Aaagh!" Eva clapped her hands together with joyous enthusiasm as Richard's two pence sent another twenty spilling into the tray at the bottom. "Well, Dr Wellar, you're the last person I would have imagined gambling on a penny arcade." Richard smiled, using his head to notion Eva to walk with him.

"There's a lot more to me than mere psychology, Eva. As much as I love my job, I don't live in it." Eva looked at the floor realising how quickly she had judged him before. Despite his demeanour reflecting the nuances of an arrogant prick, beneath the surface, he was just as human as everyone else; perhaps more human than she could ever give him credit for.

The nurse startled suddenly as a large group of young men brushed past them. Richard guided her round with this hand before whispering in her ear, "They're not all killers." Eva breathed out, laughing slightly at her nervous reaction to anything young and male.

"I'm sorry; it's just being back here." Eva shrugged her shoulders as though she didn't quite know how to complete the sentence.

"C'mon, let's go grab a hot dog." Richard skipped past her attempted explanation, realising that the nurse had probably spent far too much time explaining herself to him already.

Eva and Richard seated themselves on a small patch of grass free from trampling feet and lost pets. Eva murmured in appreciation as she tucked into the tomato sauce-laden hot dog.

"God, this stuff is so bad for you, but I love it,"

Richard nodded in agreement, professing that when his wife left him he ate nothing but takeaway for a month because he couldn't work out how to use the oven. Despite Richard's humorous portrayal of his plight, Eva didn't laugh; instead she gazed at him with pity. "That must have been hard," Richard smiled at his own misfortune. "They say nothing lasts forever, and besides, I've got two prefect boys to show for my efforts." Eva twisted shards of grass between her fingers, hesitating before she spoke.

"Well, I reckon that ex-wife of yours didn't realise what she had," Richard said nothing to her comment; instead, he looked at her deeply and said everything he wanted to with a glance. Eva jumped up from the grass as though she had burnt herself. "C'mon," she said, clapping her hands together, "I want to go on the Waltzers." Richard looked at her with an intense stare of horror as he stood up. "You know there's a reason why those damn things are called Waltzers, and it's nothing to do with the dance."

"Don't be such a cry baby" Eva laughed, her cheeky remark was enough to make Richard reluctantly agree to join the queue. Eva watched the excited screams of people with anticipation; there was an odd feeling of excitement in her stomach, a feeling that had eluded her for a long time. Eva was so engrossed that she hardly noticed her companion's persistent tugging on her arm.

"Eva, don't move suddenly, just quickly and quietly walk around the back of the waltzers," Richard whispered intensely. Eva stopped breathing for a second as her excitement turned to fear. The two lovers weaved in and out of the crowd like snakes, finally stopping at the back of the waltzer attraction, where the crowds were minimal.

"What's wrong?" Eva breathed at Richard, her chin already trembling.

"There are two men in the park. I think I've seen them before; they don't look like they are here to enjoy the fete."

"Oh God, the police?" Eva twitched nervously peering around to view the crowds.

"No, I don't think so. They are wearing pretty nice suits to be just simple police officers, and I think one of them is wearing an ear piece." Eva breathed out moaning under her breath, her trembling progressing its way down to her legs. "I think it's time we left. Perhaps another hotel for the night might be a good idea; they have probably already been to the flat."

Eva nodded without saying a word, her mouth had become so dry that she worried any noise she would make would be a scream.

Eva and Richard began to slowly back off from the park. They walked hand in hand, nervously trailing behind other groups of people as though they belonged to a party. Eva stumbled as she walked, her legs succumbing to the enormous amount of adrenalin surging through her veins, Richard grasped her tightly, leading her quickly as though she were an abducted child from a school. Richard glanced quickly behind him as they reached the path to the road, his gaze missing the suited man standing unassumingly on the corner. The couple walked past him, brushing the jacket of the man's suit. As Richard and Eva disappeared into the street, the man whispered into the collar of his jacket before slowly following.

Eva and Richard walked to the edges of the city, finally deciding to book into the Water Bay Arms. The pub was pretty on the outside, but had the familiar musky smell of late nights, heavy drinking, and vomit.

"I'm not sure how long we can stay here either," said Richard. "This is getting heavy, Eva. I don't know who those people are, but they are packing some serious equipment. I doubt whether it's a nice chat and a cup of tea they're after." Eva chewed at her lip as she followed Richard up the stairs to their room. Her nerves were beginning to fray, and she felt for the first time like she just wanted to lie down and give up. Richard helped Eva to the bed as he suddenly realised how ill she had become. Her breathing had become quick and erratic, and the tremors in her legs had proceeded to her hands, making them quake and jump. Richard sat beside her on the bed, stroking his hands through her hair. Carefully, he wiped away the sweat from her pale skin. Eva stared at him like the woman on the train had stared. Her gaze was distant, cold, and dead. The psychiatrist wished he had access to some sedatives, but instead he calmed her the old-fashioned way, with comforting soft words and gentle strokes; eventually, Eva fell asleep.

CHAPTER NINE

Eva turned to look at the sleeping Richard lying beside her. He was so attractive in his slumber, and just for a second, Eva felt the warm comfort that she had once experienced with Adam. That feeling had been so precious to her, to know that she would always be comforted by his strong embrace. Since Adam's death, she had thought that she would never experience that feeling again. Now that it was here, she almost wished it wasn't.

Eva crept silently from the bed; carefully, she reclaimed her clothes that were strewn ungracefully across the kitchen floor. As she dressed, she prayed that the decision she was about to make was the correct one. It felt almost like another betrayal, like she were betraying the trust that he had placed in her. It seemed apparent that, just like Adam, she was running away. Eva chewed the inside of her cheek as she glanced back at her sleeping lover. She couldn't bear to be responsible for the death of another, especially someone she had come to value so dearly. Leaving was the only way she knew how to protect him. Eva quickly pulled out a page from her tattered notebook. Scrawling like she only had seconds left to live, she wrote:

I can't bear the thought that when you're with me your life is in danger. I'm going to sort this out, and when it's all over, I'll come and find you. I promise.

All my Love,

Eva hurriedly slipped on her jacket as she saw the first rays of sun creep over the city limits. Taking one last glance at Richard, she left the hotel, hoping beyond all hope that it wasn't for the last time.

The night's previous rain had soaked the city streets into a shimmering canvas of wet concrete and tar. The air was still and unexpectedly warm, hinting at the impossible early emergence of summer. Despite the dark reality of her situation, Eva felt curiously fresh, like she had finally awoken from a nightmare that had never ended. Walking with an urgent sense of purpose, Eva crossed the street. The Water Bay Arms was in what Eva regarded as the posh end of town, although the untidiness of the pub and its rooms suggested otherwise. Blackwater University was a good hour's walk in exactly the opposite direction. Glancing at her watch, Eva realised that time wasn't an issue since it was only just past 6 a.m.

Eva continued to walk briskly down the streets, despite the fact that she had ample time. Eva felt more secure when she was walking at speed. The early morning traffic signalled the beginning of a work day, and Eva thought of Richard, wondering how he would react to her sudden disappearance. It was this nauseating feeling of loss that triggered Eva to take a small detour on her way to the university. The sudden dawning that she would have to face her demons was more than just a revelation. Just as much as she needed to lay to rest her guilt surrounding Adam's death, she also had to face the reality of her false angel. The consequences of this meeting could only have two outcomes, either she would live or she would die, and as much as she loved Adam, she wasn't quite ready to join him yet.

Standing as they always did, the large black iron gates of the cemetery greeted Eva with the same solemn bow she had become accustomed to. "It's good to see you again, too," Eva whispered to the gate as it whined a welcome when she forced it open. Feeling a warm familiarity, Eva relaxed as she walked along the loosely chipped path to the grave side. "Four more inmates," Eva whispered as she registered the freshly dug ground of new graves. It seemed almost a macabre habit that she had inherited from coming to the graveyard so often. Yet it was intended as such, just a respectful acknowledgement of those who would join Adam in heaven. Eva was not so convinced that heaven was something that could be easily achieved. It appeared that the destiny of the dead was not to live on in an afterlife designed for eternal happiness, but to spawn the beginnings of another being, a being Eva was not sure she was ready to accept.

The nurse felt a sense of bitter relief as she wandered up to the site of Adam's grave. Since her attack in the park, she had been unable to come here. It was like a fortress in her mind that she imagined was impenetrable. Eva knew that she had a battle ahead of her, and she wanted to win at least one before she had to face it.

"Hello, Adam," Eva whispered as she slowly approached his grave stone. The flowers she had left nearly three months ago were all but gone, and she gently moved away the litter of dead leaves that had gathered. She glanced around and noticed the vibrancy of fresh flowers left by loved ones, Adam's grave looked bare and stark in comparison. "I'm sorry I haven't been here in such a long time. I won't ever forget you; it's just that I was scared." Eva sucked at her bottom lip as a lonely tear ran over it like a mouse over a counter. "You will always be everything to me, but I must live my life as well. I think you would have wanted that." Removing her leather jacket, she placed it on the wet grass in front of his headstone. Sitting crossed-legged upon it, Eva began to tell Adam of the fantastical happenings of the past three months.

CHAPTER TEN

Sitting in the silence of his room, Richard read Eva's scrawled note. Letting it fall from his fingers, he rubbed his tongue over his teeth, almost as though he were stifling a cry from within his stomach. Feeling nauseous, Richard washed his face in the bathroom sink, the sudden splash of cold water on his skin served only to shock him back to the reality of his situation. The psychiatrist was awoken from his dark pondering by the persistent vibrations of his mobile phone. Scrambling around the living room, he finally located his abandoned suit jacket with the phone inside. Richard recognised Andrew's number and hesitated before answering.

"Jesus Christ, Richard! What the fuck is going on?" Andrew almost screamed down the phone to the psychiatrist before Richard had the chance to say hello.

"I'm not sure you'd believe me if I had the chance to explain," Richard answered his friend, with a tone that suggested he wouldn't have believed himself.

"Well, you better come up with something quick because you and that girl are on hot list at the station."

"What?" Richard's one-word response sparked another ramble of sentences from Andrew, and the psychiatrist rubbed his forehead in dazed confusion.

"We know you and Eva were the last two people to see the hotelier alive, and given the nature of his injuries—" Richard broke into Andrew's breathless sentence, "Look, that man committed suicide; we just happened to be there when he did." There was a short period of silence on the receiver as if both parties had exhausted their supply of words.

"And there's Louise," said Andrew.

"Louise?" Richard's response was instantaneous. "What about Louise?" Andrew breathed heavily down the receiver. "She's dead, Richard. The warden found her this morning with a pencil sticking out of her neck."

Richard sat down heavily on the couch, his eyes flickering with the emotion of the moment. "I saw her last night," he whispered back silently.

"Yes, we know, and we know that girl was with you, too."

"Andrew?" Richard paused for a second as he tried to think. "I need your help." Andrew stuttered as he breathed a muffled response. "C'mon, man. It's bad enough; I'm warning you in advance, let alone helping you." Richard stood up nervously pacing the floor. "You owe me, Andrew. Please, just five minutes of your time, that's all I'm asking." Andrew paused, chewing over the Psychiatrist's words he mumbled, "Yeah, I owe you."

ANDREW

Andrew looked down at his desk as though there were some hidden answers in the wood waiting to leap out at him. The middle-aged Chief Inspector had been in the force nearly twenty two years, and he lived for it. There was something that made him feel intensely proud when he asserted his authority. It wasn't the need for control either, just a sense of belonging that he had not found anywhere else. It meant so much to him that he would do almost anything to protect it. Helping Richard in the way that he was doing threatened that, and he resented the psychiatrist for making him do it. He also resented those above him who would insist on his involvement in this case, and all the others. His real job had become a hobby, whilst the job he did in secret took over everything. Andrew owed Richard, and he owed him big time.

It was a big enough debt to force him to put aside his loyalty to the force. The Chief rose from his chair in the crowded office and made his way towards the doors and the street outside, Andrew would make sure that this favour was the last one, and perhaps even the last job he would do for the government; he had helped them enough already.

Andrew grumbled to himself as he flicked up the collar of his beige jacket. The rain had been as persistent as it was cold, and the officer was sick of the grey clouds and dismal conditions. Andrew loved the sun; in fact he was a sun fanatic. The greyness of autumn and winter gave him Seasonal Affective Disorder and he hated the fact that for six months of the year he was almost permanently miserable. It had gotten so bad recently that his doctor had prescribed him anti-depressants to help lighten his moods. Still, he had two weeks of leave to take yet, and Rome had been his choice of holiday destination. Just seven weeks, three days, and a few hours before that plane would take off and deliver him into the sun. With that thought in mind, Andrew slipped into the comfortable seat of his four by four. Not exactly designed for city living, but he loved its robustness and besides he could afford it. Leaning into the foot well of the passenger seat, Andrew grabbed at his CD collection; the left side of his shirt slipped down over his collar bone to reveal a large and jagged scar. Almost instinctively but without really being aware, the Chief put his shirt back into its proper position. Listening intently to Led Zeppelin's "Early Days", Andrew drove with speed to Richard's house. The chief knew perfectly well that he wanted to avoid being seen at his former psychiatrist's, and a Grand Jeep Cherokee was not the subtlest of vehicles to do this.

Richard hovered around the windows, waiting for any sign of Andrew. As the Jeep pulled into the car park, Richard was already at the door to his flat.

"This better be good, mate, because I am going to be walking over hot coals for this."

The psychiatrist nodded his head, leading Andrew back through to the kitchen where he poured them both a glass of his reserve whiskey. Richard took a deep breath and said, "I can't tell you everything. To be honest, it's so fucked up I doubt you would believe me anyway." Andrew shook his head, putting down his glass of whiskey. "Listen, I've supported you as much as I can, but now people are dead and there has to be an explanation."

Richard looked up at his friend in a way that suggested he dare not try to explain. "Eva and Louise both saw something, something that is dangerous, and not..." Richard swilled the whiskey glass round in his hand as he thought of the appropriate word, "... not entirely human." Andrew raised his eyebrows as though Richard had just told him that the Queen Mother had risen from the dead.

"Look," Richard persuaded, rolling his eyes as he received the response he had expected. "Look at these drawings." Richard spread out the pictures that Eva and Louise had both drawn. "And look at the newspaper clippings that Eva collected." Andrew flicked through the paperwork and tossed them back down, the psychiatrist caught a faint glimmer of recollection in Andrew's eyes, and for a second, he wondered if his police friend had seen them before.

"Richard, this is all just coincidence; this is not evidence of the supernatural." Richard pulled off the bandages from his fingers. "No, but this is very real, and this is what happens when you meet one of these things." He shoved his hand into the officer's face whilst pointing with the other at the drawings. Richard frowned for a second as he remembered his mobile phone. "I took pictures of the wall at the B & B; I haven't looked at them yet." Richard reached for his camera phone, quickly running through the pictures. "Look at this." Richard handed to the phone to Andrew,

"I've seen this, Richard; it was all over the walls," Richard nodded in confirmation, "Yes, but did you read what it said? Did you think about what it could mean?" Andrew frowned again, re-reading the somewhat garbled messages strewn on the wall. "You cannot deny us life." Andrew screwed his face up, tilting his head in recognition that the message was not your average suicide note.

"Here, look at these words. I know they mean something, and I'm just about to find out what they mean," Richard almost shouted, reaching for his laptop on the table. Andrew moaned whilst dragging his hands down his face. "I know what those words mean: it's called 'the transmigration of the soul,' quite popular in some Indian and Buddhist cultures." Richard frowned to himself as he typed the words into Wikipedia. "That's a strange thing for a police officer to be aware of, isn't it?" Andrew raised his eyebrows, quickly dismissing Richard's comments. "I travel." Richard did not pay much attention to Andrew's response and read the definition of the words from the Wikipedia page out loud. *"Fundamental to some Greek philosophers, it relates to the entire universal process that gives rise to the cycle of life, death and rebirth, the changing from one life to the next, it's almost like a form of reincarnation."* The psychiatrist laughed mildly under his breath. "My God, I think Eva was onto something here."

"You know, Richard?" said Andrew. "You are probably the most level-headed, straight-down-the-line person I know, and now, now you're asking me to believe in what?" Richard shook his head retrieving his phone. "Not what, who." Richard picked back up his glass as he paced the floor. "I think Eva might be right. She thinks that these things are real, real beings living beside us, but we just never see them."

"Well, why are you seeing them now?" Andrew's response was abrupt and to the point. "Both Eva and Louise had near-death experiences, and so did everyone in those newspaper clippings. It's almost as if they are being punished for coming back."

Andrew laughed in disbelief, "Are you getting all religious on me, Richard?"

"No, no, in fact, quite the opposite. I'm talking about real science here. I think these beings need us to die, and when we don't when we're supposed to, they get pretty pissed off."

Raising his eyebrows once again, Andrew continued to stare at the blank wall in front of him. Richard eyed him curiously. Andrew chewed on the inside of his cheek as though he were attempting to hide something, or at least trying not so say what was on his mind.

"I need your help, Andrew, whether you believe me or not, Eva's in trouble; those things are going to catch her eventually. And in the mean time they are pretty much wiping out others she meets along the way. Trust me, I've met one." Waving his injured hand again, Richard sat himself heavily on the couch. Andrew sighed and closed his eyes; his gut told him that Richard had become too close; it also told him that the psychiatrist could not be fobbed off for too much longer. The most trustworthy, straight-down-the-line guy he knew, and he was mumbling some ridiculous story about some kind of supernatural being. Andrew knew that for Richard to believe in the supernatural meant that he had all the facts, and those facts spelled out the truth. Andrew rotated the whiskey glass in his hand. Either he was going to cover it all up and suggest that this was nothing more than the psycho ramblings of his deranged girlfriend, or he was going to have to confess to knowing more than he claimed.

"You know people say that all psychiatrists are a bit mixed-up upstairs?" Andrew almost shouted at Richard from across the open-plan kitchen. Richard waved his glass in response retorting, "You're only mad if you don't know it."

"God damn it." Andrew rolled his eyes. If this were anyone else, he would turn his back, march straight out to his Jeep, and forget he even knew the guy. Richard wasn't just any guy, though. Andrew rubbed at the scar on his chest; Richard had saved his mind and his job.

Three years ago, Andrew had had what he considered to be the perfect life. A lovely three-bedroom cottage on the outskirts of town, and the most beautiful fiancée he had could ever have hoped to be with. Sarah was a jewel in his life; he worshipped the ground she walked on. He also loved his work. He had dreamt of being a police officer since he was a small boy, and he thought he had everything. Sarah wasn't as enthusiastic about Andrew's job. It kept him away for long periods of time, and she was constantly worried about his safety. Andrew ignored her from the start, reassuring her with the same repetitive comments every night. Blinded by his love for the force, he failed to see the descent in Sarah's happiness until it was too late. On March 27th Andrew found himself in a position that would change his life forever. Two armed boys had attempted to rob the store he was doing his shopping in; rather than call for back up, Andrew had attempted to stop the criminals himself. He did not do a bad job although he had failed to see the kitchen knife that the younger of the two boys had concealed in his jacket pocket. In his opinion, his wounds weren't that bad really, just a couple of hundred stitches and a blood transfusion, yet for Sarah, it was the last straw. Andrew left the hospital seven days later to find his lovely little cottage in the countryside stripped of everything that had been Sarah; all that was left was a wide screen television, his favourite recliner, and the complete box set of the "X Files". The loss of Sarah had been a blow that he wasn't expecting, and he couldn't cope with the empty feeling that swallowed him up in a consuming darkness. Andrew began to make mistakes. Sometimes he wouldn't even turn up for work, and finally, his bad decisions ended up in the near death of a colleague. Andrew was put on suspension and ordered to see a psychiatrist; the psychiatrist was Richard.

If Andrew were to be honest, he found Richard to be an arrogant suit and tie. It aggravated him that his future was to be placed in the hands of a man who appeared to have no balls and even less of a personality. Regardless of what Andrew thought about him, the man was good at his job. The suspended Chief was less than happy to talk about issues he considered personal, but Richard's persistent chats every session soon prised the information Andrew was hiding into the open. After three months, Andrew was still having sessions with Richard, and the psychiatrist knew that his patient was still harbouring deep pain that would affect his job. Andrew, unable to work and alone, was suffering more with each passing week. Richard made the decision to sign Andrew as fit to go back to work, despite the fact that in his professional opinion he was far from it.

"I'm doing this because I think you need to work, and because I think it's the only thing you have left that you love," Richard spoke to Andrew as a teacher would to a small boy. "I really don't want to be facing a board of enquiry when you go back and kill someone." Andrew had accepted the psychiatrist's comments with respect; he had given him his job back and a new chance at life. Andrew owed him, and he wasn't going to let him down if he could help it.

"Richard," Andrew whispered sheepishly over the top of his whiskey glass, "there's something I need to tell you."

CHAPTER ELEVEN

Eva smiled as she proudly walked through the large wooden doors of Blackwater University. It had been nearly five years since she had left the university, and she still felt a sense of pride at having been a student in one of the county's most prestigious further education institutions. The musty smell of ancient books and paperwork struck the graduate as she walked with confidence onto the highly polished marble floor of the foyer. The university felt like a safe environment, full of facts and real life. Eva had reason to be confident when she entered these walls; she had graduated with distinction. This university had helped her choose the direction that she was to follow, and although she knew that that direction had been lost in the past few months, she had a nagging feeling that the university would once again place her on the right path.

Professor Stanford belonged to the physics department of the university. It was an area of study that had not sparked an interest in Eva, so she found herself entering a section of the institution that she had never seen before. Eva found herself giggling to herself and shaking her head as the glass swing doors revealed a realm only a Star Trek fanatic would love. A large poster graced the entrance, and Eva frowned as she attempted to decipher its meaning. "Warp Drive Fact or Fantasy?" Eva rolled her eyes, before thinking that her own experiences suggested something just as extraordinary. The graduate nurse preferred not to be stereotypical in her awareness of new people, but the group of students hovering outside the professor's office begged a stereotypical label.

Whilst clearly being young adults, they dressed like middle-aged college lecturers. Shirts and corduroy trousers seemed favourable amongst the males, whilst three-quarter length skirts and shirt blouses seemed to be the in thing for the girls. Eva insisted generally on good make up and neat hair, and wasn't particularly bothered about fashion, but she knew that there was no way in hell that she would ever be seen in one of those get-ups. As the students filed neatly in the classroom like worker ants, Eva hovered outside, unsure whether her arrival had been badly timed.

"Yes, this could be your class."

Eva spun round with a start as a tall, lanky, balding man with a white overcoat and brogue shoes peered at her from above the rim of his plastic-rimmed glasses.

"Erm, actually, I'm here to talk to you for a few minutes, Professor Stanford" Eva said sheepishly, suddenly feeling like she was indeed back in the classroom.

"Right, well, I have a class, but I suppose they can be getting on with something if it's urgent." Eva nodded her head enthusiastically, and the professor disappeared for a few seconds as he left instructions with his class. "My office is just up the corridor." The professor gestured with his hand for Eva to lead the way, although she struggled to keep up with his long pacing strides, and felt as though she were awkwardly speed walking her way down the corridor.

The professor's office was not exactly what the nurse had expected, and she marvelled at the expensively decorated room. Professor Stanford appeared to like his luxuries, and the nurse felt rather out of place as she gingerly sat down on the green leather sofa. Sitting in a wooden swivel chair in front of an extensive library of books, the professor took off his glasses.

"Now, how can I help you today?"

Eva stuttered for a second as she began. "I-I … w-was asked to talk to you by Louise Turnbull. I think that you know something that might help me." The professor screwed his face up for a second as he racked his brain for the name.

"Ah, Louise, yes. I believe she's incarcerated now."

Eva bit her lip. "I'm afraid she's dead, professor. I need to know what she meant by 'ask you.'" The professor raised his bushy, unmanaged eyebrows in shock for a second before shaking his head. "I'm not sure what she meant; she did talk to me at length about energy particles and the like. Aside from that, we didn't really converse that much; she was a complicated girl, to be sure."

Eva nodded her head, aware that the professor did not have the immediate answer that she required. Eva wasn't sure what she had expected, but the hope was there that the professor was going to hand her a folder with all the answers she needed.

"I know you have a class waiting, professor, but could you please tell me what Louise was enquiring about specifically? It might be really important." The professor pulled a surprised face and nodded. "Well, Miss Turnbull seemed entirely preoccupied by what happens to the body's energy when it dies." Eva breathed in as she suddenly realised that perhaps Louise was onto something. "What does happen?" The professor clasped his hands together. "As I'm sure you're probably aware, energy cannot be destroyed. It can be stretched, compressed, or even transferred from one structure to another." Eva shuffled forward on her chair as his sentence grabbed her attention. "Transferred?"

"Yes, when the body dies, it produces a vapour, a kind of energy, which is made up of sub-atomic molecular cells. It's even possible to smell this vapour, if you're close enough to the deceased that is." Eva closed her eyes as she attempted to absorb all the information. The professor gestured with his hands, "It is this vapour that is capable of migrating into other living cells that mirror its former likeness; energy is fundamentally attracted to other energy molecules that pattern its own likeness." Eva licked her lips. "Like another human being or something resembling a human being?" she questioned, carefully aware that the professor seemed a little perplexed by her interest.

138

"Yes, I suppose so."

Eva leaned forward as though she were about to whisper a deadly secret. "Can you stop it?" The professor leaned back in his chair. "This sounds remarkably like the questions Louise was trying to find answers for. As I told her, energy cannot be destroyed, every cell has a memory and memory is pure energy." The professor stood up from his chair. "I must get back to my class." Eva quickly rose from hers and nodded her head. "Of course, thank you so much for all your insight."

The professor walked with Eva back to his class; he paused for a second as he turned the door knob. "Louise seemed very interested in the fact that some people claim to recall secrets and memories that were once held by the deceased in question. Intuition and memory are always intimately linked." Eva smiled nodding, "Thank you, professor."

Eva fretted as she quickly walked back down the long corridors and towards the foyer. She was afraid that she might forget something that the professor had said. It seemed all so complicated, and yet in the context of her false angels, it made perfect sense. Eva racked her brain for a safe place to go. The answer to her question was obvious, and rather than exit from the building, Eva began to make her way to the stairs. It was like a blast from the past as she expertly skipped up the broad wooden stairs. She had never missed a step in the past, and she wasn't going to today. All those days she had been late for class had installed a need for speedy and accurate footing; Eva was pleased that she had not lost the skill. No other learning resource centre had the volume of books that Blackwater University boasted. It was the largest collection of educational literature in a two hundred mile radius. Often, Eva would see other students from less prestigious universities searching through the titles for the elusive book that might help them pass their studies. As the nurse walked into the large semi-circular library, she wondered why she even bothered to visit the small public one in town; this library was the library of the gods.

The nurse found a small circular table at the back of the library; it was quiet and away from the persistent keyboard tapping at the front of the room. As much as she enjoyed using technology, there was something clearer and more simplistic about good old fashioned pen and paper. When Eva wrote something down, she remembered it; when she typed it, she had forgotten what she was typing about before she had had the chance to do a spell check. The library seemed unusually quiet today; she had always remembered it in her student days, as a bustling centre of students and lecturers. Some days Eva didn't even go into the library to study; she just went to meet up and socialise with her friends. The large white signs on the walls instructing no loud talking and group gatherings suggested a possible reason why the library had returned to its original intended use. Eva grabbed a blunt pencil from her bag; cheekily snatching some blank paper from a nearby printer, she sat down to collate her thoughts.

LOUISE

•Had a near-death experience
•Contacted Professor Stanford about energy particles
•Killed people on the bus
•Committed suicide?

ME

•Had a near-death experience
•Seem to be always near to or around people who either commit suicide or are killed in accidents? - The woman on the bus, (no accident)

FALSE ANGELS

- Live on energy
- Are born when we die
- Are connected to every born human being
- Develop into adults after our death
- Will die if they do not receive the energy upon our death
- Can manipulate or enter our world in dreams, other people or as vapours?

PROFESSOR STANFORD - Suggests they cannot be killed as energy cannot be destroyed
- Subatomic particles?
- Energy as vapour (possibly what was in the petrol station)
- Energy can be manipulated, stretched, and transferred
- Memories? Energy retains the memories of its previous form. Can the false angels remember the pasts of those who once lived?????

Eva stopped for a second as she re-read her own notes. The nurse put her head in her hands as she forced herself to remember the coma-induced dream she had recalled during her recuperation. Adam. His name reverberated around her skull for a moment as she realised that perhaps the vision of him had a real meaning, not just a jumble of disjointed memories her brain had formed to deal with the trauma. Perhaps his false angel was out there. Eva bit at her lip as she contemplated the thought that Adam wasn't really dead; he was one of them, an angel.

Suddenly the nurse began to feel a deep sense of confusion. She had invested so much of her time in figuring out what these things were and ultimately how to stop them. Now, Eva wasn't sure if she was right. If these beings truly were the carriers of souls and if a soul is nothing more than a collection of subatomic energy particles with memories, then there is an afterlife. The nurse unconsciously dug the tip of her pencil into the wooden surface of the table. "There is an afterlife," Eva whispered quietly into the library as though her revelation would shock the foundations of the building. For a brief second, Eva was almost willing to give her life there and then, the possibility that she could join Adam, that she would see her mum again.

The nurse shook her head, trying to dull the enthusiasm she had acquired for death. These were not the angels told in Bibles; these were living entities, living off our souls, stealing our memories. A knot of anger rose in her throat, and she struggled to contain it. What right did any being have to choose Eva's destiny? To choose when she was to die and punish her for living? Her attempts at stifling her outburst resulted in a barrage of hot tear drops, and Eva wiped them away quickly with the cuff of her sleeve. Suddenly Eva felt incredibly small; letting out a stifled giggle, she rose from her chair. With all the greatest minds in the world, with all the religious leaders and physicists, it had been Eva, a lowly nurse from Blackwater, who had discovered the existence of a new life on earth.

Eva left the library like a scientist who had discovered the meaning of the universe. Her mind buzzed with the revelation, and yet she could only think of one thing. She wanted to survive. Reaching into her bag, the nurse reached for her flat keys. She needed the comforts of her own home to come up with a plan, and she needed access to the Internet to research them. Eva thought momentarily of Richard and wondered if perhaps she should let him know what she had discovered. But she was short on time; every moment she breathed on this earth she knew that they would be following, waiting for the right moment to infiltrate her.

Running as though she were taking part in a marathon, Eva bolted down the streets of Blackwater. Passers-by leaped out of her way as she shot by them, their confused faces being lost in the urgency of the moment. Eva felt the vibrations of her mobile phone in her bag, and knowing that it could only be Richard, she ignored it. Slipping quickly and silently passed the other flat doors, she finally reached the door to her own. Eva looked about her before she entered, as though she were trying to evade a hidden killer. Quickly closing the door behind her, the nurse locked the four latches she had put on after her attack. Feeling it wasn't enough; she grabbed a wooden chair from the kitchen and placed it under the door handle. Still, she felt nervous, unsure whether she was trying to avoid humans, the entities, or both. In her stomach, she knew that no lock or chair would prevent them from gaining access.

Eva sat down in her living room; logging onto the Internet, she reached for her ashtray, still brimming with half-smoked cigarettes from the last time she had been home. Eva placed her notes from the library on the table in front of her. She knew that the professor had said that she couldn't stop energy, but she wondered if perhaps she could hinder it, stall it, and leave herself enough time to initiate her plan.

Eva sat with a cup of coffee, a cigarette, and over-arching feeling of urgency. She couldn't help but feel that she was being watched. The constant flickering of her table-top lamp suggested that she was not alone, and she shivered with expectancy. Typing quickly, she searched the net for the keywords suggested by Professor Stanford. Eva felt that she was getting nowhere as every search result confirmed that energy transference was inevitable.

The nurse racked her brain, vainly trying to rearrange her words in the search box. Finally she found something. "Of course," Eva shouted out loud as she realised that it wasn't just energy she was searching for, but a specific type of energy, electrical. Eva laughed as she considered the simplicity of it. The beings were inherently electrical in nature, and as such, Eva just had to find a way to resist the flow of electrical charge. "Insulators," Eva whispered as the answer stared out at her in the form of the rubber cabling on her mouse. Searching for "insulators," the nurse came upon the definition in Wiki Answers. *"Insulators are used to hold conductors in place, separating them from one another to form a barrier between energized parts of an electric circuit and confine the flow of current to wires or other conductive paths."*

Eva re-read the passage a few times, working out in her head where exactly she was in terms of the circuit. She needed to create a barrier between herself and the entities. When they were in her space, they created an electric circuit between her and them, and it was through this that the energy transference could take place. Eva tapped her fingers on the table top. "Why not just do it when I'm alive? Why do I need to be dead?" Eva fidgeted in her seat, her patience was fraying, and she kicked at the flickering lamp with her foot, sending it crashing to the floor. Looking at her notes, she pondered, "When I'm dead, my energy begins to leave my body like a vapour. They can't just take it; it has to be free flowing!"

Eva talked to herself like she was having a conversation with her mind. "They can manipulate us, like the way that subatomic energy particles can be stretched, but they can't directly interfere. They need my death to complete the circuit" Eva stood up as though she had just found a million dollars in her pocket. "Now it's my time to interfere." Eva looked at the lamp as she spoke her sentence, treating it like it was the very thing she was battling against.

CHAPTER TWELVE

Andrew flicked thoughtfully through all the evidence that Richard and Eva had gathered for a second time. His occasional sighs signalled to the psychiatrist that his friend couldn't help but recognise the points that he had made, however fantastical.

"Nobody at the station would believe what you're suggesting Richard, especially not the Chief Superintendent," The psychiatrist nodded his head as though he was aware of that fact. "I'm not asking them to believe me, only that Eva is not responsible for those deaths." Andrew clasped his hands together. "Well, all you need to do is come down the station and tell us exactly why you were where you were and what happened. The more you two keep running away, the more suspicious it looks when a trail of dead bodies follows behind you."

Richard stood up redialling Eva's number from his mobile phone. "Fine, we will, but you're missing the point. I think Eva's in real danger. She's not answering her phone, and I need to find her." Andrew stood up making his way to the hall as his own phone chimed out the theme from "Twin Peaks".

"Professor," said Andrew.

There was a momentary pause on the line as though the meeting of voices was neither needed nor wanted.

"Ah, Andrew, how are you?"

The Chief Inspector moved further away from the living room and the prying ears of Richard before he began. "I think we have a problem. Miss Gardiner appears to be unearthing a lot more than we thought; this isn't something that can be passed off as mere coincidence."

"Yes." Professor Stanton cleared his throat of the imaginary frog that leaped around on his palate. "She was in my office earlier, asking about the Turnbull girl. I don't believe locking this one up in a psychiatric hospital is the answer, my friend. She's smart, this one."

Andrew tapped his finger rhythmically on the end of his mobile phone. "Yes, well, she's managing to convince a rather well-respected psychiatrist of her ideas also; if he believes, anyone will." The professor breathed heavily down the phone as though he were about to have an asthma attack.

"We can't stall the facts forever, my friend," mumbled the professor. "What we need is damage control. Look after this girl, Andrew; she may be the warrior we've been waiting for." The Chief Inspector nodded down the phone in response as though his counterpart were standing right beside him. Flicking his mobile phone closed, Andrew shook his head in sarcasm. "Damage control," he whispered jokingly.

Pacing around his flat, Richard ran through his hair with frustration. The constant "tick, tick" of his wall clock served only to remind him that time was running short.

"Well, I hope you've got some clue as to where she is because my guys just busted into her flat, and she's not there," Andrew shook his head, "They had to break through four security locks and a chair to get in." Richard half-laughed as he sighed,

"Yeah, if you'd seen what we have seen, you'd want five bloody locks on your door," Richard shook his head as he tried to rack his brain.

"Was there nothing there that could help?" Andrew pulled a puzzled face,

"They said her computer was sitting on a Wikipedia page about deionised water, and it looks like she decided to leave her flat via the fire escape." Richard screwed his face up.

"Deionised water?" The psychiatrist rubbed at his face as he continued to wear down a path in his laminate flooring. "What's deionised water used for?" Andrew shrugged his shoulders.

"If I remember my physics correctly, it's used in lead acid batteries, autoclaves. I think it's a kind of insulator for automotive products, but don't quote me on that one." Richard instantly looked up from his wanderings.

"Insulator?" Andrew nodded.

"Yeah, you know it doesn't conduct electricity very well, like the rubber on your electric cables." Richard pointed a finger at Andrew with excitement.

"That's it, that's the clue. These beings are like massive electrical conductors; she must be trying to insulate herself somehow."

Andrew shrugged his shoulders, "I don't get it."

Richard ignored Andrew's last comment and rummaged around for his own computer under the piles of paperwork strewn on his desk.

"We need to find out where there's going to be large quantities of deionised water," He logged onto his laptop, quickly searching for the Blackwater Council homepage.

"Well, the hospital's bound to have some and the university; they use it for experiments, I think," Richard swung round his laptop to face Andrew,

"No, it's got to be here; she's going to need a lot of that stuff, trust me." Andrew raised his eyebrows as he read the welcome page of the Marine Aquarium Centre.

THE AQUARIUM

Eva stood with nervous trepidation in front of the Marine Aquarium. She had lived in Blackwater for nearly eight years, and yet she had never thought to visit it. Her lack of knowledge made it difficult for her to gain entry after dark, and the nurse watched warily as the security cameras did their sweep of the area. Skulking like a cat in the shadows, she slid in between the scope of the cameras. Eva pulled up the hood on her sweatshirt to mask her face, and with her back pressed firmly against the wall, she edged her way around the side of the building. The back of the aquarium seemed remarkably unprotected, Eva noted that one of the loading bay doors did not quite reach the tarmac courtyard, and she bit her lip as she pondered squeezing between the gap. Closing her eyes, the nurse crouched in the shadows. She could feel her body trembling with adrenalin; her deep erratic breaths blooming out into the frosty air like miniature clouds. "C'mon, c'mon," Eva spoke to herself in the darkness before taking three quick breaths and darting towards the open loading bay door.

Eva cursed as she lay flat on her back on the tar; there was less than a six-inch gap between the bottom of the door and the ground. Her adrenalin still pumping thick and fast, she forced her head and chest through the gap; not stopping to breathe, she dragged the rest of her body through as though the world would end if she failed in her task. Lying on the inside of the door, Eva took a few moments to compose herself. A sharp sting from her chin and knee signalled that she had not made the transition from outside incident-free, but the nurse ignored the pain as she began her search for the freshwater tank.

The loading bay she had broken into was vast. The nurse was reluctant to switch on a light, and used the illuminating glow of her mobile phone to navigate around the highly stacked boxes of shrimp and brine eggs. A small red door with a sign that read 'Staff Only' offered her an exit into the main building, and Eva breathed a sigh of relief as it opened without reluctance.

Although dark, the narrow corridors of the marine centre were faintly lit with the subtle glow of small coloured lights situated underneath the fish tanks. The nurse wished that she were there for a different reason. It would have been pleasant to wander around staring at the fish as a visitor, rather than as a criminal fighting for her life. Eva grimaced as her phone vibrated' it created an awkward intrusion into the peacefulness of the aquarium. The nurse could almost feel the fish looking with annoyance at her rudeness. Eva switched off the phone. She was secretly pleased at Richard's persistent attempts at contact, but she knew that he couldn't help her. The marine centre was vast, one corridor led to another, with multiple branches leading to different tourist attractions. Eva felt as though she were a rat in a maze, and began to feel frustration as she struggled to find what she was looking for. A large glass tunnel led Eva through an underwater exhibit, and she smiled as its exit revealed a sign pointing towards the fresh water aquarium.

The marine centre like most of Blackwater's institutions was famous for its grandness. In this case, it boasted the largest fresh water marine tank in the country. Eva marvelled at the giant circular glass bowl that stood before her. Suddenly, she became aware of the task that she had set herself. This was more than just a task. If it went pear-shaped, then it would almost certainly result in her death, another apparent suicide in Blackwater's logbook of dead citizens. Removing her shoes and jacket, the nurse stepped cautiously towards the tank. A large information plaque hung from two silver chains attached to the roof, and Eva nodded with confirmation as she read exactly what she had hoped for. *"This tank contains purified water. Purified water is used in fresh water and marine aquaria as it does not contain impurities such as copper and chlorine, and keeps the fish free from disease."* As the nurse gingerly climbed the steel ladder to the top of the tank, she prayed that her research had been correct. Purified water was described as a dialectic insulator with electrical conductivity of not more than 10μ s/cm. Eva hoped that its poor conductivity would keep them at bay long enough for her to try and make contact with Adam.

Eva let out a whimpering cry as the cold water in the tank immersed her feet. It was freezing, like ice water, and it caused instant cramping pains to shoot up the backs of her calves. The nurse began to rethink her plan, as the cold deepness of the tank hovered below her like a watery grave. Eva shook her head. Aware of her own cowardice, she began to climb back up the ladder towards the edge of the tank. Before the nurse could reach the top, a series of small spark like explosions broke out in the marine centre. Eva looked with confusion as the fish in the tank began darting around in the water like miniature arrows. The subtle warming glow that illuminated the aquarium became dull like an extinguishing flame as the lights beneath them went out one by one. Eva looked about in panic, and before she was reduced to total darkness, she dived into the tank. The nurse sank to the bottom, like a lead balloon, as the shock paralysed her freezing body. Her senses dulled by the immersion of water, she felt nothing, only the pounding of her heart relieved the silence. Eva opened her eyes to a well of total darkness. The numbing water forced her to close them again, and the nurse realised that her time was short. Quietening her mind, Eva allowed her thoughts to wander.

Outside the tank, a number of crystalline spheres hovered around the glass. They resembled miniature snowflakes and clung to the tank as if they had become stuck to a frozen lake. The darkness of the freshwater aquarium was once again replaced by the subtle glow of tiny lights. A bioluminescence so bright in its core, that it could outshine a hundred watt bulb. As they clung to the tank's glass frame, they began to smother its surface in a membrane of blue electrostatic charges. Occasionally, as one entity connected with another, an electric arc would fan out into the room, imitating the solar flares of the sun. Inside the protection of her dielectric water bath, Eva remained unaware of the danger lurking just outside her glass protectorate.

The nurse explored the recesses of her own mind, as she had done in her dream. She struggled to focus, as her body suffered from lack of oxygen and the deep cold that surrounded her limbs. Eva felt powerless to stop herself from letting go. Her heartbeat had become nothing more than an intermittent echo, and she began to realise how tired she had become. Reasoning with her failing consciousness, she accepted the fact that it was okay to let go. She had done enough; they couldn't take her soul in here. Drifting like a piece of fossil wood in the water, the nurse sank slowly towards the bottom of the tank.

ADAM

"You know what you're doing really isn't fair."

Eva opened her eyes as a familiar voice struck into her consciousness.

"Adam," Eva whispered, then smiled as she saw the comforting glow of his eyes on hers.

"No, I'm not Adam. I'm Chrydle. Adam is a part of me, but he is not me."

Eva frowned as she struggled to believe that the face so recognisable before her was not the man she had loved.

"You come into my world and try to force me to die, and then you kill those around me. I don't think you understand the meaning of the word fair," said Eva with a flash of aggression, partly because she felt threatened and partly because she was forced to face Adam's death again.

"You deny us the right to live," Chrydle hissed. "We are dying because of you; the pod designed for your life has already begun to die. You are responsible."

Eva shook her head, "Every being has the right to live, even you, but not at the expense of another, I cannot allow you to destroy life for the sake of your own." Eva turned away from the entity that had now relinquished its human form and returned to its natural crystal state.

"It is the way it has always been," Chrydle murmered. "Your kind live longer, while ours perish, but no more; we will restore the balance of life."

Eva stopped waving her arms around in the water as the being behind her hissed into the blue glow surrounding them. Turning to face it, Eva smiled, "Perhaps it's time we came into your world. It won't be long before every human being on the planet knows about your kind, and when they do, you will understand what the phrase a 'fight for survival' really means." A crackle like the sound of crumpling tin foil broke out around them.

"You're dying," said Chrydle. The entity circled Eva like a lion stalking its prey.

Eva nodded. "I know, and this is one soul you will not be collecting." Eva laughed, directing her sarcasm as strongly as she could at the being before her. "Adam," Eva spoke purposefully into the blue. "I love you". There was a moment of pause as the entity seemed to become confused with her comment, and just for a second, Eva saw the warmth of her lover's eyes, once again. Closing her own, and feeling fulfilled, Eva drifted into the veil of darkness that swept into the blue.

Andrew and Richard burst in to the freshwater aquarium like hungry dogs waiting for their supper. "What the fuck is that?" Andrew stopped still as the crystalline structures attached to the tank drifted from its glass surface into the room. The Chief Inspector ducked as the tiny balls of light flew over his head like bullets, disappearing into the walls of the building. "Were those orbs?" Andrew looked with shock at the psychiatrist, who was already making his way up the ladder of the aquarium tank.

"C-c-call an ambulance, and be quick!" Richard stuttered with fear as he dived into the water to retrieve Eva, who drifted unconsciously on the bottom. Andrew frowned with dazed uncertainty as he dialled for the ambulance. He looked about him in trepidation as he did. Dragging the cold and pale nurse from the tank, Richard began to resuscitate her. Andrew took over the compressions as Richard breathed long and deep into her lungs.

"C'mon, don't give up on me now, not after all of this, not now," Richard pleaded with Eva as her wet body lay motionless on the marina floor. The sound of the ambulance could be heard in the distance, and Richard closed his eyes, praying that he had not been too late.

CHAPTER THIRTEEN

"Perhaps it's about time you came back to work instead of insisting on being a patient. I have to say, I'd much rather you were doing my bidding, than me doing yours, Nurse Gardiner."

Eva peered through her half-closed eyes and managed a partial smile at the sister hovering above her.

"I have to say, Eva, you seem to have bagged yourself a rather nice psychiatrist." Her former boss winked, motioning with her shoulder down the corridor. "He hasn't left your side since you were brought in; thought I was going to have to make him up a bed!" The sister chuckled as she left Eva, jingling her keys as she closed the door behind her.

A subtle breeze from the open window in Eva's hospital room glided past the nurse's face, and she breathed in cautiously. Eva shuddered as she pulled the nasal drip from her nose. The familiar smell of Dettol signalled that the hospital cleaners had finished their rounds. The nurse smirked to herself as she dragged her groggy body up into a sitting position.

"Cheated you twice," she whispered with a sense of triumph as she attempted to focus properly on her surroundings. A blanket of warm sun pushed through the curtains, and the nurse realised that it had been days since she had basked in its golden glow. Oddly and without logical reasoning, Eva felt lighter than she had in months. It was as though all that had drowned her in blackness had been swept away with the dust, to be forgotten and ignored. She woke with no painful memories; no shadow of a presence lurking in her consciousness, just clarity of judgement that made breathing easy.

"Hey, you!"

Eva grinned with enthusiasm as Richard walked casually through the door with a bouquet of flowers tucked under his arm. Richard strode up with an immature swagger that made Eva giggle like a schoolgirl.

"Well, my angel of Mercy, looks like you've survived again," Richard whispered as he leaned forward to kiss her on the forehead. "I expect I'll be going to prison for this," the nurse grimaced under her breath.

"Well, that's the great thing about knowing people in the right departments. Andrew said he thinks he can come up with something to get you off the hook, although … it appears you're back on my psychiatric list for attempted suicide!" Eva laughed sarcastically under her breath. "Yeah, well, this is one soul those bastards aren't going to get. Well, not yet anyway."

Eva smiled as her psychologist and lover placed himself in the seat beside her bed. There was a momentary pause as he took a breath to speak. "It seems that you and I are not alone in this strange mystery." Eva frowned as Richard rolled his eyes in disbelief at his own words. Patting Eva's knee, Richard looked intensely into her eyes as though what he was about to say would be too much for her to comprehend. "We are not the first to encounter these beings. In fact, we are two among thousands." The nurse pulled herself up into a sitting position on the bed. "The trouble is, very few people have ever lived to talk about them." Eva rubbed her face with her hands, still feeling groggy from her extended sleep.

"How do you know this?" The nurse shook her head in a daze. "I think that these people might be better equipped to tell us that," Eva looked up as a faint squeak from the door to her room signalled the entrance of Andrew and Professor Stanford. The nurse pulled up the covers on her bed to hide her bare legs as the two men approached.

"I thought you might like these," Andrew smiled.

"They're beautiful," Eva whispered in warm appreciation as Andrew handed her a large bunch of white lilies. Professor Stanford filled a vase with water and winked at Eva as he arranged them on her bedside table.

"I should have known the first time I laid eyes on you that you're a survivor," Professor Stanford laughed. Eva bit her lip, "I'd really like to know what's going on and who you and they are."

Professor Stanford leaned on the window ledge staring out at the hospital gardens.

"We don't have a name for them," He stared across the grounds. "They are in natural and physical terms scavengers of the dead, and in Biblical terms … angels."

Eva breathed out as she recognised the simplicity of it.

"These beings have coexisted with us since the very dawn of man," the professor continued. "As we die, the energy particles that are dissipated by our dying cells are collected by them. For these beings, our energy is their life force, their blood so to speak. Without it, they die."

Eva held the frown that had crept upon her face. "If this is true and they really have been on earth as long as man, then why aren't they public knowledge?"

The professor laughed with an undertone of sarcasm. "They are known to some. If you happen to be religious, then they are the angels that carry your soul to heaven. If you're not, then they are the ghosts of dead relatives and friends seen in dark corners." Eva raised her eyebrows and reached for a glass of water on the table; Andrew passed the glass to her, saving the nurse the effort of the stretch.

"As you and Richard have noticed, Eva, things are not as smooth running as they once were," Andrew remarked cautiously. Eva smirked in reply to his obvious observation.

"No shit. I've been hounded and hunted like a wild fox since my attack." Professor Stanford nodded, leaving the window ledge behind to stand at the foot of the bed.

"The problem is that the balance between our existence and theirs has begun to lose this delicate balance." Eva shook her head again,

"I don't understand." The professor smiled as he saw the nurse's confusion.

"Its people like you, institutes like the one we are in, and good men like Andrew over there that are causing the problem." The professor stroked his moustache as though calming his own thoughts. "People are living longer. They are surviving things that they never would have in the past; our own natural evolution has developed technologies to prolong human life. Whilst we evolve, these beings remain stagnant; our medical and technological advances are quite literally killing their species." Eva nodded reaching for Richard's hand.

"So they are coming to collect what they need to survive,"

"Exactly." The professor pointed his finger at Eva, like he would a student answering a correct question. Richard looked up from his pondering stare at the floor to break into the conversation.

"So what is being done about this? I mean who knows about them?" Andrew shrugged his shoulders,

"Not many, a few people in the government whom we work for, and, of course, the Vatican."

"The Vatican?" Richard nearly shouted as he voiced his amused shock. Andrew half-heartedly laughed in response to Richard's reaction.

"Yeah, well, what better proof of God than living entities masquerading as angels? Besides, the notion of a different species on this planet would involve the reinterpretation and writing of the oldest book in the world, not an idea the church much cares for."

There was a momentary pause as Richard and Eva realised the religious ramifications if such a revelation were to come to light. A guttural cough from the professor broke the silence, and he turned away from the bed motioning Andrew to do the same.

"What we have discussed is not to be vocalised to anyone else, ever," Eva and Richard looked up as the tone became obviously more authoritative in nature.

"We could certainly use some more hands, and no one has as much detailed experience with the entities as you two." Eva looked up with a hint of fear. "Don't worry, Miss Gardiner, the entity that came for your energy has surely died by now; I doubt if you will be chased again."

Eva smiled vaguely in response as she watched the two men make a silent and quick exit from the room. The nurse sat, clutching Richard's hand like it was her only connection to reality. The room they both sat in seemed oddly close, as though there just wasn't enough space for them to be comfortable. Eva looked at Richard whilst continuing to bite her lip.

"I'm not sure how to feel, if we fight them, then we become responsible for the death of a species as old as our own. If we don't, then we are condemning people who have been given a second chance at life a possible early death." The nurse shook her head to clear the cotton wool manifesting in her brain. "There's so much that we don't know yet." Richard lifted Eva's chin with his finger, "Then we will find out together."

THE CAVERN

The large unmarked room at Blackwater University was once again sporting its highly polished wooden table. The traditional seating arrangements had been altered to suit the occasion. Professor Stanford and Andrew sat together at the bottom; the rest of the committee seated themselves at either side of them to form a short semicircle. At the head of the table sat one man, his heavy black suit and neatly pressed tie reflecting his importance.

Secretary of State William Schneider cleared his throat before standing up. "Last night at approximately 3 a.m., thirty-eight people were killed on the New Heights Bridge. A young pregnant woman single-handedly armed and detonated six explosive devices. Police reports indicated that the woman was shouting 'Save me from the blue angels.' The Secretary paced the carpet in front of the table before leaning to look at the group. "This situation has now gone beyond our control, gentlemen. The time has come to take action."

2 YEARS LATER...

CHAPTER FOURTEEN

Shards of luminescent light broke through the ceiling of the crystal cavern. Andrew pressed his back firmly against a wall of smoky Quartz, the constant vibrating of the monitor strapped to his arm signalled the eminent danger he was about to face. Agent Hollands closed his eyes, the persistent sweat dripping from his brow had begun to cloud his vision and he could feel his heartbeat skipping with his mounting anxiety. "Come on, Andrew," he whispered to himself between gritted teeth. "You've been in tighter squeezes than this." The agent peered cautiously around the sharp edges of the crystal, he was running out of time, he had to find somewhere safe to wait for them to wake him up, somewhere where the blue angels wouldn't see his leaking aura.

Andrew darted towards a large crystalline rock two feet from where he had been hiding. The thick density of its structure offered some protection against his failing fluidic suit. Andrew laid on his back, squeezing into the small gap between the floor of the cavern and the roof of the rock, he rhythmically made fists with his hands. "Left, Right, Left, Right," he spoke to himself inside his head as he tried to combat the searing wave of claustrophobia which enveloped him like glue. Andrew grimaced with frustration as a violet hue began to seep from his armpits into the blue haze that surrounded him. The absence of persistent vibrating from his arm concluded that his fluidic suit had finally failed. The agent tried to stay as small as possible underneath his crystal rock roof, his breathing stuttered as he struggled to control his anxiety. "Come on, come on, wake me up, wake me up!" Andrew almost cried the words under his breath as he watched the violet sprays of his own energy leak into the blue atmosphere like a drop of blood in a saucer of milk. Andrew tried to withdraw further under the rock as a familiar smell permeated through the static air. They were coming.

His body shook like a tall tower in the midst of an earthquake. The agent struggled to evade the burning acidity as its singed his nostrils, and he breathed awkwardly through his mouth.

"Crap, crap, crap, crap!" Andrew hissed between his trembling lips, droplets of spittle sprayed unceremoniously onto his unshaven chin. The agent had never felt fear so intense in his life; it was coupled with a raging anger that threatened to implode his heart. "Fuck!" Andrew recoiled whimpering, the smell was so intense that he began to vomit inside the helmet of his suit. The visor became clouded from the contents of his stomach, but the vomit and pooling tears in his eyes could not shield him from the source of his fear.

"Andrew," the whisper was cold and sure, reverberating in his ears like a cast iron drum. "Andrew," the agent stopped trembling, his body became limp as though the adrenalin in his veins had evaporated like water in a shallow puddle. He could feel the entities burning through his soul, it singed like a candle held to thin parchment, and like the parchment he too was burning, burning with fear, melting into thin ashes.

"Agent Hollands!" Andrew's body shook back and forth as his shoulders were roughly shaken. "Agent?" Andrew's hands wildly grasped at his head as several other agents attempted to remove his vomit sodden helmet. Becoming suddenly aware, Andrew pushed aside the medical team.

"Where were you?" Andrew shouted angrily at the concerned faces of those who stood around him. He pushed them aside as he awkwardly leapt from the recovery bed.

"The stimulant didn't work." An older man approached Andrew; he walked with an authority that suggested his position in the team. "We had to give you nearly three times the standard dose," He whispered with an urgent anger in Andrew's ear. "You told me you'd quit, I can't protect you if you lie to me, I refuse to be held responsible for your demise." The agent swung round in quick response, turning his head away from the onlookers he hoarsely whispered back. "What the hell does that mean?" The head of the medical team turned away before quickly replying.

"Quit taking the shit Andrew, or quit doing this job, I'm not going to cover for you anymore." Andrew took a shallow breath in as the doctor walked away. Grabbing at his jacket, he reached into the pocket for his packet of cigarettes, lighting it deliberately before he left the building.

The cold November air circulated around the back of the institution, pluming Andrew's cigarette smoke into spiralling grey clouds. He scratched at the stubble on his face as his ectopic heart beat made him fidget with anxiety.

"I heard there was a bit of trouble?" The agent jumped, spinning around in alarm as he was jolted from his pondering.

"Christ Eva! You scared the shit out of me!"

"Sorry," Eva whispered sympathetically as she seated herself next to her friend. "Mind if I?" Andrew shook his head, shaking the packet of cigarettes as she deftly took one from the silver packet.

"These things will kill you, you know?" He winked back at her.

"So Richard keeps telling me," she winked back as she lit the cigarette, blowing her own smoke into Andrew's cloud. "Correct me if I'm wrong, but there's not much out there that doesn't." There was a cautious silence between them, as though a certain question was begging to be asked but neither wanted to answer it. Finally as Eva drew her last breath upon her dying cigarette she spoke. "Dammit Andrew, what is going on? These past few months you've—" Eva stopped as she searched for the right words to describe her concern. "You've become so dark, so distant." Andrew stubbed his cigarette butt out on the floor before abruptly standing up.

"I'm getting a bit old for this kind of nonsense, Eva, I feel thin, like paper," he nodded at her as he spoke as if to reinforce his feelings. "I want a normal life again, not a life spent chasing after demons in some half dead reality." Eva looked at the floor, she understood how he felt more than she cared to admit, and yet she felt a certain sense of obligation to the cause, almost like she owed humanity a debt that she would never repay. "Look I'll see you later; I'm gonna try sleep my mood off." He offered Eva a warm wink as he left her sitting on the cobbled floor. The agent watched him leave, shuddering as a sudden prickling sensation rose the hairs on her arms, Eva brushed it off shaking her head.

"Daft cow," she mumbled angrily to herself as she made her way down the corridor to her office. "Spooking yourself!" Eva tossed the door closed as she slumped onto her swivel chair, she swung lazily from side to side on the seat as she grasped at her forehead. This was normally the result of thinking too much about the job, there was so much to think about and nobody could be blamed for being a little clouded upstairs when forced to face the realities of what they were doing, of what they knew.

Eva began gnawing vigorously at the top third of her pencil, rotating it around her mouth as though she were loosening the graphite bone marrow inside. It was a habit she had developed during arduous long hours at university and one that accessorised her character. Once again, her nerves were bothering her, she could feel the twitchiness of her body and she felt it necessary to slurp at endless cups of chamomile tea. It tasted like shit, but had a wonderful knack of soothing her troubled mind.

Andrew's behaviour was indeed becoming more and more erratic, confused. Since Eva had first met him, she had never witnessed such turmoil in his personality. He had almost developed a 'nervous anger' that snapped out of him like elastic at random intervals. At first Eva thought it was just the pressure, their jobs at 'The Cavern' were unique, isolated in nature, and so very, very treacherous. No other human being had been where they had ventured, no other human had learned their secrets and had lived to protect those who remained oblivious. Only those at the brink of their own mortality had seen the static realm, and yet here, at The Cavern, it was the job of people like Andrew and Eva to walk, explore and most importantly to avoid detection, in a realm filled only with the scattered remnants of human life and the energy-hungry beings who dwelt there. It wasn't just a bad dream; it was a nightmare, a living nightmare that was brought to life every time they went to work. Richard was right; this was not a job that could be left behind when one went home every night. It followed you like a bad odour, a frightening reality that reminded you that the invisible eyes we feel on us in those eerie dark moments were real, and they were waiting for us to make that one mistake that would lead to our death.

"Agent Gardiner," Eva looked up from her highly polished walnut desk. "Have you got a minute" Eva nodded with some surprise as she rose from her seated position. It was unusual for the doctor to engage her in any length of conversation, let alone to request a discussion. 'The Pompous Ass' as Eva regarded him was far too self-important to want to do anything other than his job at his usual unrelenting impeccable standard. Eva followed him somewhat cautiously into his own office, meetings such as this usually resulted in a berating of some kind and the agent just wasn't in the mood for another lecture on following 'proper procedures'. Folding her arms as she had often done whilst being confronted by the sister at Mercy Hospital, Eva waited for the sermon to begin. The doctor paced in an awkwardly edgy fashion upon the heavy pile of his red office carpet. Eva chewed the inside of her lip as she watched him. There was a peculiar sense of anger in his stride, yet underneath that bubbled a nervousness that belittled his professional character.

"You and Andrew have been friends for quite some time now haven't you?" Eva looked up somewhat surprised by the doctor's question, not least because he had referred to Andrew by name rather than by agent.

"Uh, huh," Eva nodded her head, "I've known him as long as I've been working here." The doctor offered agent Gardiner a difficult smile as he edged himself onto the swivel chair behind his desk.

"You must have noticed that he's been behaving oddly of late." The doctor licked his lips in subtle defensiveness as he spoke. Eva almost laughed at his comment.

"Of course he has, anybody doing our job has the right to act a little strangely don't you think?" Eva shook her head at the doctor's apparent attack of Andrew's behaviour, despite the fact that she had become aware of it herself, she began to feel like she were being coerced into slander.

"No," the doctor ran a hand through his wispy grey hair. "It's more than that, I thought that perhaps since you appeared to be the closest to him, that he may have confided in you." Eva rubbed at her hands with an emerging sense of anxiety.

"Confided what?" she shook her head with an intended rush of vigour. The doctor stared at her for a few minutes although he doubted her sincerity. "Agent Hollands has been abusing a class A drug for quite some time now I believe, Ketamine, if you want to be precise." Eva dropped her hands to her side in shock.

"What?" She almost shouted into his face and he stood up from his desk in a renewed attempt at professionalism.

"I've known about it for a few months, we have been finding it difficult to awake Agent Hollands from the chemical coma." The doctor clicked on the mouse at his computer removing it from its sleep mode. "At first I wondered if his body was beginning to reject the drugs we use to keep you agents asleep, and then I realised that higher doses of the stimulant brought him round, actually nearly three times the dose of normal stimulant." Eva looked at the floor swallowing as she felt a sudden pang of shame for her colleague. "As a nurse, you will be aware that a drug like Ketamine is also a suppressant, making the job of waking him from the coma even harder for the stimulant that we administer" Agent Gardiner felt the skin on her cheek bones begin to flush and she shuffled her feet on the carpet. For the first time in a long time, she struggled for words, there appeared to be nothing she could say in answer. The doctor seated himself back behind his desk. "I took a blood test this morning and the results confirmed my suspicions" Eva squinted at the results on the computer screen, her mind had begun to feel decidedly numb. "Look, I can keep these with me for just now" Eva looked up at the doctor as he offered a meek olive branch. "As much as I loathe Andrew, I believe he's a good agent, and a good man" Eva nodded to confirm the doctor's estimations. "Talk to him, because I can't keep his secret for much longer, one of these days the volume of stimulant needed will be too much, and it will kill him, I don't want to be held responsible for his mistakes" Eva stood up straight, she stared at the doctor for a second before quietly leaving his office.

Eva drove home slowly, she felt a strange coldness prickling at the back of her neck, she rubbed at it with her hand as though she could warm away the tension. Richard had warned her that the job was too dangerous, he had pleaded with her to stay away from their realm, but Eva was insatiably curious. They had chased her, hunted her and now she wanted to hunt them, in their world, under her terms. Eva cranked up the heating in the car, she so desperately wanted to feel warm and safe again, but the truth of Andrew's drug abuse had thrown her into a confused turmoil. Andrew had always been so steady, so reliable, like an old Rolls Royce engine, purring quietly behind the excited fear of the world. She struck at the steering wheel with the heel of her palm. "Damn you!" She cursed under her breath. Despite the difficulty of her job, over the months she had found a comfortable understanding of what she did, and why she did it, in fact, some mornings she actually looked forward to work. She had begun to feel like a pioneer, exploring boundaries only dreamed of in the most fantastical of books. She was the explorer, the first to see another world, and the first to walk upon it. There was an overwhelming sense of pride in that truth and that sense of pride drowned the danger in a vacuole of purpose. Andrew, Eva, and the other agents had unique characters, most of the others were single and lived at The Cavern on a permanent basis, Andrew still had his own place to which he returned to every night and Eva, Eva had Richard, and she loved their sanctuary on the outskirts of town, far enough away to be home, but close enough to remind her of her purpose.

The agent breathed slowly in as she silently turned the key in the lock of their apartment, normally she couldn't wait to burst through the door, but tonight she felt a little edgy. Eva couldn't hold back her smile however as she gazed upon her fiancée in the kitchen. Richard's demeanour was one of pride, as he quickly leaned against the kitchen counter.

"Sweet or savoury?" Eva stifled a laugh as she watched her fiancée toss home-made pancakes skilfully in the frying pan. Agent Gardiner pulled an exaggerated thoughtful face as she slinked towards him.

"Sweet" she whispered seductively into his ear whilst stroking his waistline. Through his own choice, Richard's involvement at The Cavern was kept to a minimum. He did not share Eva's need to investigate the static realm, and often he found their intrusion upon the beings world reckless. He supported all of Eva's decisions however and had chosen to remain in his original position as a psychiatrist working comfortably from their spacious home in the modern corner of Blackwater. Eva's impressive salary was more than they needed, but Richard felt he wanted to maintain his professional position and of course provide amply for the two children he had already had. Eva had not been disappointed at Richard's decision, the home they had built together provided her with a safe zone, a place where she could let the adrenalin in her blood stream fade without the worry that she may have to fight or run. It was a place of normality, of humanity and most importantly of love.

Richard winced with pretend pain as he scooped a large spoon of double cream onto his plate. Eva smiled with jealousy, Richard never appeared to gain weight whilst she had become awkwardly aware that her waistline was thickening.

"You need to stop cooking such tempting food, I'm getting fat." Richard laughed at Eva's woeful comment.

"You do keep choosing the sweet option rather than the savoury" Agent Gardiner nodded in appreciation of his comments, "Stop offering it to me then!" She smiled at him in a somewhat sarcastic fashion "There was some trouble today in the lab," Eva twisted the fork around her fingers awkwardly as she waited a response from Richard, the psychiatrist continued to eat his pancakes as though she had not spoken. "It involved Andrew," Eva raised her voice slightly to re-assert the importance of her attempted conversation. Richard put down his fork wiping away loose dribbles of cream with his napkin.

"Andrew?" Eva nodded slowly, "The doc said that they had been having trouble waking Andrew from the coma" Richard shook his head, "I'm not surprised, human beings are not supposed to be comatose on a daily basis." Eva began to chew again at her already shredded cheek. "The doc took some blood from him this morning and found high doses of Ketamine in his sample" Richard threw down his napkin, rubbing at his face with frustration. "For god's sake did nobody notice that something was going on? You know I said that it was just a matter of time before somebody cracked." Eva screwed up her face, "C'mon Richard, you can't expect people like us to make the biggest discovery of all time and not want to explore it? Besides, it's not about us, it's about protecting the people we love from murderous beings who have no mercy for anyone." Richard raised his eyebrows in a manner that suggested Eva's stupidity. "Has anybody stopped to think that perhaps they too are protecting themselves?" Eva swallowed the last remnants of her food, washing it down with a large mouthful of Jacob's Creek before continuing. "What do you mean?" Richard sighed reluctantly, and paused for a second as though his true thoughts were hard to realise. "If they have been co-existing with us for as long as we think they have, then don't you think that they have developed just as complex a society as ours? In terms of their social and personal interrelations?" Eva pulled a reluctant face; Richard shifted his position on the sofa to face her. "Look, I'm not saying that what they are doing isn't wrong, of course it is, I'm just trying to understand it from their point of view, they may be protecting their own families in just the same way that we protect ours" Eva swallowed, it was difficult for her to think of them as anything other than crazed demons and she quickly changed the subject back to Andrew. "The doc said that he would keep the results to himself for now, but he's refusing to cover for him much longer, we need to talk to him, before he goes back under." Richard nodded his head as he replaced the cap on the bottle of wine. "I'll pop into the cavern tomorrow, see if I can coerce him into talking." Eva smirked quietly to herself, in a strange way despite Andrew and Richard's history, she felt that she knew the agent better than anyone, and she felt almost disappointed that he had chosen not to confide in her.

Eva stared at the ceiling of their romantically rouge-painted bedroom. Richard's rhythmical snoring did little to lull her mind to sleep and she fidgeted nervously under the covers. Richard's comment regarding the nature of the energy beings existence had unnerved her. The former nurse had failed to consider anything other than her burning hatred of them. She couldn't help but blame them, even for those whose time would come regardless of the medicines and doctors that surrounded them. Her friend Edna, her mother, and maybe even Adam. He was so young, so very young and she had loved him so much. She hated him for leaving her; it was more palatable for her to think that they had driven him to suicide rather than to think that he could have betrayed her in such a cruel manner. Eva shook her head against her own thoughts, warm tears had begun to seep uncontrollably down the sides of her cheeks and she hastily wiped them away lest the sleeping Richard should notice her turmoil.

Eva shivered suddenly as a thought passed through her mind. The former nurse had changed so much since her first encounter with the static realm; she used to be so diligent, so in tune with the people that surrounded her, the people that were once her responsibility to help. Now? Now she could hardly recognise herself, her make-up had remained the same, but beneath the caked-on foundation, a cold hard crust had developed, and as much as she hated it, she needed it. Eva twisted at her lips as she dissected her own personality, it was true that she had become a much stronger person than the Eva of the past, but it was also true that she had lost her compassion. The former nurse had never hated anything or anyone in her life, she had a strong dislike for blue cheese and country music but the placidity of her nature overwhelmed any aggression that she may have felt. It appeared that the last two years had done more than change her career and explode her bank balance.

Eva slipped carefully out from underneath her silken bed sheets; silently she tiptoed across the crimson carpet and across the hall into the kitchen. She winced with annoyance as her rummaging in the cupboard caused a jar of sundried tomatoes to topple noisily on the shelf. She quickly opened the cigarettes she had skilfully hidden behind the tub of 'Smash' and haphazardly hung out of the kitchen window. Eva had almost managed to quit the cancer sticks, she tended to reserve it for the hours she spent at work, but tonight her urge to smoke suppressed her desire to keep their home smoke free.

The garden was remarkably calm, the last few November days had been cloaked in a heavy blanket of freezing rain and sharp gusts of Northerly wind. The garden looked slightly overgrown, the scruffy looking gardener they employed to maintain it had not been in to tend it for over a week, and loose, broken, wind-damaged branches and brown leaves scattered over it like brown sugar on crème caramel. Despite this, Eva found herself relaxing into its secret beauty. It was an enclosed garden away from the prying eyes of the world, a small patch of green in a developing grey city. The agent wiggled her toes as she dangled them out of the window. The still calm air nursed a sharp frost which had already begun to crystallize the fine mist of evening dew on the edges of the lawn. Eva took a last quick draw of her cigarette before flicking it out of the window and withdrawing back into the warmth of the kitchen. She shuddered unexpectedly as she carefully closed the window, the same prickling sensation had begun to tease the hairs on the back of her neck again, and the agent found herself rubbing it reverently with her hand. Eva scowled in the moonlit darkness of her kitchen, suddenly she felt edgy, frightened, like a rabbit in a den of foxes. She pushed her back close against the kitchen cupboards almost as though she were evading someone's gaze. Eva tried to steady her breathing, but the persistent flickering from the solar powered lanterns in the garden told Eva that she had more to worry about than a rapid pulse and shuddering breaths.

CHAPTER FIFTEEN

"Damn!" Eva rubbed her face with the back of her hand as she dazedly threw back the oriental black silk duvet. The memories of the hour after her late night cigarette were marred by fretful disorientated conversation with Richard which, according to Eva's screwed up memory of the event, culminated in the psychiatrist giving his fiancée something that was sure to make her sleep. The former nurse groaned as she rolled over onto her stomach, she had definitely slept like a rock, but there was a dull cloudiness in her head that suggested it had not been natural. Eva quickly lifted her head from the feather pillow as she realised that Richard had already left. She scrambled from beneath the covers and then abruptly sat back down again as she realised that no amount of rushing was going to impact on the outcome of the day.

Eva dragged herself through to the kitchen. Her taste buds craved for the earthy flavours of English Breakfast tea and she began to salivate as she prepared her cup. The agent flicked on the kettle and then jumped back in alarm as a flurry of sparks shot out from the switch. "Bastard fake angels," Eva growled as she threw the kettle into the bin, resorting to boiling a pan of water on the stove instead. The agent sat on her bar stool overlooking the garden. She blew at the hot steam which rose from her tea, watching it cloud the cold window like frost on a lake. She tutted as she scribbled a note to the gardener. "Please replace all the solar lights" Eva knew that like the kettle, microwave and anything else electrical that had happened to have been plugged in and switched on last night, the solar lights would be burned out and useless. The agent couldn't help but feel pissed off and defensive that they had managed to invade her home. Despite her job, it made no sense that they would have followed her here. The fluidic suits protected them as they explored the static realm, they were nothing more than shadows, passing flickers of disguised energy searching vainly for anything that might give them an edge in the secret war. Eva flicked her pen rhythmically off the counter. They knew her, much more intimately than she knew herself, but the being that was meant for her energy had died years ago, and up until now, she had never seen them go after an individual's energy twice. It appeared that every single human being had a blue angel counterpart, but if the counterpart did not receive the energy from the human in time, then the being simply died and the human was left alone. Eva sipped carefully at her hot tea, now that her counterpart was dead, she was denied the chance to live again in their realm, but after very little consideration, Eva had concluded that she was much happier living one life as a human than a second life as one of them.

THE CAVERN

Richard parked the silver Mercedes in the Aquarium car park. He dropped down the glove compartment and sighed with annoyance as he searched for his key-card. It was only occasionally that he used it to attend the monthly debriefings. The psychiatrist preferred to contribute in a minimalistic fashion to the work at The Cavern. The aquarium was bustling in its usual manner with bus-loads of eager school children cheerfully following the guide with excited faces and pointless questions. Richard dodged past them, quickly flashing his key card at a security guard before entering a door marked 'Staff Only'. A large silver elevator door stood less than a foot away from the entrance that Richard had just opened, and he grappled with his card as he attempted to slot it into the inconspicuous slit on the wall. Despite its hidden nature, the elevator was surprisingly large inside, brightly lit with four spot lights and decorated in a hideous cream and lime-striped outfit. Richard rubbed at his stomach, breathing out heavily as the lift began to slide smoothly downwards. No matter how big the lift was, he couldn't help but feel claustrophobic. In any other circumstance, the psychiatrist would have chosen to take the stairs, but at a mile underground, The Cavern was just a little too deep for a leisurely stroll. Richard closed his eyes inside the metal cylinder, it took only twenty five seconds to reach the ground floor of The Cavern, but those few seconds were always the most uncomfortable of his life.

The elevator door opened out onto a large oval shaped room. The smoothly polished black and white chequered floor glared uncomfortably back at the eyes and Richard quickly made his way across it to the front desk. "Hi Michael" Richard smiled reluctantly to the neatly suited receptionist behind the front desk.

"Hey Richard, another debriefing?" The receptionist quizzed the psychiatrist with surprise, it had only been two weeks since the last one.

"No, not this time." The psychiatrist raised his eyebrows as if to suggest that he were not here for anything important. "Have you seen Agent Hollands today?" The receptionist slid back expertly on his swivel chair, typing Andrew's name into the computer as though he had done it a million times before.

"He's supposed to be here, but he hasn't checked in yet, actually that's the fourth time he's been late this month" Richard nodded his head, "Well you know Andrew, always was a bit lazy" The psychiatrist played down Michael's comment before thanking him and heading off down the left corridor to the lab.

The Cavern was arranged in a spider like formation, the central body was oval, and contained the elevators, main reception, and the garish black and white chequered floor. Eight corridors branched from the central access, each travelling for the same distance of ten metres before opening out into individual rooms. There were five offices, one of which was Eva's but that she also shared with the other agents who travelled to the static realm. Professor Stanton, The doctor and occasionally the Minister of State occupied the other three. One room was empty, but like the other four was also encapsulated by a thin wall of purified water. The building of The Cavern underneath the aquarium had originally been Eva's idea. The purified water acted as an internal defence against any attempt made by the beings to enter the walls of the institution. It created a barrier between them and any other biological entities within the space, the poor conductivity of the water prevented the creation of conductive pathways from which the beings could commence their energy transference and essentially coerce their host. Despite The Caverns intended purpose, Richard had always thought of its structure as being remarkably beautiful. It gave the illusion of walking inside a giant air bubble at the bottom of the ocean, the only thing missing was the sea life, unfortunately the absence of which, was enough to remind the psychiatrist that he was actually a mile and a half underneath the aquarium surrounded by an envelope of battery water.

"Dr Wellar?" Richard looked up as he walked down the seventh corridor. The doctor stood with his hand outstretched ready to welcome the psychiatrist into his lab. Richard smiled as he warmly took the doctors hand.

"Good to see you again Mark," Richard was undoubtedly the only other person from The Cavern that the doctor showed a slight appreciation for. 'A mutual understanding of educational credibility' was his one line response to a jibe made by Andrew at the last Christmas party. Richard followed Mark into the vast laboratory; it was the only other room in The Cavern that was bigger than the central access. The lab also boasted a double screen of purified water within its walls separated by six-inch thick, toughened glass. Richard had never enjoyed being at The Cavern, but the modern, well laid out instruments and equipment made it an appealing place to work. Everything was in easy reach and yet there still appeared to be enough room to swing two cats by the tail. The doctor motioned Richard to seat himself at a large triangular table, the centre of which boasted a square touch screen computer. Richard eyed it suspiciously as though the technology were alien to him.

"Eva told me about what's been happening with Andrew, I was wondering if I might be able to help" Mark laughed in an almost sarcastic fashion and the psychiatrist frowned at the unusual response.

"I'm afraid it's a bit more serious than I had initially thought, there's more than drug addiction going on." The doctor responded with an almost jittery composure and Richard began to feel his stomach lining twitch with nervousness. "What do you mean?" The doctor motioned at Richard to follow him into an adjacent room. Four table-like beds were arranged in a circular formation, the heads of which met in the centre to form an empty diamond shape. Blood pressure, cardiac response and brain wave monitoring equipment were positioned to the right of each shiny metal bed. Richard swallowed hard as he entered the room; it was so clinical, so cold and impersonal. It reminded him of a hospital morgue and the thought of his fiancée lying there with her mind roaming around some alien realm chilled him to his core. Richard hovered uncomfortably in the door way, and the doctor sensing his unease collected a fluidic suit from the locker and returned with Richard to the triangular table.

"Do you know what this is?" Richard shrugged his shoulders, nodding his head as he took the suit from Mark.

"It's a fluidic suit, it protects the body whilst the brain is in the static realm?" The doctor slowly nodded his head at the psychiatrist's crude evaluation of the highly sophisticated body wear.

"The suit works in a similar fashion as The Cavern does – fresh uncontaminated purified water is pumped slowly throughout the entire body of the suit." The doctor pulled out a rectangular-shaped box from the silver lining in the arm of the suit. "These are stimulators, they act a little bit like nerves, sending information about the condition of the suit directly to the brain, where it is interpreted in the dream state of the

176

agent." Richard breathed out as he made his first physical evaluation of the equipment. He had heard Eva ranting on about the ingenious design, but he had not cared to examine it himself. Upon closer inspection, the psychiatrist could not deny that his fiancée had been correct in her admiration of the suit. A paper-thin yet flexible membrane carried the purified water around the lining. Sensors from the arms, legs and chest spread out through the suit like blood vessels in the skin, they made contact with the body inside, through an equally thin rubber clear compound which stuck closely the occupant like a blood thirsty leech. The head of the suit resembled a diver's facemask, carefully mixed amounts of oxygen and fentanyl helped to keep the agent in a coma, the oxygen content of the mixture slowly increasing as the stimulant was administered to promote the awakening. The cooled, purified water slowing the body functions whilst the mind was in the static realm and then slowly heating to aid in the recovery process. Richard reluctantly smiled as he handed the suit back to the doctor.

"It is pretty impressive," Mark nodded his head as he took back the suit, plugging a USB cable into the sensor in the arm he brought up a diagnostic programme on the computer. "It is when it's used correctly," Richard stood up leaning over the computer screen

"I'm not sure what you're getting at." The doctor pointed at the results from the diagnostics test on the computer screen.

"This suit is Andrew's, he was wearing it yesterday." Richard peered into the centre of the table recoiling back slowly into his seat as he attempted to digest the meaning of the words.

"Complete failure?" Michael nodded "Yep" he threw the suit on the floor before scratching harshly at the back of his head. "For some reason, Andrew didn't switch on the pump that circulates fresh purified water through the suit, he was pretty much running on empty the entire time he was in the realm." Richard nibbled at the skin surrounding his fingernails as the doctor continued. "The suit registered a complete failure twelve minutes after he entered, Richard, he was in there for forty three minutes, and he was not protected."

"What?" Richard stared at the doctor as though he had delivered him a bomb. "Well, where is he? We have to find him." The psychiatrist stood up as though he were about to spring into action. The doctor shrugged his shoulders.

"I don't know, he hasn't turned up, he's not answering his phone, Professor Stanton is out looking for him now." Richard nodded his head as he drew a sweating palm across his face. "Who else knows?" Mark shook his head, "No one yet, the professor was hoping he might get to him first." Richard acknowledged his response and began walking out of the lab.

"Richard?" the psychiatrist turned round to face Mark.

"If the MOD find out about this, they will take him out." Richard swallowed as the reality of the doctors words struck home. "Then let's find him first." The doctor nodded his agreement,

"Good luck," he murmured after Richard as the psychiatrist quickly made his way out of the room and back towards the car park.

Richard gnawed with brutal efficiency at the skin surrounding his nails. Eva's encounter with them last night deeply burned in his mind. This was the first encounter with the beings outside of their realm, that either Eva or him had had since they joined the cavern. The psychiatrist was convinced that Andrew's exposure to them had something to do with last night's appearance, what worried him more, was that they had decided to make themselves known to Eva, and not Andrew. Richard fumbled with his phone as he tried to connect his Bluetooth, cursing loudly as his lack of attention to the road ahead caused him to break sharply at the junction. The psychiatrist tapped his bleeding fingers on the steering wheel with frustration as Eva failed to pick up his call. "C'mon, C'mon," Richard tutted impatiently as he immediately tried to call her again. The familiar 'click' of connection spurred him into action and he instantly began talking. "Eva listen, Andrew's—" before the psychiatrist could finish his sentence, a high pitched whistle, like the feedback from a microphone blared through the Bluetooth into his eardrum. Richard blinked in pain as his eyes filled up with water, bringing the car to a screaming halt on the pavement he ripped the Bluetooth from his ear, clutching at the side of his head as if he had suffered a gunshot wound. Richard breathed in deeply as he attempted to subdue the nausea rising quickly in the back of his throat, his head felt white hot with a burning heat that threatened to boil his brain. The psychiatrist sat slumped over his steering wheel for nearly twenty minutes before his thoughts became lucid again. In the silence of the car he could think of only one thing. Eva.

CO – ERCION

"Hello?" Eva sighed as she threw down her mobile phone. The silence on the other end frustrated her and she shook her head with annoyance. Richard had this annoying habit of calling her when he had little or no signal and the resulting conversation was often not comprehendible or marred with debilitating periods of eerie silence. Her desire to know if Richard had spoken with Andrew was enough to quell her annoyance however, and she reached for the house phone to call him back. Eva rolled her eyes as Richard's mobile went straight to answer phone and she rubbed heavily at the dull pain throbbing at the base of her neck.

The agent grabbed her lighter and the last remaining cigarette she had in her packet and made her way to the patio. Eva shivered, sinking deeply into her woollen roll neck jumper as her breath made small, silver smoke filled clouds in the air. The agent squirmed in the cast iron garden chair. The frozen metal was like tiny shards of razor blade poking through her thin pyjama bottoms. Eva frowned, looking down at the patio table as a glimmer caught her eye. The white painted iron table was beautifully encrusted with a snowflake pattern of ice crystals. Their geometric design was captivating if not daunting in its mathematical perfection. The agent stared as a flash of light bounced from each crystal in a glowing wave, spiralling clockwise from where she sat. Eva looked up at the heavy grey sky above her, searching with confusion for the source of light. The mid-November morning offered no sunlight and yet Eva could feel a subtle heat beneath the pads of her fingertips as she rested them upon the edges of the table. A vague vibration accompanied the heat, and as the agent watched she realised that it synchronised perfectly with the waves of light reflecting brightly from the frozen ice crystals.

It was beautiful. Eva stared hypnotized, as the gap between the waves slowly began to decrease, quickly becoming a regular pulse which shook the table like a persistent heavy drum beat. Everything surrounding the agent became dull, silenced by the overwhelming power of the rhythmical waves of light. Eva's head twitched randomly as the suffocating vibrations choked her windpipe. Her eyes watering with a mixture of tears and cold dryness as her gaze remained fixed on the table, she struggled to regain control. Suddenly from the space within the centre of the table a shockwave burst out towards Eva, it boomed with a flash of light so intense it drowned the light of day. The agent was propelled backward with the force of an exploding bomb, a dense mixture of sound, vibration and light filled the garden. The remaining leaves from the trees and bushes fell to the ground instantly, surrounding the agent's body on the grass like a memorial wreath. An odd period of silence followed, as though all the creatures in the world had simply stopped, as if everything had stopped, an eternal moment of quiet within the eye of the storm. Eva lay motionless on the ground.

A sudden violent intake of breath awoke her dormant body and she coughed repeatedly into the wet grass. Agent Gardiner groaned as she slowly attempted to move her aching legs. Her ribs popped under her skin as though they had been forcefully pushed into her chest. Sitting up, Eva nursed her bruised and broken skin, her body felt as though she had been struck by a wrecking ball and her head felt strangely compressed as though her skull had been packed with heavy cotton wadding.

A gentle light breeze circulated around the garden, it whipped up the fallen leaves and the eerie period of silence was finally broken. Eva stumbled as she awkwardly picked herself up from the ground, her attempts to stay balanced were thwarted by sharp fragments of the obliterated iron table. Eva raised a hand to her head as she cautiously looked round at the carnage surrounding her. It was almost too much for her to deal with and she half-heartedly attempted to subdue her sobs.

Despite the destroyed table, Eva could sense as she dazedly gazed around the garden that something wasn't quite right. At first she couldn't put her finger on it, something seemed wrong, and the former nurse began to wonder if she had hit her head in the fall. Eva calmed herself, closing her eyes she shut out the world as she regained control of herself and her situation. As the agent opened her eyes again she quickly pinpointed the source of her anxieties.

Richard and Eva's garden was arranged in an elongated oval shape, the patio was just off to the left of the living room and served as a nice seating area to view the stone wishing well and ornamental rockery. A beautifully manicured lawn carpeted the centre of the garden edged with evenly spaced solar lights. The smallest portion of the oval garden was made up of this very well maintained and loved show piece. The other two thirds right up to the boundary of the garden was rambling with fruit trees, bushes and wild herbs. For Richard, this was his favourite part of the garden, he preferred the wild freedom to Eva's crisp lines and perfection. It was in her fiancée's part of the garden that the agent caught sight of her unease.

The largest tree in the garden was an apple tree, its tall spindly branches dominated the skyline, and Eva often wondered how those branches managed to support the weight of all the apples, but as she soon realised, the brittle-looking wood was stronger than it looked. Eva made her way towards the fruit bushes, the branches of the apple tree seemed oddly bowed, bent downwards towards the ground as if someone were swinging from its branches. The agent peered cautiously between the thorny bushes of the overgrown raspberry and as she did so, she fell to her knees in shock.

Dangling like a rabbit on a butcher's hook was Andrew, his head hung heavily to the right revealing the grey electric cable he had used to tie around his neck. The branches of the apple tree creaked under his weight as the breeze brushed past his sagging legs.

"NO!" Eva cried into the sharp thorns of the fruit bush, and for the second time that morning, the garden fell silent.

CHAPTER SIXTEEN

"I'm fine," Eva brushed away the attentions of the medical staff, as they vainly attempted to dress her many wounds. Agent Gardiner stared blankly into her garden as Professor Stanton and the doctor removed Andrew's body from the apple tree. Eva closed her eyes as the branch continued to stoop awkwardly from the trunk. Before Eva could gather her thoughts, the sanctity of her home and garden became violated by the comings and goings of agents, some of which she had never even met before dressed amusingly in the skin-tight fluidic suits. Eva smirked in her head as she sat inside her own bubble of thought. Andrew would have found this scene particularly laughable.

The former nurse smiled as she turned her head, she could almost feel his presence next to her, and she acknowledged him as she had always done.

"What have you done my old friend?" she whispered. The indefinite period of silence that swallowed Eva's mind, blinded her to the bustling chaos of the morning. She sat remarkably calmly in her open plan living room. Agents, flashed past like insects caught in the light, but Eva's eyes held a solemn glaze that reflected nothing but her own secret tears. The agent could sense the subtle layers of her own pain; her heartbreak was sandwiched between an upper crust of hollow emptiness, almost as though she had fallen into a wormhole without the energy nor will to escape. Underneath was a bitter crust of ferocious anger, it spat out like a feral child in chains and Eva almost worried at the prospect of it breaking loose. The former nurse had been here before, and she burned at the fact that she should find herself here again. She had lost enough, why? Because some sick demonic life form felt it had the right to strip the life from them like they didn't matter. Eva bit at her lip grimacing slightly as the warm taste of iron crept upon her tongue.

"It's payback time," Eva spoke aloud as she stood up.

"Where are you going?" The professor shouted after her from across the room. She looked back, pausing for a second before answering. "I just need some air," he nodded after her as she grabbed her jacket and headed for the door.

Agent Gardiner walked in a brisk determined manner as she made her way back to The Cavern. Her anger was overwhelming, and she fought to ignore the pit of hatred that stained her thoughts. Eva pulled the collar of her jacket up around her neck, suddenly conscious that her scratched face was still raw with the freshness of her injuries. It took forty minutes for the former nurse to walk briskly back to the car park of the aquarium. Those forty minutes flashed past in her mind in a whirlwind of repetitive angry rants and vengeful ponderings. The agent blindly sidestepped the tow truck carrying Richard's car, it wasn't until she swung open the aquarium doors that she realised it was there.

Eva paused for a second, breathing in heavily as her mind suddenly came back to the present. The agent looked down at her feet in embarrassment as her dishevelled hair and battered skin attracted the eyes of a young girl who tugged frustrated at her mother's jacket in the foyer. Eva turned away from her attentions, quickly scurrying through the 'staff only' doors to the hidden elevator. The agent closed her eyes, pressing her back firmly against the back of the door as she searched inside her jacket for the keycard. Eva rushed herself through the sliding doors as they opened, wiggling her foot impatiently as she watched the doors slowly close. In the safety and silence of the enclosed elevator, Eva let out an angry scream, followed quickly by strong stomach wrenching sobs. For a few moments she lost herself in the chaos of her emotions, but the ping of the elevator reaching the ground level brought Eva abruptly back from her loss of control and she quickly wiped away her tears, straightening her jacket like she was wearing a military uniform. Eva walked out onto the black and white foyer, avoiding everyone she could as she made her way towards the offices.

"Eva" The agent spun round as she recognised the voice. "Richard" Eva allowed herself to sink into his embrace, his familiar smell comforted her and she fought the urge to sink back into her tearful episode.

"Andrew's dead" she whispered into his shoulder and he pulled her away from him so that he could see her face.

"I know, Mark just told me, he didn't tell me you had been hurt" Richard ran a finger over his fiancée's face, and Eva smiled at his concern.

"I'm ok, it's just scratches" Eva chewed at her already swollen lips. "In our garden" Richard pulled her back close swallowing back his own anxiety.

"I think we might be in trouble" Eva looked up from their embrace, "Andrew's suit failed, they got to him and they tried to attack me earlier" Agent Gardiner nodded her head

"Something strange happened to me before I found Andrew, that's how I got these scratches, they physically manipulated the environment around me Richard, something has changed and we need to find out what it is"

The atmosphere in The Cavern had become suddenly alive. The normal calm silence of the building became polluted with the noise of drafted agents and the persistent ringing of phones. Eva and Richard skulked around the lab, Andrew's body lay in the trauma room, a plain white sheet shrouding his snapped neck and glazed over eyes. Eva paced back and forth across the room, intermittently glancing at her fallen comrade. Richard watched her nervously from a chair.

"Eva I think that perhaps you should step back a little" The agent flashed an angry look at her fiancée. "Step back? Richard are you crazy? Your friend ... my friend, committed suicide in our garden, we have both been attacked, and you want me to step back?" Richard shrugged his shoulders a look of doubt blanching his expression. "I don't want to lose you." The psychiatrist pointed at her, returning his finger to his lips as though he were preventing himself from saying any more. "You had to die before they left you alone last time, and here we are again, what are you going to have to do this time?" Eva clenched her fists as she paced. "But it's too late already, they are here, Richard, do you think that they are just going to ignore us if we ignore them?" Eva shook her head as she walked toward him. "Richard, this is war, we can't just walk away when they cut a little too deep, we have been on the defensive for nearly two years, it's time to make a stand"

"I completely agree." Eva jumped in alarm as the minister of state walked casually into the room followed closely by Professor Stanton.

"Sir." Eva stood straight nodding her respects whilst Richard remained seated and unimpressed.

"You are right, of course, Agent Gardiner, everything we have done in the past twenty four months has been about gathering Intel and designing defences. In those past eighteen months the number of deaths suspected as being entity controlled has risen to three thousand plus, and that's just in this country" Eva nodded her head as though she already knew. "Reports coming in worldwide take that figure to tens of thousands, currently this is the only cavern, but there are cavern's being built as we speak in Germany, Italy and America, we hope to have them up and running by the end of the month." Richard let out a whistle.

"So it really is war …" The minister nodded his head.

"Yes, and I think it's about time we brought this war to them" The finely suited man offered Agent Hollands body a sympathetic glance as he turned to leave the lab. "I think those bastards have taken enough from the human race" Eva smiled to herself as she watched the minister leave the room. Finally someone had the right idea.

CONSEQUENCES

From that moment on, The Cavern took on a completely different feel. It wasn't just noisy, it had taken on a regimented military attitude. Eva found herself helping the doctor to train new agents for crossing into the realm, only it was no longer for exploration, it was for seeking ways to kill. Eva found herself struggling to begin with, she had spent so much of her young career trying to save lives, and now she was trying to take them, although she hadn't managed to convince herself that the entities actually qualified as life. Richard remained as he always had been, hovering on the outskirts of The Cavern, neither a part of it nor absent from it, he spent his time mentoring the new agents, not to aid them in their killing, but to help them deal with the consequences of the lives they took. To deal with the emotions of what was ultimately murder. The psychiatrist; despite his attempts to remain at arms-length, found himself being dragged along with the military goals of the cavern, and he watched Eva being dragged along with it. In his own mind he couldn't justify what they were doing, there was something inhuman about the strange particle weapons that were being developed in the labs, weapons designed to tear apart a species that they knew barely nothing about. Richard wondered if Andrew's life was worth the attempted genocide of a species, if anyone's life was, but at the present time, it seemed to be all anyone could focus on.

Eva and Richard barely talked about work away from The Cavern. They both had severely conflicting opinions about the war they were helping to wage, and after the third argument that had almost ended in separation, they decided to keep their personal and private lives as far apart from one another as they could outside of the cavern.

The psychiatrist worried, and he worried a lot. His fiancée had lost the spark that had once glinted in her eyes, she had become dull, lustreless. Every day that she came home from that place, she wore a smile that had been painted on during the journey home. Richard didn't know the details about what it was she did when she was in the realm, but the sullen guilt-ridden look of fear in her eyes was enough to tell him that the tests on the new particle weapon had been successful. Eva was no longer a nurse, nor an explorer; she was a judge and an executioner. It came as no surprise to him that she avoided any and all conflict outside of work. She wouldn't even argue a parking ticket. All of her energy had gone into hating them, she had to hate them, it was the only way she could kill them, and it was all the hatred she had. Richard didn't question her attitude, or her lack of guile for the normal things in life. Just like the garden which she never walked in anymore, she had become alone, cold and withered. A small Guardian of light in a perpetual landscape of black.

In some ways, Andrew's suicide had brought forward a new era to The Cavern that had been brewing quietly in the background for some time. His death had almost humiliated those in power to finally take the plunge into an intense secret war. A war covert, and hidden behind falsely labelled doors and blackened out windows. The Minister of state made routine appearances to Blackwater. The new addition of a military protected corridor to the railway station, allowed the more important members of the government to come and go without public detection. The military unrest in the middle east appeared to slip down the list of 'objectives to pursue' as the addition of family photographs and personal belongings to the minister's office at The Cavern suggested that he would be spending more time down there than in his office topside.

Richard sat quietly through the traditional monthly meetings. Eva had become the front runner and consistently led the meetings alongside Professor Stanton. The psychiatrist found himself marvelling at how easy she took charge of every situation. She thrived under pressure, in fact, she almost demanded it. Before the end of the first six month campaign against the Static Realm, Eva had been promoted.

The silence of their woeful conversation eventually became too much to bear. The passions that had so easily found themselves wrapped around the excitement of the chase had begun to fade as Eva and Richard prevented themselves from being a part of it together. What was intended to protect their relationship against the turmoil of conflicting opinion regarding the static realm ended up causing its demise. Richard watched the staleness of their relationship transgress into a stagnant pool of half-hearted attempts at humour, followed by long periods of tense unease and silence. The psychiatrist had been here before, he knew what was coming, the problem was that he had never felt such hollow pain at the truth and obvious reality of their separation. He knew he loved her, with every molecule of his being; he loved her. He longed to smell her perfume, touch her hair, hold her hand; and as she walked out of their home with her overnight bag in one hand and a tear slowly rolling down her cheek, he felt himself crumble, he knew he would never be the same again without her.

CHAPTER SEVENTEEN

The psychiatrist rolled the half empty whiskey glass from one palm to the other. He hadn't touched the stuff in nearly two years, but lately the occasional glass of red wine just hadn't seemed enough. Richard could hardly agree that he was enjoying it, in fact its bitter smoky taste did nothing but enrage his palette. Still, old habits die hard, and with no-one there to discourage him, the psychiatrist let his will power wane with his empty lust for life.

The incredibly spacious apartment that he and Eva had shared was nothing more than an empty carcass with only the psychiatrist residing within it. There had been no discussion as to who was moving out, Eva had simply packed her bags and moved into The Cavern. It was true that her life revolved around that place, it owned every part of her, and now it even owned her wardrobe.

Richard dismissively pushed aside some patient notes as he sank heavily back into his black leather couch. It had become apparent in recent months that he was not the only member of The Cavern who struggled with the extermination of an entire species. A species, which, unknown or not, were the arbitrators of the world's belief in an afterlife. In many of the situations that he came across with his patients, Richard shared their turmoil in attempting to rationalise a logical evaluation of the events. If these beings truly were a part of the human condition; of human existence, then they must surely be a part of the human evolutionary process as well. In being so; if this evolution is a natural one, then who is to say that they are not intended to be the bringers of an afterlife? If we exterminate them, then might we not be exterminating our own gods? Our own heaven?

Richard put down his glasses, despite the cotton wool feeling he had achieved in his troubled mind, the half empty bottle of Lagavulin had finally given rise to heavy indigestion. Only the passing of occasional acid bearing burps reminded him that he was not having a heart attack. The psychiatrist picked up his glasses again, rubbing his face as he stretched out to pick up his patients notes. 'Agent Helena Camille' – her name was inherently French in its pronunciation, and Richard pondered as to her religious background. Despite his persistent attempts to enquire about her belief systems, she appeared reluctant to divulge it. The psychiatrist found it difficult to get to the root cause of the problems without knowing all the 'ins' and 'outs' of the case, although as he half smirked to himself, her problems were obviously religious in origin, and he would be worried if she didn't have an issue with murder.

Richard flicked through the file to a section that he had been returning to again and again. Reading it continuously as he did, was of no meaningful help to his patient, rather it had become a haunting backdrop to his own mental conflictions. It was the truth, it was undeniable, it was the very act that the one person in the world he loved more than anything in the world (aside from his boys) committed every time she entered their world; and for Richard, it remained painfully unforgiveable. '…seventeen confirmed killings, ten suspected and six wounded'. Those words, plain in their black and white sterility, and far too easily understood.

HOLLANDS TRUTH

The gardener shook his head in disgust as he slowly made his way around the garden scratching his heavily tanned balding head with his pencil; he tutted with annoyance as the list of horticultural violations forced him to turn over a new page in his notebook: 'Too much money and not enough common'. Eva and Richard rarely saw their gardener; since Eva had left the psychiatrist had taken to leaving notes and signed pay cheques on the patio paving. The lack of polite communication between house owner and gardener had become something of the 'norm' and in reality was probably for the best since 'Tom', the gardener, cared little for his employers, and even less for their reckless attempts at horticultural pursuits.

Tom muttered angrily to himself as he stood underneath the crippled apple tree. Its wounded branch split by the weight of Andrew's body; clung onto the main trunk with a few desperate shards of wood. Tom sighed with pity, stroking the branch as though he could soothe its pain.

"And I suppose this was the result of one of those hammocks!" The gardener almost shouted his fury as he used his pocket knife to put the branch out of its misery and remove it from the scene. The heavy trail of footprints across the lawn and the occasional shard of broken glass from the patio table told Tom a different story to the one that actually happened, but Tom wasn't interested in stories, just plants and soil.

The gardener sat down with his back against Eva's stone sundial, despite the coldness of the air, he found himself mopping his sweating brow with a less than white handkerchief. Tom frowned with puzzlement as his hand scratched against something sharp in his pocket as he replaced his handkerchief. The gardener got down on his hands and knees with curiosity as he saw the corner of something white poke out between the crumbling, frost-damaged mortar of the stone built sundial. Tom looked up, peering through the patio windows to see if anyone was looking before he removed the object from the stone plinth. The gardener's curiosity was short lived as he instantly recognised that he was holding a letter. It's damp and somewhat hard crinkled edges suggested that it had been stuck in the wall for a while, and Tom hesitated as he decided whether to return it back to the sundial.

Despite the gardener's lack of interest for his fellow human beings, he had a keen sense for deep thought and the somewhat faded name of 'Eva' on the front of the letter suggested that it was meant for the lady of the house, and it wouldn't be right if that lady didn't get a chance to read it. Tom stood up; after quickly brushing himself down he scribbled a note on his white pad before shoving it, and the letter, through the patio door behind a sleeping Richard on the couch. "It's not going to be cheap to fix this garden," Tom said to himself as he left the residence.

Richard started out of his whiskey-induced sleep as he heard the familiar 'click, click' of the patio door. The possibility that someone may have entered his house took second precedence as he realised that he had spilled a half glass of whiskey on his crotch. Without even checking the patio, the psychiatrist made his way to the bedroom to change his clothes. He moaned to himself with annoyance as a dull thud in his temples threatened to interfere with his morning schedule. Richard threw his whiskey-stained clothes into the hamper. The old familiar smell of the night before reminded Richard why he had left those drunken habits behind; and he immediately turned from his bedroom to the bathroom to reach for his toothbrush. As the psychiatrist re-entered the open plan living room he suddenly remembered what had awoken him in the first place. Richard rubbed his eyes with some annoyance as he instantly recognised the scrawling illegible writing of the gardener. The psychiatrist was convinced that, Tom knew nothing of good manners; still, having said that, he was the best bloody gardener they had ever had.

Richard bent down to pick up the note and then paused slightly as he caught sight of the letter. "Eva" Richard spoke her name aloud as he read the front of the envelope. Sitting himself firmly back into his alcohol-stained couch, he held the letter in his hand. The psychiatrist rotated the crisp weather-beaten paper around in his fingers, he paused for a second, licking his lips before continuing its rotation. Ten minutes elapsed before Richard finally flipped it over and gently teased the closed envelope. The numerous frosty nights had deteriorated the flimsy glue and the bond between the paper broke almost instantly. Richard sighed with relief as though it made his nosiness less criminal. As the psychiatrist unfolded the still crisp white Basildon Bond paper, his hands began to shake. The straight up and down formation of the letters, the way every 'y' had a curly tail crossed with just a little slant to the right. This handwriting was unmistakeable, it belonged to Andrew. Drawing a hand down his slightly pale face, Richard drew in a breath as he read.

"My dearest Eva,

You and Richard have been my closest friends, and yet I have found myself wandering paths that have taken me away from our goals. I understand your hatred Eva, but I also understand your fire, and your compassion. I hope you can use those most honourable of qualities to see past our fear of them, to see what I have seen, and maybe you and Richard could continue my work. I had never thought that in all my days in this world, in this job, that I would ever be witness to a crueller and darker extermination. Even in the blackest chasms of my mind, in the coldest reaches of my imagination, have I ever been witness to such pain; to such suffering. One cannot possibly imagine or speculate what it must be like to endure such a weapon. Our superiors tell us they feel nothing, that they are amalgamations of energy particles with no soul. No emotion. Do you truly believe that Eva?, I have seen their reactions, listened to their distorted, amplified cracks and bangs and screams, I hear them in my dreams, and I know you hear them too. Do you know what the weapon actually does? I'm sure you have an idea, or perhaps like the others it's easier to forget the science and just think of the war. This weapon is designed to slowly tear apart their cohesiveness. It rips the particles of energy apart like a child pulling away Velcro. The process is slow, it takes nearly ten minutes for the beings to lose their cohesion. They crumble, into thousands of tiny grains of sand, like a castle on the beach dried out from the sun's heat. I have never used the weapon for more than a few seconds, I expect that surprises you; the great Agent Hollands will not kill. To be honest, I'd rather be in Afghanistan killing my own kind than in a realm I've barely begun to understand and with information I know to be inaccurate. It doesn't take a genius to recognise the suffering of another, even if that other is not human. We are soldiers you and I Eva, and we have a duty to perform to protect our fellow kind. They have committed atrocities in our world and now we find ourselves committing atrocities in theirs. If this is the beginning of a new future for us, then I suggest that it is a future that will be short lived. Our search for other forms of life has been found right under our own skin, and yet we are destroying it, just like we destroy our religions, our hopes and in the end even our own dreams. We are the demons that burn the angels in heaven. We are the minions of darkness, help me stop this Eva, help me protect the Guardians of Light"

Richard scowled as he gently placed the letter and the opened envelope upon the coffee table. His heart was racing, and he struggled to regulate his breathing. In an oddly cold fashion, Richard almost felt vindicated, he was right, and Andrew knew he was. The static realm was not full of murderous demons from some hellish electric dimension. They were conscious, thinking, sentient beings. The information The Cavern so proudly based their work on was wrong.

Richard grabbed a pad of paper and a pencil from the kitchen counter. At the bottom of his letter to Eva, Andrew had written two words, 'Cautious Path' The psychiatrist grabbed his keys, stuffing the letter firmly into the inside pocket of his jacket he headed for the door. He had to find Eva, and there was only one place she would be.

CHAPTER EIGHTEEN

Eva swung recklessly on her swivel chair. Her office had become her home and it had begun to look as though a squatter had moved in unannounced. What little personal belongings she had taken from their home lay dotted haphazardly about the room. Like her, they looked awkwardly out of place. Consciously or not, Agent Gardiner had left nearly all of her trinkets and small personal objects with Richard, somewhere in her own mind it was as though she had left the noblest part of herself with him. The person she really was, not the agent construct she was so desperately trying to emulate.

The chair came back down with a thump onto the floor and Eva sighed as she twiddled with the pens on the desk. There was a lot to be said about her previous life as a nurse at the hospital. Yes it was mundane, occasionally even disheartening; but at least it was straightforward and perhaps more importantly it was innocent. Despite her drive and new found confidence, there were occasions when Eva longed to be back in the long marble floored corridors of Mercy. There was a stark difference between cleaning up the mess and being the person who had caused the mess in the first place.

Eva grumbled to herself as she carefully tiptoed around the jumbled objects on the floor to make her way to the coffee machine. If there was one thing she needed to do, it was to move out of her office. She had intended it only as a temporary arrangement; and yet she found herself finding excuses not to look for other accommodation. The excuses had been starting to wear thin of late and the disdainful glances of Professor Stanton as he dodged her jumbled up piles of clothes on the floor suggested that her welcome was also beginning to wear thin.

Despite the fact that to all intent and purposes her relationship with Richard had ended, she preferred to think of it as being 'on hold' The act of actually looking for somewhere else to live might suggest some kind of finale; and Eva didn't particularly like that thought. 'End' was such a one stop word, and agent Gardiner preferred the thought that there might still be some room for negotiation in their relationship. Richard's feelings about what Eva did for The Cavern were quite plain, and Agent Gardiner had no intention of persuading him otherwise. Her own feelings on the matter where not so clear cut and heavily coloured by hatred. Eva was convinced that The Caverns campaign and her own involvement were justified and necessary. She was in her view 'defending humanity against those who would wish to destroy it' and until another method was designed to dispose of their enemy however cruel and harsh that method was; it would never the less be necessary.

Eva couldn't help but enjoy the feeling that she was in control. So much of her younger life had been spent obeying the whims of others, and when she wasn't doing that, she was trying to heal those who could not be healed. The agent was almost resentful of certain aspects of her past, and she almost wished that 'they' whoever 'they' were, could see her now. At The Cavern, she was in control, in control of her team, in control of a variety of decisions made in the field, and perhaps more importantly to her; in control of herself. She chose to do what she did, and she would choose when she chose to stop doing it.

The phone on Eva's desk blurted out into the silence of her office/bedroom, and the agent grimaced at its persistent high pitched ring. She hated it, the noise reminded her of the first flat she had shared with Adam, with its dark damp walls and hideous flower-patterned carpets. Needless to say, everyone knew that if they called Eva in her office, she would have it answered by the second ring. If only as she aptly put it 'to shut the bloody thing up'

"Agent Gardiner," Eva spoke quickly and confidently down the receiver.

"Hey, Eva, its Michael at reception, listen, Richards making his way down to you, thought you might like the heads up." Eva closed her eyes in mild annoyance at the information and nodded down the receiver to confirm his thought,

"Cheers Michael." The agent tugged at her hair with panic as she looked at the random untidiness of her office. The last thing she wanted was for Richard to think she wasn't organised and well planned with her arrangements, despite her mild obsession with work and The Cavern, she still had a heavy dose of pride, and ex fiancée or not, she still wanted to look good when she was around him.

Eva quickly kicked her clothes underneath the desk, having only enough time to throw herself into the swivel chair before Richard rudely opened her door without knocking.

"Hey." The psychiatrist blundered into the office, closing the door behind him as though he were trying to keep out a flood.

"Hi," Eva responded cautiously as Richard's unusual behaviour caught her strangely off guard. The psychiatrist peered around the room for a second and Eva purposefully ignored his curious glances at her abode.

"Erm, Listen, Tom found this in the garden" Richard paused for a second as he decided whether lying to Eva was a wise move. "It was sort of open, and I kind of read it." The psychiatrist bit his lip in response to Eva's raised eyebrows as he handed her the letter. "It's important, it's from Andrew," Eva looked up at Richard as her annoyance about his intrusion dissipated into irrelevance. The agent stood up from her desk, clutching the letter as though she had been handed a newborn. Standing with her back to Richard she opened the weather-beaten paper and read. The psychiatrist wasn't quite sure what he was expecting from Eva, but her response was almost unbelievably alien in its straightforward plainness.

"Well, he really was suffering from some severe psychological issues wasn't he?" Richard said nothing in response to her statement; in truth he was having difficulty processing her blunt lack of care. Eva placed the letter back onto her desk before re-seating herself into the swivel chair. "I mean, he obviously didn't like this job, I just never thought that he would commit suicide over it." Eva laughed as she talked, in an ironic way she couldn't quite believe what she was saying. It was almost as though some huge defensive wall had sprung up between her devotion to The Cavern and her true innermost feelings. She couldn't show both, and she could only protect one. The psychiatrist blinked in an almost dumbfounded disbelief at what he was hearing.

"Looks like The Cavern's claimed its second victim" Richard allowed his arms to strike his legs as though they were made of lead.

"What?" Eva shrugged her shoulders to suggest that she remained oblivious to his hidden connotations. Richard span round angrily to face her; there was a volatile frustration in his face and Eva was taken aback by the fear response that it stimulated in her.

"You can't win a war when you know nothing about your enemy." The psychiatrist pointed at her as he did when he was chastising one of his sons. "And you certainly can't win a war that you know nothing about yourself." Eva rotated her jaw in an attempt to subdue her tears as the psychiatrist angrily slammed the door as he left. The agent pursed her lips, deftly swiping away the tears from her cheek with angry embarrassment. She hated it that he felt vindicated enough to talk to her in such a manner. She hated it even more that she couldn't quite explain her own behaviour. She loved Andrew, she loved him like a brother, and yet it was apparent she couldn't even put aside her own convictions to understand his letter. To truly read it.

"Fuck," Eva cursed under her breath as she struggled to deal with the emotion of the moment. For a second she wondered if she knew herself at all. The old Eva was so timid, so damned straight-laced. She needed the tenacity this war had given her; maybe she even needed 'them'.

"This is bloody ridiculous." Eva snatched at the letter on the table, grabbing her cigarettes from the drawer she pulled on her jacket and made her way out into the corridor; carefully sliding the letter into the inside pocket of her jacket. She tentatively smiled at Michael on the reception desk as she passed.

"I'm just going for a quick walk, I've got my mobile if anyone needs me" Michael smiled sympathetically at her; it was no secret about her and Richard.

Agent Gardiner waited until she was a good few blocks away from the aquarium before she reached inside her jacket pocket for the letter. Smoking a cigarette as she walked, she re-read the letter, and then she read it again and again. She had this burning need to feel anger for Andrew, his letter suggested that she was wrong, that they were all wrong; that everything she had believed and worked towards in the past two years had been based on a false stereotype – a stereotype that in part at least, she had helped create; Eva tutt-tutted to herself, shaking her head and heavily sighing as she slowly meandered down the streets.

"Goddam you, Andrew!" Agent Gardiner scrunched at the letter in her hand, resisting the urge to throw it away as though it had never existed. It would be so much easier just to forget the ramblings of a suicidal man, to forget the possibility that there was more than just the enemy, more than just the killing; but she knew that she could not forget him, he had been her friend, their friend and she could no more forget him than she could forget Adam or Edna.

Regardless of her burning desire to ignore his ideas, Eva trusted him, in the past she had trusted him with her life; it was only right now that she would trust him with her future.

The power of her fond memories for her fallen comrade reminded the agent of the responsibilities she had once held dear. Those responsibilities were outside of The Cavern, outside of work. Eva opened out the letter she had screwed up in so much anger, replacing it inside the pocket of her jacket with a calm affection before heading for the only place she thought she could be herself; Home.

Eva peered cautiously through the front door. Her house key dangled loosely from her thumb and she began to feel as though she were breaking and entering her own property. She had only been away from their home a couple of months, and yet she felt oddly uncomfortable.

"Hello?" Eva called out tentatively as she made her way towards the kitchen and living-room. The agent breathed in as she heard a muffled response, biting her lip with a sense of trepidation as she poked her head around the door. "Sorry," Eva stuttered to a startled Richard half dozing on the couch. "I used my key to let myself in, I hope that's OK?" The psychiatrist jumped up as though someone had shoved a pin through his trouser seat.

"Of course, it's actually your house." Eva smiled shyly at his welcome pointing to the kettle in an attempt to make the situation more comfortable.

"Just the usual for me," Eva laughed at Richard's unbelievable ability to slip back into the ropes of old times. Eva carefully peered around as he made them both cups of coffee. There was an odd stale smell in the house as though none of the windows had been opened since she'd left, and the agent couldn't help but notice the empty bottle of whiskey sat unceremoniously next to the bin. It was a curious feeling, but she felt almost comforted that Richard had fallen back into old habits. It meant that he needed her, and however selfish, it gave her a warm feeling in her stomach.

Eva and Richard sat next to each other on the couch. Agent Gardiner deliberately sat with her back facing the patio windows. The garden had become much more than just a garden. It was a place of loss and sorrow. She had often wondered why Andrew had chosen their home to end his life. The three of them spent so many relaxed evenings on the patio, but those memories would always be marred by his death, and it had since become a place that she felt she would never enter again. Eva placed the letter, now slightly worse for wear, on the coffee table in front of them. They both stared blankly at it for a few moments; it was so small and looked so insignificant, yet from a friend that meant so much. Richard sighed as he placed his coffee mug on the table to pick up the letter.

"Did you see the two words on the bottom?" Eva frowned shaking her head as Richard pointed them out.

"Cautious Path," Agent Gardiner whispered them aloud as she read. "You know I didn't even notice them." Eva shrugged her shoulders in disbelief at her own blindness.

"There's enough in that letter to grab anyone's attention." Richard offered her a welcomed excuse as he reached for the laptop. "I think they might be passwords, but for some reason I can't logon to the system" Richard's statement was almost a question, as though he expected Eva to know the answer. Agent Gardiner nodded her head as she pulled the laptop towards her.

"The security for the mainframe has been updated, this is the wrong address," Richard pulled a face and Eva smiled her response. "That's what you get for not keeping up with the monthly meetings." The psychiatrist shrugged his shoulders, cocking his head to one side as if to suggest that was nothing unusual.

Eva tapped the edges of the laptop impatiently with her fingertips. The password enabled security logon came up on the main screen and Eva paused for a second as she began entering her own username and password.

"No, don't logon as you, logon as Andrew." Richard stood up hovering over her shoulder as he watched the screen. Eva nodded her head as her own thoughts crossed his.

"I don't even know if his username is still active, they usually get removed from the system after death." She looked up at Richard with a mixture of hope and mourning. He nodded his head with encouragement.

"Go on, try it anyway." Eva quickly entered Andrew's username which was a simple birthdate followed by a personal identification number. His password was simple; it was the same password that he used for everything, 'Sarah'.

"Yes," Agent Gardiner exclaimed out loud as Agent Hollands homepage popped up on screen. Eva's face darkened slightly as the familiarity of the bright, neatly organised screen was replaced by a dark blue background with two small rectangular cursor boxes. "He must have added his own security; I've never seen this before." Richard reached onto the coffee table for the letter.

"He was a smart man." The psychiatrist pointed to the two isolated words on the bottom of the letter and Eva obediently typed 'cautious' into the top cursor box followed by 'path' in the second. For a moment or two Eva wondered if perhaps she had made a mistake. "Give it a minute." Richard spoke with an optimism that paid off as a block of six folders appeared in the top left hand corner of the screen. Eva fidgeted slightly in her seat.

"This is going to sound really odd, but I feel kind of excited." Eva laughed at her own ridiculous sounding statement. The psychiatrist placed a hand on her shoulder, gently squeezing it he replied.

"It's a bit like old times eh?" Eva nodded; in truth, their discovery had sparked a little bit of the old nurse Gardiner back into action. She felt excited, almost hyperactive at the thought that they had discovered something new; something else that The Cavern was unaware of. It was almost as though she had discovered the energy beings all over again, and as she stared at the folders in front of her, her hands began to shake.

"He hasn't named any of the files." Eva looked up at Richard, her statement was obvious and he knew that she was asking him for direction. Richard sighed dragging a hand down his face.

"Wow" He exclaimed with disbelief in his voice. "Erm, just open the top left and then we will work consecutively after that," Eva nodded. "What have you been up to, my old friend?" Richard looked up as he asked the question, but he knew that the answers were in those folders. The everyday normality of their otherwise uneventful living room was heavily tainted with a nervous expectancy. Eva and Richard stared at the laptop screen as though it was an alien technology.

"Right," Eva took a deep breath as she ran her finger over the scroll pad. "Top left it is." Neither the agent nor the psychiatrist knew quite what they were expecting, but the unassuming small beige folder in the top left of the screen marked 'generation 1' suddenly opened up to reveal nearly a hundred further files, all of which contained enough information to keep the pair busy for hours. "What the hell is this?" Eva questioned the computer screen as though the answer would just suddenly appear.

"They look like personnel files." Richard pointed over her shoulder to individually named files.

"Look; Campbell, Forester, Muchausen, Ricci; those are all surnames" Eva clicked on the Forester file displaying a range of family photographs, birth certificates and electoral register forms.

"Why would he be storing information of this nature? None of these people are familiar; well, they don't work at the cavern that's for sure." Eva shrugged her shoulders exiting the file and opening the one called 'Ricci'. Richard shook his head as he explored the file.

"You wouldn't know this person, well unless you were in your eighties" Eva frowned as she focused her attention on the date of birth of 'Mrs Charlotte Ann Ricci' born in Chester on the seventeenth of April 1932. Eva began shaking her head,

"Richard, I'm just not getting this; why the hell would he be collecting information on people who are already dead?" Dead; the word rang out into the living room like a church bell on a frosty white morning. Eva looked at Richard with an almost desperate urgency. The answer was on the tip of her tongue and her mind burned with aching need to answer her own questions.

"Look at this," Richard took over the laptop moving the cursor as he illustrated his findings. "Each folder is given a generation number and then opposite is a folder with a generation number and letter" Eva moved her head in closer to Richard as she stared at the screen, the familiar smell of his favourite aftershave made her stomach tingle and she swallowed hard against the sensation. "I think if we open generation 1b it's going to look pretty different." The psychiatrist's assumption was correct. The folder marked generation '1b' was still under the name of 'Forester' but next to the name behind a forward slash was the word 'Ferushi' "Forester/Ferushi" Richard whispered as he looked closer at the file. "Ferushi; second generation Forester, energised on the third of March 1982, due to expire on the twenty fifth of September 2022."

"Oh my God," Eva exclaimed in disbelief as she understood its meaning. "Mark Forester died on the third of March 1982 from Cancer, that's exactly when this 'Fersuhi' energised?" Richard nodded his head, laughing at the annoying simplicity of the situation.

"It's pretty simple really, these beings are us, in another form perhaps yes; but the name 'Ferushi', I'm guessing is derived from the human name 'Forester'" Eva rubbed her forehead with the back of her palm.

"Are you talking about an ancestral name?"

The psychiatrist nodded, slowly continuing the nod he began to digest his own trail of thought. "Yes, I think so. Look, this 'Ferushi' already has an expiry date, a time of death I suppose, so I bet that on the same date another generation 'Forester' is due to be born." Eva stood up behind Richard.

"A life cycle," she whispered as she made her way across the room to the kitchen to light a cigarette. "This means that for every human generation, there's a generation between us, in their realm and that generation brings on the third human generation and so forth; Shit ..." Eva blew out her cigarette smoke in an almost instant panic. "But that means that any disruption to the beings in the static realm would disrupt the next generation of humans." Richard nodded his head.

"Yes and vice versa, we are literally killing off a branch of our own species, perhaps even the route to our next generation"

"Oh my God!" Agent Gardiner threw her cigarette out of the window. "We have to stop the next shift, before they enter the realm." Eva rushed about the room trying to gather her belongings. Richard grabbed at her arms to stop her.

"Wait, we don't know enough yet, for a start these beings have been attacking us a lot longer, we need to know why, and secondly Andrew told no-one about this, not even us, he died before we found this information, let's not ruin all his hard work before we know who we can trust." Eva breathed out in a stuttering fashion.

"Shit," she repeated herself as she grabbed another cigarette from her waning packet. Richard returned to his laptop.

"There are literally hundreds of surnames in here, Jesus," Richard breathed out as he came across something that grabbed his immediate attention.

"What?" Eva broke her own house rules and wandered into the living room with the cigarette still burning between her fingers.

"Most of these human names are like the static beings, they have a date of expiry too, in the future, I can literally see the exact date when all of these individuals are going to die" Eva trembled slightly as she sucked on her cigarette.

"That's why he didn't tell anyone, can you imagine if people knew the date that they were going to die?" Richard nodded.

"I think Andrew knew that his time was up, I think he chose his own route."

Eva closed her eyes, a tight knot had formed in the back of her throat and she swallowed against the pain of it. "There are so many variables in life," she whispered, attempting to subdue the persistent quaver in her voice. "Accidents, misfortunes" Richard screwed up his face in response.

"Are there? This world exists on such a delicate balance of events and consequences, of deaths and re-births; you'd think that there would have to be a plan in there somewhere"

"God?" Eva questioned the psychiatrist as though he had suggested something implausible.

"Perhaps God is more natural than we all thought; nothing beats a well-laid-out and executed plan, Eva, and there's nothing supernatural about Mother Nature."

"Jesus." The agent walked back into the kitchen searching for the alcohol she felt sure Richard had stashed away.

"Top right," Richard gestured with his eyebrows offering Eva an apologetic smile.

"We will talk about this later." She waved the bottle of Famous Grouse at him whilst grabbing a couple of glasses. "There must be some overlap in the generations though?" Eva frowned as she tried to work out the math.

"Yes, if the grandmother dies and begins again as a new entity in the static realm, it would make sense that it would be the great granddaughter who is reborn from the death of the static being." Eva raised her eyebrows at Richard's statement.

"But some great grandparents are still alive when that generation is being born," Richard drank deeply into his whiskey glass.

"Yeah, but it wouldn't have been like that a hundred years ago, it's really only in the last century that our medical advancements have allowed us to live so long." Eva coughed at the harshness of the Grouse.

"Our own medical and technological advances are allowing us to live beyond our dates; we are literally cheating the system and the beings from the static realm are being denied the energy they need to reproduce, but we already knew that was the problem." Eva drew a hand over her face shaking her head as she thought. "But we still reproduce in the way that we always have, we don't need them to survive, we just get a second chance at heaven." Richard nodded his head.

"No, but they need us; and in all honesty, Eva, we have no idea what the consequences of destroying a species that have lived symbiotically with us for generations will be."

Eva grimaced as she threw the last of the whiskey down her throat. "What happens when you kill the bees?" She put her glass down heavily on the table, staring out at her long forgotten garden like she could see the mysteries of the world panned out on her sundial. "I can't believe that he did all this by himself, someone else must have known what he knew, if only to help him document it." Eva continued to stare out of the window. The agent was intensely angry with herself for becoming so closed and so single-minded in her hatred for the static realm that a man she considered to be one of her closest friends dared not confide in her. "It should have been us," Eva whispered back at her ex with a feebleness that she had not displayed in months. Richard placed a hand on her shoulder, gently turning her body into his own. Eva did not refuse, but deeply buried her face in his chest.

"You thought you were doing the right thing, they attacked you on a personal level, Eva; how could you have reacted? How would anyone else react?" Despite Richard's attempts to settle her conscience, Agent Gardiner found herself chewing on her own humiliation. Her own naïve stupidity had belittled the courage of her former character and she ached to set things right. "We need to find out if anyone else knows." Richard nodded, stroking her head as though she were one of his children. "Dr Jackson?" She lifted her head looking up at the psychiatrist for some kind of approval. "I bet it's the doctor, I bet he knows." Richard drew his jaw down as though he wasn't in entire agreement.

"Really? Mark? I thought those two hated each other." Eva smiled,

"They did, but it doesn't mean that Andrew didn't trust him, the doctor knew about the drugs, maybe he also knows what caused Andrew to take them in the first place." Richard reached for the bottle of whiskey again and then changed his mind as he caught the look on his former fiancée's face.

"It's a pretty big risk Eva, we can't just come right out and ask him." Eva shook her head,

"No, but I can use a trigger, if he knows what I'm talking about then he's bound to show some kind of response, and if not then I just look like a babbling idiot." Richard laughed,

"You? Surely not." Agent Gardiner cocked her head,

"You would be surprised how insane I've become lately" Richard ignored her comment aware of her own immediate self-loathing.

"So what are you going to say as your trigger?" Eva licked her lips, "I don't know, generation one?" Richard nodded his head, "Yeah, but it sounds too scientific, especially if he knows nothing about it, the man is a genius he's bound to want to know where you got the statement 'generation one' from." Eva waved her hands around the room as she thought. "Ok, what about Andrew's password, 'cautious path?' at least I can attempt to use that in a sentence."

"Yeah, I think that might be your best bet, I'd go with that" Richard wandered back over to the laptop. "I'm going to save this data onto a memory key, just in case 'The Cavern' decides to remove Andrew's login from the system."

"That's a good idea, you keep it; I reckon it's safest with you." Richard didn't argue, he couldn't help but feel flattered that her trust in him had remained unfaltering despite their disagreements.

CHAPTER NINETEEN

Richard drove Eva and himself back to the aquarium. There was an awkward moment as they slipped into the discreetly hidden elevator, that perhaps they shouldn't appear out of the lift together. Eva, annoyed with the strange uneasiness, announced into the quiet tension of the lift.

"Jesus Christ, we're colleagues, Richard, this is ridiculous." The psychiatrist coughed a half laugh as he agreed that the worry of what others might think was a juvenile concern. "Besides, it wasn't that long ago we were banging each other, and I doubt whether it will be long before we are again." Eva straightened herself up as she stepped out into the foyer and Richard stared after her with a mixture of confused humour and relief.

Despite Eva's concerns about being seen in such close proximity to her ex-partner, she marched up to the reception desk with the same sturdy confidence she displayed in her normal working day.

"Hey" Eva leaned over the desk at Michael. "Is the good doctor in today?" Michael stared past Eva at Richard who was ambling up slowly behind her. Michael glanced up at Agent Gardiner with a curious look of puzzlement on his face. Eva ignored his feeble attempts to gain inside knowledge and simply smiled in response. "Mark?"

"Oh yes, yes, hang on a minute." Michael jumped slightly as Richard also made his presence felt by leaning over the table.

"Hi, Michael."

The receptionist stuttered his response, "Hi, and Erm, yes, the doctor is training some of the new agents on the fluidic suits today, he's in lab one." Eva nodded her head as she walked away.

"Riveting stuff eh?" Richard offered Michael a wry smile as he gently jogged away to catch up with Eva. Michael frowned, drumming his fingers on the desk as he watched after them. He wasn't the brightest agent in the bunch, but he could tell when something was a foot.

Eva and Richard peered around the lab door into a room crowded with new and existing agents. It was fairly simple to spot the fledglings from the seasoned personnel as they all stared at the fluidic suits as if they had been handed an alien embryo. Richard gestured to Eva that for now at least she should go in by herself, and he hovered slightly uncomfortably in the corridor. Agent Gardiner discreetly entered the lab, taking care to avoid disrupting the eager agents from their learning. The doctor caught sight of her vain attempts at tip toe walking and gestured her to move to the front of the lab beside himself. Eva re-adjusted back into agent mode and confidently took her place beside him.

"Most of you will already recognise Agent Gardiner as your team leader in the static realm, for those of you who don't, this is the agent you report to, she is not only your boss but quite possibly the person who will save your life should the need arise; No one knows the static beings or their realm better than this woman." Eva smiled, laughing slightly as if to brush off some of the needless compliments.

"It's good to see you all here, I'm sure as the good doctor has already told you, this is no ordinary assignment," Eva began to walk around the rows of agents, sitting like obedient puppies in their plastic chairs. "This job isn't just dangerous, it's quite literally life-threatening, male or female, you need to have balls; and if you haven't? Then you need to be mighty quick at growing them, because I don't have the time to wait for you." Eva made sure she was standing at the back of the class, looking at the doctor before she continued. "As you will all find out tomorrow, you need to have your eyes and your ears open at all times whilst in the static realm, and if you don't know what to do, do as the doctor always suggests and take the cautious path." Agent Gardiner looked directly at her colleague as she said the last two words of Andrew's password. A sudden flicker of recognition passed the doctor's face and Richard smiled as he looked through the glass into the lab. Eva wasn't just a pretty face, she was smart, too.

"Right" The doctor flapped his arms around as though he were swatting a fly. "I think that's enough for today, take your suits away with you, and bring them back in time tomorrow morning so I can get them ready for the realm." The doctor offered his students a wry smile as they began filing out of the lab, clutching at their fluidic suits like children holding candy. Eva waited at the back of the lab until the last fledgling agent had left before quietly and curiously eyeing Dr Mark Jackson. The doctor licked his lips.

"Well what can I do for you today, Agent Gardiner?" Eva smiled, rubbing her hands together to reiterate the fact that she was getting at something.

"I was thinking that you might be able to assist me with something, you know perhaps something to keep me on that cautious path?" Dr Jackson sat down heavily on his desk.

"So…" He paused for a second, almost as though he were gathering courage before he spoke, Dr Jackson looked Eva in the eye, "Are you here to have me arrested, or are you here to learn the truth?" Before Eva could answer the door to the lab opened and Richard wandered casually in.

"As you know, doctor, the truth is the only cause worth dying for."

Mark looked at the floor, tapping his foot irregularly on the white tiled slabs as though he were sending a secret Morse Code message.

ANCESTRAL GUARDIANS

"Well," Mark rubbed his brow, "Andrew damned well thought it was." The doctor ambled over to his desk, his movements were weak, almost lifeless in their integrity, and for a second, Eva wondered if he might fall. "You know I've been waiting for this day for three months, not sure whether the steadfast Agent Gardiner was going to trade me in for a promotion" Mark laughed and Eva swallowed against his bitterness.

"I've been … slightly blinded by my own hatred." Eva bypassed his curious stare as she choked on her own stubborn pride. Mark smiled, his face relaxing slightly as he appreciated her humility.

"So how did you come across our research?" Richard walked over to the doctor's desk sliding the memory key towards him. "Andrew left us a note, only he hid it so well, we've only just discovered it." Mark snorted, rolling his eyes as if he had expected nothing else.

"Typical Andrew, if he wasn't one step ahead, he was two steps behind." Eva raised her eyebrows at Mark's comment; it appeared that Mark Jackson's bitterness extended beyond Agent Gardiner. The doctor leaned back in his chair and it creaked angrily; placing his hands behind his head he took a deep breath before elaborating. "About a year ago, Andrew died of a self-induced drug overdose." Eva and Richard looked at each other as though the doctor had lost his mind, Mark smiled and continued. "Don't ask me why he did it, or why he even started using, because I can't tell you and I doubt whether he could either, whatever the reason, he took a cocktail of shit and by the time that I found him he was dead." Eva continued to stare blankly at the doctor as though he were speaking a language she was unfamiliar with. Dr Jackson began laughing almost as if he disbelieved himself. "Well he was dead, for a couple of minutes at least, I was just about to zip the body bag up when the arrogant twat sat up."

Dr Jackson began laughing again, Richard watched him carefully, trying to decide whether the tear rolling down his cheek was as a result of his laughter or genuine despair. "Thing is, it wasn't quite Andrew's time to die, his juvenile host entity was too young to accept his energy transference, so they simply sent him back." Mark slapped the desk with his hands as though he had said something that only a fool would be ignorant of. Eva pulled up a chair suddenly feeling that she needed to sit down.

"That's what we saw in those files wasn't it? The beings, did you call them Guardians?" Mark nodded,

"That's the name that they are referred to in their world" Eva nodded back, "They are generationally related to us?" Eva looked towards Richard to back up her trail of thought, and the psychiatrist took the opportunity to speak.

"It looked as though it was only every third generation?" Mark began nodding his head in confirmation.

"Yes, they have a longer life span than ours; one generation of their species spans approximately two of ours." Eva chewed her lip as she began asking a question she really wasn't sure that she wanted to know the answer to.

"And they are related to us?" Dr Jackson screwed up his face, tilting his head slightly as he analysed her comment. "I'm afraid it's not quite as simple as that, in a crude sense, yes, they literally are a part of our own family tree, but they also contain a unique part of us as individuals" Eva looked at Richard with an almost humorous, dumb-founded look on her face. "As you discovered yourself Eva, each living cell retains a memory of the life it has been a part of, and it is this energy that the static beings, or Guardians as they call themselves, absorb in order to initiate their own life cycles." Mark looked intently at Eva, "They hold our memories, an imprint of the lives we live right here perhaps even our souls all mixed up as part of their own psych, and not just ours but our great grandparents and every third generation prior to that." Richard leaned forward, the enormity of the facts fascinated, even excited him.

"They even have a derivative of our human names, Richard looked at Eva with a sense of enlightenment. "Just as we said before, 'Forester' and 'Ferushi'." Eva nodded, for some reason she was beginning to feel more and more overwhelmed. There was nothing more acrid than the taste of wrong-doing, The agent reminded herself again as she had been doing repeatedly for the past twelve hours, that she had been killing entities that were the reflections of every human being on the planet. She had been sentencing her friends, her family her neighbours to an eternal end, no second chance, no heaven. Eva swallowed against the bitterness on her tongue and the intense emotions that had begun to crumble her steel framework.

"So when I saw Adam, it was actually him?" Richard offered her a quick glance as she returned to biting her lip.

"There will have been elements of Adam's life that the static being could remember, his relationship with you perhaps," Eva nodded. "That's maybe why they chose Adam's ancestral being to approach you, to strike more of a chord, have more of an impact" Eva nodded raising her eyebrows. "What about me? It was clear that I was supposed to die in the attack in the park, but I didn't, so my ancestral being is dead right?" The doctor looked at Richard almost as though he didn't want to answer, or rather didn't know how to answer.

"To be honest, Eva, I'm not sure, if I were to hazard a guess, I would suggest that your ancestral line will die whenever you do." Eva said nothing, she wasn't sure what it all meant, but it left a cold empty feeling in her heart that made her stomach churn. "When your great grandmother's or indeed grandfather's entity died, the information coded in those cells was transferred into the next developing human foetus, that was you, when you were supposed to die, two years ago; that information would have been passed onto the developing Guardian infant … who would have passed it on two generations down the line to the next kin in your family tree" Eva shook her head as a thought entered her mind. "But not every human female will have a child; there are some of us that can't, what happens when there are no further generations to pass information on to?" Mark shrugged his shoulders as though that was something he had never considered.

"Well, I'm only guessing, but everything dies right? There is an eventual closure to everything, it's worth considering that such an event may be the natural end for the human and Guardian family tree." Mark waved his arms around as another thought entered his mind. "Maybe that's why twins seem to know what's happening to each other when they are miles apart, or even just other siblings, it would make sense if they were sharing each other's souls, so to speak"

"I don't have any brothers or sisters" Eva broke in as if to add weight to her own non-existent future. Mark looked at Richard and offered him a grin. "No, Eva, but that doesn't mean that you won't have children." Eva blushed slightly as her and Richard's gaze met. The psychiatrist stood up and began walking around the lab, breaking the awkward moment of embarrassment.

"In that case, Eva would pass on her genetic code and cell memories to her children, her soul if you will; onto her offspring, whilst she may be missing out on an afterlife after her death, she is certainly not ending her ancestral line" The doctor twiddled the memory key around between his fingers as Richard spoke.

"And I believe it's here that we come to the problem." Mark tapped the plastic stick onto his table. "We are cheating the plan laid out for us, we are living beyond our planned death dates, ignoring the cycle of life which we have been following for generations; as a result of this, we are slowly killing off a symbiotic species." Mark paused for a second before continuing, "And what's the price? Well quite frankly it appears to be nothing more than the loss of an afterlife that we have all forgotten by the time our coded information has been passed onto the next human foetus" Richard stared out of the lab window, rubbing his chin he sighed before speaking.

"Ignoring the moral, religious and ethical implications of what you've just said, it appears that the human race could comfortably survive without them?" The doctor stood up joining Richard at the lab window.

"Obviously we have no idea what the long term implications would be, but from a simple biological front, the loss of the static realm isn't going to prevent humans from pro-creating." The doctor shrugged his shoulders as he commented, to reassert the needlessness of the static realm. Eva began bouncing her leg up and down with a tense uneasiness, she whispered adding, "What is a human being without a soul?" Richard and Mark looked at each other, neither one had an answer to her question.

Agent Gardiner suddenly stood from her chair, the gloominess of their conversation had begun to weigh down on her and she stood up as if to remove the heaviness from her shoulders. "But how did all this come to light, and what does it have to do with Andrew?" Eva directed her question to the doctor and walked over to join the two men at the lab window, but quickly changed her mind as she caught sight of Michael hovering around in the corridor outside. Mark also caught sight of the wandering, curious agent and issued a warning glance to Richard to also move away from the window. As the three sat around the hexagonal computer table, Mark began to cautiously talk, lowering his voice and tone to avoid any unwanted interest.

"Andrew's experience was similar to your own first encounter with the beings, Eva, but the motive was different." The doctor clasped his hands together as he considered his words. "These beings are not simple-minded energy particles acting on basic reflexes for survival, they are as socially, emotionally and organisationally advanced as we are" Eva momentarily lifted her eyebrows, but she could tell from the look on Richard's face, that this revelation came as no great surprise to him. For Eva, however, whilst she had never denied their intelligence she had failed to consider the humanity of their social structure. The doctor laughed continuing with his explanation.

"We are dealing with a species that share most of our own social attributes and ideas, it's almost like looking at a static reflection of our own society" The doctor took a short quick breath as though he was eager to blurt the rest out. "When Andrew crossed over he wasn't met by some hellish blue spark of energy trying to drain his soul, but by an intelligent peaceful being, this entity explained the basic facts of their existence, it gave him answers that could not be obtained by taking up arms, but … More importantly … It delivered him a message before returning him back." Eva sat forward as though someone had shoved a gun in her back.

"What message?" She whispered urgently.

Mark looked down at his clasped hands, "It told him that there was good and bad in every society, right and wrong. The same applies to the static realm, whilst beings like the one who approached Andrew are content to live peaceful lives; there are others who resent the human race, and our evolutionary progress, which is slowly causing the destruction of their lives." Eva sat back heavily in her chair, between hands that covered her face she whispered.

"It was trying to warn us."

Mark nodded in response, "Yes, myself and Andrew believe that something is coming, something big and I doubt very much whether fluidic suits and deionised water will stop it."

Eva shuddered, "So it is as I thought, they are coming into our world to collect the energy from those who haven't died, to feed their own life cycles."

The doctor nodded in agreement before responding, "Yes, but it's not going to be long before they start getting greedy; before Andrew crossed over he managed to secure some information from beings sympathetic to natural evolution, this information suggested that the entities have come up with a way to store human energy, until it was needed, this way, they don't have to wait for their human relative counterpart to depart before procreating one of their own species … oh, and their proper name is Guardians, not static beings or whatever we have been calling them."

Richard laughed awkwardly as he spoke, "Guardians? Interesting term considering you are talking about them using some form of human purgatory to imprison our energy." Mark breathed out and whistled unexpectedly from between his clamped teeth. "I don't know about you two, but I would rather live one life with a soul that died with me, than two with a soul stuck in a glass jar in an alien world"

CHAPTER TWENTY

Eva woke between the familiar sheets of their large double bed. Richard slept silently to the right of her and she couldn't help but feel a comfortable sense of completion. Eva carefully slipped out from beneath the bed covers and smiled to herself as the nagging back pain she had been experiencing had vanished. Her office in The Cavern had been a much welcomed home when she had needed it, but the single air bed which continuously deflated during the night was taking its toll on her spine.

Agent Gardiner breathed in deeply as she walked into the kitchen. The early morning sun had found its way through the gaps in the blinds, and Eva smiled as her feet touched the slightly sun warmed tiles of the floor. It was so strange and she could hardly explain it, but despite everything she had learned yesterday, the agent felt so much lighter, almost as though a thick veil of misunderstanding had been removed from her mind. Warming her hands around a freshly made cup of coffee, Eva peered with slight hesitation into the garden. She paused for a second as her eyes caught the familiar outline of the sundial, and then like a child catching her first glimpse of the summer sun, she grabbed her dressing gown and darted out onto the patio. As her feet touched the cold stone of the patio slabs she stopped, suddenly overwhelmed by the memories of the last time she had set foot there. Eva closed her eyes, moist with the intensity of her emotion. Breathing in she allowed the fresh scents of the dewy garden to melt away the poignant images, and she collapsed into her garden chair.

Agent Gardiner sat staring fixedly out into the garden. Deliberately she avoided any thought, any conscious recall of moments past or present. It felt as though she had been sitting on the patio chair for hours, slowly glancing around as she had done the first time she had laid eyes upon it. The noise of Richard's mobile phone disrupted the moment, and Eva blinked as she rapidly came back to reality. Despite the interruption, the agent smiled as she stood up. Her garden belonged again, and she mentally fixed a date with a bottle of wine.

"Eva," Richard stuck his head around the patio door, "You've got that class today remember? Mark just called to remind you to drop off your fluidic suit."

"Shit," Eva ran a hand over her face. "I forgot about that, why didn't he call me?" Richard shrugged his shoulders,

"Maybe he did, he obviously just assumed that we would be together" Agent Gardiner murmured a disgruntled response and Richard looked taken aback by her annoyed muttering. Eva felt his eyes watching her and she quickly realised her mistake.

"I didn't mean anything by that," she smiled as she walked over to the psychiatrist placing a hand on his cheek. "It's just really aggravating when everyone knows your business, it makes keeping secrets very difficult." Eva looked meaningfully at Richard as she said the last two words and he nodded in appreciation of her thoughts.

"At least it was Mark, he knows everything we do." Eva nodded, pulling on her jeans and jumper.

"I'd better get going," Eva said reluctantly, the psychiatrist leaned into her, gently kissing her lips.

"Be careful," he whispered with authority in her ear and agent Gardiner stifled a laugh shaking her head.

"Well, I won't be killing any Guardians, that's for damn sure." The psychiatrist smiled cautiously in return, there was an odd sense of darkness in her words, since she had killed hundreds prior to this day. Eva looked down at her fidgeting hands as she fumbled with the car keys; swallowing as the dryness in her mouth hindered her voice. "I'll s-see you l-later" she stammered back at him as she quickly left the room.

Agent Gardiner drove slowly to The Cavern. For the first time since she and Richard had become part of the government organisation, she felt trepidation at walking through the doors. The annoyed rasping from a car horn behind her reminded the agent that the lights had turned green and she crunched the gearbox into second as she unsteadily took off again. Her driving skills reflected her waning confidence, and as she approached the aquarium, Eva chose to leave the car on the side street rather than her usual bold parking spot in the car park. "God damn it!" Agent Gardiner growled angrily to herself as her old anxiety related ectopic heart beat made its presence known. Eva straightened herself up as best she could on the way down the elevator. As she stepped out into the foyer wearing a crudely faked smile, the agent wished reverently that she could go back to her old job at Mercy; there were no secrets at the hospital, just a thin line which separated the living from the dead, which right now was at least preferable to the merciless killing at The Cavern.

"Sleep in?" Eva frowned to see Michael lazily leaning over his desk like he owned the rights of its manufacture.

"No," Eva retorted, pausing slightly with irritation at his presumptuous remark. "I don't believe I have a set time for starting and finishing work," she offered him a raised eyebrow as if to re-assert her authority over him and walked steadily passed his desk. Agent Gardiner couldn't quite put her finger on the problem, but the eager young receptionist appeared to be acting well above his station of late.

The low rumblings of excited chatter caught Eva's attention as she made her way down to the laboratory. The agent rolled her eyes, sighing. She could understand their excitement, few would ever get the chance to see another world, but she also knew what awaited them in the realm of static electricity and vengeful Guardians. For a second or two, Eva pondered with the idea of telling these new agents the truth, perhaps she could avoid future needless deaths, but as she strode with false confidence towards the crowd, a sense of reality washed over her and she knew that for today at least, she would be teaching business as usual.

Dr Jackson offered Eva a sympathetic smile as he readied her fluidic suit for the realm. The agents were organised into groups of five, and Eva sighed at the prospect of having to make three trips in one day. Eva could feel a sense of apprehension from her class as they gathered around the cartwheel shaped alignment of metal beds in the medical lab. There was nothing cosy about this room, nothing welcoming, only the cold sterility of shining steel, white walls and medical resuscitation equipment graced the deionised water encapsulated room. As Agent Gardiner quickly reminded them, they would never be more vulnerable than when they were unconscious in the static realm, not only were they open to attack on an unconscious level, but their bodies were also at risk, lying like beef on a butcher's board in their own world.

"Hence the three glass walls of de-ionised water" she offered them a wink after her statement which was met with some cautious laughter.

The doctor travelled around each agent one at a time, fixing blood pressure monitoring equipment, heart rate detectors and issuing them the relaxant which would stimulate the drug induced coma necessary for static realm penetration. He approached Eva last, and as he pushed the drug into her vein he whispered carefully into her ear. "I'm sorry you have to do this, try to be yourself." Eva blinked weakly as his message just had time to register before her pupils dilated and she left conscious thought.

Eva shuddered slightly as she opened her eyes. The sensation of entering the realm was not unlike the falling dream encountered when the brain falls asleep before the body does. The agent curled her toes inside her suit; she had found it to be a quick way of ridding herself from the imbalance.

Eva glanced quickly around her, the other agents stood awkwardly still in the Catherine wheel shape, many of them swaying as though they were on the deck of a ship.

"Take your time, the transition into the static realm can be a little disorientating." Eva waited in silence for a few minutes until her students had stopped swaying. "Just talk as you normally would back home, there's no need to be quiet" Eva projected her voice loudly as she spoke as if to make her point.

"Won't they hear us?" A young female agent began to walk cautiously towards Eva, her fear obvious in her body language. Agent Gardiner put a hand on her shoulder in reassurance. "It's agent Parker right?" The young girl nodded her head.

"Holly," she replied shakily.

"OK, Holly, listen, the static beings can't hear us because we are operating on a different frequency from them, our suits change the way that our natural electrical field vibrates, they can't detect our vibrations either on a visual or sonic level," Eva patted the young agent on the back, and Holly breathed out relaxing a little. "Having said that," Eva turned to face the rest of the agents making sure that they were all paying attention. "This suit is your life, if it becomes damaged, your electrical vibration will begin to seep out into the frequency of the static realm, you can't miss a damaged suit; it leaks a vibrant purple hue, pretty obvious in a blue atmosphere" Eva turned away attempting to mask an amused smile as she watched the agents anxiously scrutinising each-other's fluidic suits.

"Agent Gardiner!" Eva spun round at the shout and motioned her students to move forward as a Guardian moved close to their position.

"It's beautiful!" Holly whispered as she watched the being glide through the static atmosphere with a grace known only to angels.

"Yes," Eva's reply harboured a note of sadness, and the experienced agent took a moment to study the Guardians in a new light, away from the hatred she had wallowed in for so long. Eva motioned to her students to gather around, "The Guardians vibrate at a frequency which is in harmony with the realm in which they live, look how their bodies seem to float in and out of visual acuity, they are almost like jellyfish in the ocean, transparent yet defined by these striking blue zigzagging lines," Eva pointed to the Guardian which was less than a metre away, highlighting different parts of its body with her finger, tracing its outline with perfection, almost as though she were admiring it.

"Guardians? Is that what we call them?" A male agent approached, and Eva realised her mistake, fortunately she did not need to answer him as his confidence was bursting through his attention span. "What would happen if I touched it?" The eager young man outstretched his hand as though to pass it through the entity's body. Agent Gardiner calmly grabbed his hand, quickly returning it back to his side.

"Agent Turner, right?" Eva questioned her student who responded with a quick nod. "Well, Turner, have you ever had that feeling that someone has walked over your grave? You know, that sudden icy cold chill that makes the hairs on the back of your neck stand up?"

Agent Turner nodded in recognition of her statement and then added, "Haven't we all felt that?" Eva watched as the rest of the students all began nodding their heads in agreement.

"Then you should know that every time you have felt that sensation, one of these beings has just walked straight through you, they don't need a suit to be present in our world, they are made of energy and can choose to be visible if they want to be, in fact I think it would be safe to say that many of the ghost stories and sightings that are so prevalent in our society could be down to these beings." Agent Turner stretched out his hand again as he began speaking,

"So if I touched it, then it would just give it the creeps right?" The agent leaned forward and Eva quickly intervened again, returning his hand slightly more aggressively to his side.

"You forget, Agent Turner, we are at war, these beings can recognise a fluctuation in their electrical field just as easy as we can, if you had touched the entity, then it would have instantly recognised our presence, and before you would have even known it, this place would be swarming with static beings; they might not be able to see us, but it doesn't stop them hunting us down." Agent Gardiner finished her sentence making sure that the confident agent had fully understood her before she relinquished her grip on his hand. Agent Turner murmured an apologetic mumble before stepping backwards toward his colleagues.

"What exactly is our mission in the static realm?" Another male agent spoke up and Eva nodded her head, frowning slightly as though the question was in some way difficult to answer.

"Six months ago, I would have told you that our mission was reconnaissance, learn as much as you can about the realm, the beings, and the environment; however, that mission has since changed, the static beings are making more of a presence in our world, and they are influencing human beings to kill others or themselves, the Minister of State has decided that it is time to take affirmative action, and by that I mean to kill any static being on sight whilst in the realm." Agent Gardiner held her hands up as she saw several of the agents reach for the unusual looking weapons strapped to their shoulders. "I think that for today at least, you should be getting used to the environment, and the entities, before you start blowing them or yourselves to pieces."

Agent Parker squinted at the gun in her hand.

"I wouldn't even know how to fire this thing," she laughed cautiously as she scrutinised the odd silver cylinder and curious digital panelling on the gun.

"I was going to save the weapons lessons for the laboratory; I believe our first trip should be about getting used to the realm." Agent Gardiner beckoned to the other agents to follow her as she began to walk towards the crystalline structures up ahead.

"Agent Gardiner?" An agent that had previously remained silent spoke up and Eva stopped to allow him to catch up. "I don't remember having this weapon when we are at the lab." The confused looking agent glanced warily at the gun, flicking it with his finger as though it had a disease.

Eva nodded her head, "That's because you didn't have it, remember that our bodies are still physically back in the lab, our unconscious minds are here, on a completely different level; the bio-suits that you are all wearing are designed to emit a small electrical pulse which allows them to register the same electrical patterns produced by the brain whilst we are in this chemically induced coma, hence why we appear to be wearing a fluidic suit here whilst also wearing it back in the lab. The weapons are slightly different, they are manufactured from a virtual particle, although this one is really in the jurisdiction of Doctor Jackson, but as far as I'm aware, it has something to do with 'The Time, Energy and Certainty Principle'." Eva met the dumbfounded looks of her students with a chuckle, "Yeah, well let's move onto these." Eva quickly changed the subject and moved towards a large beige crystal.

The agent looked carefully around them, several more Guardians had begun to move towards the vicinity of the group, and although their movements did not indicate that they were aware of the agents' presence, Eva eyed them with caution.

"This is what we call a crystalline diode," Eva patted the large beige crystal affectionately as she spoke. "These beauties are a natural part of the static realm environment, they are dotted around all over the place, sometimes in small clusters, individually or in massive forests, they come in all different shapes and sizes, but perhaps more importantly, they are also are unwitting allies" Several agents came up to touch the crystals and a gasp of surprise broke out amongst the group as the agents felt a warm vibration pass through their hands. "It's the crystals," Eva answered the puzzled looks on their faces. "They seem to vibrate internally, and not only that, but they allow energy to flow one way but not the other, in the same manner that a diode works, which is why we call them crystalline diodes. If your suit is damaged and you're leaking energy into the static realm, it's possible to use these babies as shields until the doctor can get you out, providing of course you've worked out which way the energy is flowing."

Eva and the agents spent some time exploring an outcrop of crystalline diodes which had formed a small but densely populated crystal forest. As a child Eva had imagined that this was what the centre of the earth was like, just as described in one of her favourite books, but she had never dreamt of actually seeing it. Eva felt the look of awe on her students faces oddly satisfying, she had seen these diodes a thousand times, but every time was just as amazing as the first. Letting her attention wane slightly, agent Gardiner entered the forest with her students.

"Agent Gardiner, look at this one!" Holly appeared from behind an enormously tall diode, unlike the vast majority of the other crystals it sported a vibrant purple haze.

"It's beautiful isn't it?" Eva remarked as she walked over to her student. "There are not very many of these giant purple ones, to be honest we don't know why they are different to all the rest" Eva spoke lowly to Holly as she stroked the crystal, almost as though she were respecting its privacy.

"Perhaps it's the diamond in the bucket of quartz," Holly replied with a sympathetic smile in understanding of Eva's obvious humility for the diode forest.

Agent Gardiner and her students wandered freely around the diodes, chatting amongst themselves as though they were visiting an art gallery. It was only when Eva began feeling a familiar sense of foreboding that she realised she had forgotten her duties and her mission.

"Shit!" Eva cursed loudly, and her sudden outburst alerted her students to the danger that Eva had become acutely aware of. Outside of the diode forest, the familiar blue of the static atmosphere was oddly distorted, thickly warped by fleeting images and the zipping of blue lines.

"I think it might be time for a crash course on how to use these weapons." Agent Turner removed the gun from his shoulder, but Eva shook her head in response.

"No, no, we haven't got time, I have to get you lot out of here now." Eva tried to tone down the panic in her voice, but the urgency of her beckoning to the others quickly made it apparent that the situation was dire. "There's no way we can all get out of this forest without one of them detecting us, there must be at least twenty of them out there." Eva looked back over her shoulder at the fleeting shadows. "It's almost as though they knew we were here," Eva whispered under her breath and Holly whispered urgently back.

"How could that happen? I thought they couldn't hear us?" Holly croaked back.

"They can't," Eva quickly replied and then shook her head dismissively as though she didn't have time to discuss it further. "On the top of your arm, there's a small orange push button, it's a panic alarm, it will let the doctor know that you need to be brought back urgently, all of you, push that button now!" Eva shouted the command with a stern voice.

"What about you?" Holly replied after triggering her alarm.

"It takes time to bring an individual back, approximately four minutes per person, I need to make sure that you guys get back before I do, don't worry the doc will bring me back just as soon as you guys wake up in the lab"

Agent Gardiner and her five students moved further into the dense crystals, within four minutes of pushing their alarms the first agent had already dissipated. There were some alarmed jumps from the group as the first of their colleagues vanished, and Eva quickly stepped in to calm them.

"It's OK, the doctor is pushing the meds to wake you, soon you will all wake up in the lab," Eva breathed a sigh of relief as Holly became the next to leave the realm. Agent Gardiner had developed a fondness for the girl, in a way, she reminded her of her own much younger self.

"Agent Gardiner, I think we should begin moving again," Turner shouted as he pointed directly over her shoulder and Eva turned to see a Guardian move quickly and silently into the crystalline forest.

"OK, listen," Eva spoke with urgency to her colleague. "Just avoid it, get out of its way, don't touch it and don't let it touch you."

Eva watched with rising anxiety as several more Guardians began to enter the forest. The agent moved between her slowly vanishing students, ushering the remaining ones away from the approaching danger. Turner was the last to return to the lab and Eva offered him a reassuring wink as he began to de-materialise. The agent breathed out as the last of her students returned safely and she turned round to push her own panic button. Out of nowhere, like a ghost on a cool breeze, Eva found herself turning into the face of a Guardian. Leaping back, she instinctively grabbed at the particle weapon on her shoulder; but before she had even had the chance to turn it on; the Guardian had grabbed her.

Eva breathed in suddenly, her breath whistling between her teeth as she felt the painful burn of static electricity singe her skin. The agent pulled away, jabbing her arm back, but quickly gave up as the pain intensified in her lower arm. Eva glanced up into the shifting blue lines of the Guardian's gaze.

"I am not here to harm you."

Eva swallowed with gratitude as the static being let go of its painful grip on her arm.

"How did you find us?" Eva stood back, her heart pounding as though she were having a cardiac arrest. Despite the Guardian's assurance, Eva was terrified.

"There are things you don't know about our world, we have ways of seeing you, even if you are well hidden"

Eva frowned, glancing around her she realised that they were now the only two in the crystalline forest. The agent was struggling with the urge to reach for her weapon, but somewhere in the back of her mind, she could hear Andrew urging her to stay calm.

"Why are you talking to me? What are you doing?" Eva spoke quietly between her trembling lips and the Guardian softened in its appearance, it resembled the angelic beauty that she had first witnessed all those years ago.

Turning to stand beside her, the Guardian led her away from the purple diode before continuing, "We do not all agree with conflict, I amongst others are objectors of this battle between are species, and I will help you, if you will help us." Eva let go of the weapon on her shoulder, "Andrew was helping you wasn't he?" the Guardian nodded, "Andrew's lineage is that of the leaders, he takes his place as one of us now, amongst the rulers of our race." Eva couldn't help but laugh, it was a mixture of relief and also amusement that Agent Hollands would now find himself in such a position.

"Our time is short, I must show you what you need to know" Eva jumped, squealing with shock as the Guardian resumed its tight grip upon both her arms. The agent stood paralysed in its grip, her eyes wide with fear as the entity pulled her towards itself, in the blink of a second she had been engulfed. The air was so think around her throat and mouth that she began to whoop with panicked breaths. Closing her eyes she steadied herself, "It's OK, it's OK," Eva whispered under her breath as she slowly became accustomed to the heavily static sodden atmosphere.

"I need to show you." The voice of the Guardian boomed from all angles and it was as though Eva was floating in a womb; the noise of the world outside reverberating around her watery bath.

The agent felt a weightlessness lift her mind; she was almost detached from her body, drifting like a cobweb on the breeze. A sudden rush of imagery flooded her and the agent gasped at the intensity of it. Silvery sac-like pods flashed before her face, a brilliant light emanating from within. Eva watched the lights grow dimmer until the pods fell to the ground, withered and lifeless. Sadness befell her, but before she could think too much about what she had witnessed a second image appeared. A large beige diode, at least ten times the size of those she had seen before, but this one was different, it looked as though it were alive inside. As the agent peered closer to the fleeting movements from within, she let out a startled cry.

A face – an anguished face – and not one, but thousands. They darted, confused like flies in the light inside the hollowed out diode. Eva reached out, desperate to try and subdue their terrified expressions. The agent began to feel a sense of extreme anxiety, her breaths quickened and she suddenly felt herself spiralling out of control. Eva was desperate to help them, but it was just an image, the closer she dragged herself to them, the further away she became. "Stop, please stop," the agent blurted out, her head was beginning to pound with a drumming pain, and her eyes had begun to feel like burned out holes in the bright flashing atmosphere.

"Agent Gardiner!" Eva thrashed around on the table as the doctor and several of her students attempted to pin her down. "What's going on?" Holly questioned the doctor as she restrained Eva's waving arm. "Erm, I'm not sure, I think it might be an unexpected reaction to the drugs." Dr Jackson cursed under his breath as he attempted to subdue Eva. "I think I'm going to need to sedate her"

Eva could hear the doctor in the lab, she knew exactly where she was but the agent was struggling to break free from the Guardian's grasp on her mind. "No," Eva managed to half cry out and the doctor leaned into her face. "You need to come back to us, agent, right now." Eva heard his voice again, it was like a shout through cotton wool, but she grasped onto it, teasing herself away from the images and the light. Sucking in air like it was the first breath she had ever taken. Eva sat bolt upright on the steel bed. Her blood-shot, tear-moistened eyes met the terrified gazes of her students and the agent tried to choke back her shock.

"I'm OK, I'm OK," she held her hands out as Dr Jackson shone his torch light into the pupils of her eyes.

"What happened?" he whispered under his breath and Eva turned away from the stares of the fledglings.

"I saw it all, the Guardian showed me images, I think I know what they are doing," she hissed back before rubbing her head wearily. Dr Jackson nodded before cautiously turning to face the onlookers in the room.

"This is a dangerous job, and I'm sorry to say that incidents like this happen not too irregularly. Agent Gardiner will be fine, but please bear in mind that whilst you're in the realm, there are no certainties." The fledglings filed cautiously out of the med-lab, mumbling in low voices and concerned tones. Dr Jackson looked at the floor as Eva peeled off her fluidic suit without shame, coughing lightly, Mark handed her a dressing gown. "What did you see?" the doctor questioned her as he turned around again.

"I saw their young, so many of them are dying, but unfortunately for us, they've come up with a way to prevent it." Now dressed, Eva swung back round to face Mark. "They have a holding cell, some kind of prison in a crystal diode, they seem to be storing human energy, almost harvesting it." Eva whispered under her breath despite the fact there was no need. "I saw faces, Mark, human faces, they were suffering, lost." Agent Gardiner bit at her lip as she recalled the scene. "It's almost as though these people are being held as spares, for the pods that don't get the human energy they need to grow."

Dr Jackson rubbed at his face as he thought about the situation, "It doesn't make much sense, surely that would screw up with their own generational lineage?"

Eva sighed as she swung her legs from the edge of the table, "Wait," the agent paused slowly raising her hand as a thought came to her mind. "What if these people have already died? I mean, like me, they've cheated the cycle, the Guardian meant for them has already perished, so, essentially, these humans are spare, their energy is spare."

The doctor nodded his head, running a hand through his greasy hair. "If that's the case, then there will surely be a chance that we can pinpoint who could be next on their list as a target."

CHAPTER TWENTY-ONE

Richard stared at the glaring screen of Eva's laptop; he knew that the answer to his question was right there, in those unassuming beige folders. The problem was, he was too afraid to look. The psychiatrist nibbled at the already bleeding skin surrounding his cuticles, he had an odd feeling, almost as though he knew the answer already, but it was there; it was just there staring him in the face, the psychiatrist swore; standing up he walked over to the whiskey cabinet, looking at his reflection in the glass as though it might give him the answer he wanted. Richard felt the intensity of his feelings well up in his eyes, he firmly believed that no human being should know when they are going to die, but if you could find out, wouldn't you look?

"This is fucking stupid!" the psychiatrist laughed as he found himself pacing the room like a school boy awaiting a chastising from the teacher. Richard had seen his family name in folder three whilst he and Eva were scrolling through that morning, she hadn't noticed, and Richard had failed to enlighten her. Since then, he had been logging on and off the computer for hours, so tempted, but so terribly afraid to learn the truth. No amount of reasoning or false plan of action could satisfy his fear of knowing. Yet, the more he pondered the situation, the more he had this burning feeling that he already knew, that the answer was within him, not in a beige folder on the screen of a computer. With a sudden strop, Richard marched towards the laptop, quickly and deftly logging in, he opened folder three. "Wellar, Wellushi" he read his family and

Guardian name out loud, before mindlessly deleting the file. "Don't have to think about it now" he muttered to himself as he closed he laptop lid with a thud.

Eva returned to her office, stepping over the rubbish on the floor as she made her way to her desk. She sat heavily on the chair, the wheels squeaking slightly as the force pushed them into the carpet. The agent pondered her situation for a moment before noticing something strangely unusual about the drawer on her desk. Her oak desk was Victorian, everyone else had modern furniture, but Eva had chosen this desk personally, she loved the way that it oozed personality, and robustness, it had been around a lot longer than anything, or anyone, and yet it was faultless, that was until now. Peering intensely as though she required glasses, agent Gardiner rubbed her finger over the small brass lock that garnished the front of the drawer, Eva had a key, she kept it in the inside pocket of her jacket, alongside her key card. The agent chewed at the inside of her lip, a light series of score marks surrounded the key hole and Eva instantly recognised them as pick marks. Someone had picked the lock on her desk. Suddenly feeling as though she were being watched, Eva stood up; cautiously she glanced around the room. Aside from the picked lock, nothing else seemed out of the ordinary, but Eva was leaving nothing to chance, quickly opening the drawer, she retrieved the only think that was in it, stuffing Andrew's letter into the pocket of her jeans, she quickly retreated back to the med-lab, hurrying down the corridor, she stopped abruptly.

Ahead of her she could see Professor Stanford, he was talking to the doctor in the lab, normally that wouldn't have bothered her, but the appearance of the weasel like receptionist to the professors left was enough to caution Eva into another retreat back to her office. Unfortunately she was going to have to wait until the small gathering had broken up before she could leave the building, she had chosen the furthest away office, and the only one that required she walk past the med-lab to exit.

Eva hurriedly turned on her mobile phone, drumming her fingers on the desk as she waited for the Sony logo name to leave her screen. Bringing up Richard's name she quickly typed him a message, before grabbing a black bag. Stuffing as many of her clothes into it as possible she tried to clear the room. Eva stopped before putting the last of her clothes in the bag, it suddenly occurred to her that a rapid clear up of her office might look suspicious, especially since it appeared she was already under someone's scrutiny. Throwing a few random handfuls of dirty socks and tops back on the floor, she placed the black bag discreetly under her desk. Edging back out into the corridor again, Eva replaced her paranoia with a rather unsteady air of confidence, walking casually but as briskly as she could, the agent made her way past the lab and towards the reception. Eva noted the absence of Professor Stanton as she glanced in and breathed out as she made it past the first hurdle undetected.

"Finishing already? Wish I could do that" Eva grimaced as she heard the familiar and somewhat annoying voice of Michael from behind the reception desk.

"No, I'm just going to pick up my laptop, I've left it at home" the receptionist nodded raising an eyebrow and Eva felt a sudden burn of anger in her throat.

"Sign me out will you? You receptionists are good at that kind of thing." Agent Gardiner marched herself into the lift, and then wished suddenly that she had played it a little cooler. That man irritated her like a bad skin rash, and if she were right then he was also responsible for breaking into her desk, one thing she knew for sure, and that was that the weasily little receptionist was going to find himself in a big pile of shit.

Richard was already responding to Eva's text message by the time the agent had got back home. He shook his head with confusion at her as she walked in the door.

"I'm not sure what you were expecting me to find, but there's nothing unusual about Michael's personal files, he's a rookie, fresh out of training, but we all knew that." Eva screwed her face up as though she didn't quite believe Richard's words. Reaching in her pocket for Andrew's letter and the key to her desk, she pointed to them as if to her assert her feeling.

"Somebody broke into my desk, and whomever it was probably knows as much as we do about what Andrew knew and was doing. More to the point I think, is the possibility that someone might be on to us."

Richard ran a hand over his face, "Aside from withholding information, we haven't actually done anything wrong."

Eva licked her lips, "If we haven't done anything wrong, then why steal this from my desk, why not just ask for it?"

Richard shrugged his shoulders, "This information could completely change this war, alter the way that the people in charge view and judge the actions of The Cavern."

Eva sat down with a heavy thud onto the couch. "Surely that's got to be a good thing, more exploration, less killing," the agent rubbed at her forehead as though she had had enough of thinking for one day. "Not everyone likes the idea of peace, especially when there's the possibility of power sharing." Richard leaned over to pick up Andrew's letter again before continuing. "Nobody enjoys being demoted, and I doubt whether the masses could handle a species just as dominant as our own infiltrating their homes and religious beliefs."

Eva laughed with a sense of annoyance. "These beings are offering us a second chance of life, a true afterlife, one that allows the human race to continue, surely that's a revelation that calms the aggravating fear of death we all possess."

Richard smiled, rubbing her knee as though he wished her words to be true. "But it's not heaven, Eva, it's an alien existence within an alien world, it may have been so for all eternity, but it's not what we have been taught to believe, people kill for religion, Eva, and imagine what people would do to protect it."

"Fuck, what the hell are we supposed to do now? We can't exactly take on The Cavern, and I doubt whether there are many out there who will want to listen."

Eva blew out a puff of smoke as she lit a cigarette. "What about The Professor? He's pretty chummy with the minister of state, maybe we can get him to listen." Eva looked up at Richard hoping for some kind of positive response.

He met her eyes with an air of scepticism. "Really? The Professor? Andrew always said he was a bit of a dick, I'm not sure about trusting him."

Eva let out a shocked laugh; it was just like Andrew to have called someone so influential a dick. Blowing out her cigarette smoke into the room, Eva rolled her eyes as she thought, "Looks like it's just you, me and the doc."

Richard nodded and reaching for his coffee cup he added, "We could do with a plan."

THE PLAN

Eva dragged the coffee table across the floor, wincing slightly as the high pitched squeal signalled another scratch on the walnut laminate. "I think this should be enough room," she looked up at Richard who nodded his head with a slight reluctance.

"Are you sure this is a good idea? Without the lab … what if something goes wrong?"

Eva sighed with frustration, "Well, that's why we have the good doctor."

Richard smiled wryly, "C'mon, you need to help me with the bloody bath; I'm not superman."

Eva and Richard dragged the large cast iron bath into the centre of the living room, putting in the plug; Eva filled the bath with purified water.

"I'll tell you what; it's going to be cold in there." Richard swallowed in agreement, "Perhaps I should go" he looked up at her and she met his gaze with a slight laugh, "Sorry darling but you know nothing about what's over there, you wouldn't have a clue what to do, not only that but the Guardian's won't recognise you, if you don't get killed by the bad guys, then you might get yourself killed by the good guys." Richard could hardly argue, since it was perfectly clear that she was right. The psychiatrist felt oddly ashamed, almost as though he had pussied out of the static realm on conscientious grounds.

"Yeah, I suppose so."

Eva felt his unease and whispered as she readied her fluidic suit, "This isn't for everyone; your talents are with humanity."

A quick succession of raps on the door, signalled the arrival of Dr Jackson and Richard hurriedly let him in.

"I got your message, but I have to say, I think this is a bad idea."

Richard nodded his head in agreement, "That's what I said too, but try telling her that," he jabbed his thumb towards Eva, who shook her head whilst squeezing herself into the black rubber suit.

"Look, we need to find a way of working with them, Andrew had a plan, and I was a part of that plan, I know that now," Eva rubbed at the back of her neck with a strange sense of uncertainty. "Even if we can find an easier way of communication without these damned suits, and baths of purified water," Eva jabbed her thumb back at the tub, and then smiled wryly at Richard. "I'll be careful, I'm sure the good Dr Jackson will be kind enough to keep me alive whilst I'm in there"

Agent Gardiner rubbed her hands together in an attempt to distract herself from the sharp jab of the doctor's needle in her arm. With the aid of her two companions she lowered herself into the bath. Her breath instantly escaped as the cold engulfed her body. Eva closed her eyes, she wanted to be in control of the situation, as the familiar spinning blackness shrouded her mind, she realised that entering their world meant leaving control behind.

"Such meetings within our world are no longer advisable."

Eva span round to face the Guardian, "We have no choice; we must talk."

The Guardian gestured to Eva and the two made their way to the crystalline forest.

"This is the only safe place within our realm; your suits do not protect you as you thought; only the crystals in the forest mask your energy."

Eva scratched her head with a sense of dismay, "The other agents do not know that there are peaceful entities amongst you, they will kill any Guardian they see."

Eva's companion stopped, reducing in size until it was the same height as herself. The agent was fascinated by the beautiful way it re-emerged its shape. It was almost a miniature light show, complete with sparks.

"There's so much we don't know about you" Eva whispered with an air of sadness.

"There's so much we don't know about each other, our species will kill yours just as quickly, we are trying to survive and some of us will stop at nothing."

Eva swallowed, "I don't know what I am supposed to do, I doubt if my words will change the minds of those in power. What was Andrew's plan?" Eva looked up at the Guardian with a sense of hope, but its response failed to enlighten her.

"There is no plan, but it appears our battle lies within our own species first before we can begin to negotiate with each other."

Eva shook her head with a burning sense of frustration. "What am I to do?" she shouted out with torment.

"Our leader, Hollushi, or Andrew as you once knew him is the creator of our resistance, there are a great many of us opposed to this war, and together we hope to free your people and stop the aggressors of our race."

Eva nodded, "What can we do?"

The Guardian twitched suddenly as though pricked by a needle. A sudden surge of blue shot out towards Eva and the agent leapt back in alarm as the Guardian trebled in size.

"You must prepare a resistance of your own; help us and you will save your future." The Guardian's voice boomed out in a way that reflected its stature. It charged past Eva knocking her to the side, as the agent stood up she watched the Guardian zigzag towards an unseen target. A sudden brilliant flash of white ensued and Eva instantly recognised the discharge of a particle weapon. Scrambling to her feet she shouted out.

"Stop! Stop, he's not dangerous!" Her shouts were futile and the haunting scream of the entity confirmed that her words had gone unheeded. Eva launched herself forward, desperately trying to push the Guardian away from the weapon's destructive stream. The static electricity surging through her body proved too painful and Eva stared with agony at the Guardian as she watched it slowly disintegrate before her.

"Start your own rebellion." The crumbling entity hoarsely whispered at Eva before breaking apart like snapped caramel. Eva fought to control her anger dragging herself to her feet again she stormed towards the agent.

"Who the hell are you?" she shouted with fury, snatching the weapon from the agent. "Michael?" Eva said the receptionist's name with shock. "What are you doing here? You're a pen pusher not an agent."

Michael took his weapon back swinging it with ease over his shoulder. "Well, you know I guess I just fancied something different."

"What?" Eva's response was sharp and disbelieving. Michael shrugged his shoulders.

"So, how did you get here? I didn't see you in the lab?" Eva stood back, quickly checking around she dragged Michael back to the safety of the crystalline forest.

"It's none of your business how I got here, why the hell are you here? There are no training sessions for today, and I'm sure I haven't been training any receptionists for active duty." Eva spat with temper from within her suit. The image of the Guardian's demise was still fresh in her memory, and she struggled to control herself.

"You're not the only one who's been training students." Michael's reply was calm and cool. He jumped onto a toppled crystal, swinging his legs lackadaisically from the edge.

Eva said nothing, eyeing him with suspicion. "We don't come to the static realm alone, it's one of The Cavern's rules; where's the rest of your party?" Michael smiled in response, jumping back down from the crystal he pushed the alarm on his suit before slowly walking out of the forest. As he began to de-materialise he shouted over his shoulder. "You're here aren't you?"

Eva cursed as he vanished before her. "Damn you, Michael, what are you up to?"

Pushing her own alarm she waited for the doctor.

CHAPTER TWENTY-TWO

"Jesus it's cold." Eva trembled as she wrapped the blanket around herself.

"Yeah, sorry the cold water really lowers your body temperature, might be a good idea to skip the purified water bath in future" The doctor smiled with sympathy as he handed Eva a hot cup of coffee.

"That would put her at risk from the Guardians wouldn't it?" Richard questioned Mark with worry. The doctor shrugged his shoulders, "Probably no more dangerous than catching hypothermia"

Eva rubbed at her arm where the dying Guardian had touched her skin. "It hurts even though there's nothing there." She half laughed suddenly feeling overwhelmed with emotion. Richard stood behind her rubbing her back soothingly with his palms. "Your brain thinks your skin was damaged in the realm, and although your body remained here with us, your skin is still sending pain signals in response to what your mind witnessed." He whispered gently in her ear and she nodded, she knew that already, but it was comforting to be told anyway.

"That receptionist, Michael, he's up to something, I wasn't even aware that other agents were entering the realm, or that he was trained up. He saw me talking to the Guardian; I have the feeling that I'm going to be answering some serious questions." Eva looked up from her mug at Dr Jackson, as though she were expecting answers.

Dr Jackson shook his head, "There are no other people training at The Cavern, well, not at our Cavern anyway."

"Shit." Eva whispered as a realisation struck her. "I thought all the other Caverns were abroad, and nobody said anything about them being up and running."

Mark rubbed at some newly formed sweat on his brow. "It's the only explanation, there must be another facility pretty close to our own, they could be going in and out of the realm and we wouldn't even be aware of it."

"That's not good." Richard slumped himself down in a chair. "Why would they want to keep something like that a secret, I mean from us? Unless they already know that we found Andrew's research."

Eva sniffed wiping at her running nose with the back of her hand. "I have this awful feeling that we are being used, they are allowing us to continue at The Cavern, maybe they are trying to get to the leaders, and maybe we are leading them right to them."

"It's possible," Richard nodded. "If they can destroy the leaders, the government or whatever political structures they have, then it's going to be a hell of lot easier to destroy the species." The psychiatrist glanced at Mark for confirmation. "No leaders, no direction. They must know that we are meeting with the Guardians, they must also have known that Eva would be in the realm today, why else would Michael be there?"

Eva abruptly stood up, brushing off her blanket. "Someone must have told them." The agent took a step towards Mark. "Perhaps the same person who broke into my drawer," Eva glanced back at Richard as though she were trying to tell him something telepathically. "You wouldn't know anything about that, would you, Mark?"

"What?" the doctor backed away from Eva rubbing ferociously at his palm. "I don't know what you're getting at."

"Really?" Eva continued to approach him, "No one else knew that I was entering the realm today and everything we know about Andrew's research, you know, too." Eva jabbed a finger at the doctor who responded by grabbing his jacket from the chair whilst heading for the door.

"This is far bigger than you realise." Mark wiped his brow with his jacket sleeve. "Professor Stanford and the minister are just pawns compared to the real powers involved." Dr Jackson made a quick sprint for the door and Richard leapt over the couch to stop him.

"No!" Eva yelled into the room, "Let him go," she glanced at Richard who reluctantly halted his pursuit.

"You're going to get yourselves killed," Dr Jackson offered Eva as a word of warning before skulking out the door.

"We have to go, now," Richard urged at Eva before quickly grabbing his back pack and stuffing it with clothes. "Grab the laptop, charger and phones," he gestured to her as he rummaged about for his keys.

Running like escaped convicts they darted from their home and into the car. Thrashing the engine of the Mercedes, Richard span it out of the drive and onto the road. "We need a safe house, somewhere to figure out what the hell we're going to do."

Eva lit up a cigarette, sucking on it like a lollipop. "I think I might know someone" The agent grabbed her phone, hesitating for a second, she made the call.

HOLLY

"Holly, thank you so much," Eva hugged her colleague before slipping inside the house. There was an awkward moment of silence as Richard and Eva sat opposite Holly in her living room. The girl fidgeted uneasily and Eva frowned with concern.

"Listen, Holly, we don't want to get you in any trouble, perhaps it might be best if we just leave." Eva stood up but Holly immediately jumped in to stop them.

"No, stay, please, I'm just a little out of my depth you know? I mean, I'm not really sure what's going on?" Holly stuttered as she spoke and Eva smiled with sympathy.

"Let us fill you in." Eva and Richard spent the next hour filling Holly in on everything that they knew, and the couple were surprised by how little their revelations phased the girl. Eva and Richard were further taken aback when Holly disappeared and returned with the blue prints for the second Cavern.

"My dad is quite high up in the military, he's been working in the Minister's office; he gave me these so I could find a quick escape route should 'the shit hit the fan' as he puts it" Holly laughed passing the schematic to Richard. "Actually, you know I was never comfortable with killing things, anything for that matter. I trained as a diplomat not a soldier."

"Why are you at The Cavern?" Richard's curiosity got the better of him and Holly shrugged her shoulders.

"Dad wanted me to be a part of it, I think he would have secretly preferred a son to the peacekeeping humanitarian daughter he got lumbered with." Holly smiled shallowly; reaching over Richard she used a remote control to open the garage doors. "You had better get your car out of sight, they are going to be looking for it." Richard nodded his head in response.

"Have you been to the other Cavern?" Eva studied the blue prints. "It doesn't look any different to the one under the aquarium." Holly nodded her head in agreement. "It's not, except there's no stupid elevator hidden behind a covert door." The blonde-haired girl laughed again, grabbing at a cigarette packet from underneath the table, offering one to Eva before continuing. "It's actually less than a mile from here, underneath an old house." Eva shook her head in disbelief. "I can't believe I didn't know about this," Holly swallowed, pausing for a second before continuing. "The late agent Hollands, you, Richard and Professor Stanton are all coded Black"

"Black?" Eva frowned.

"It means compromised, no agent is to inform you of anything, but none of us are to interfere with what you're doing either." Holly blew out her cigarette smoke, stubbing the butt end into the ashtray.

"When did this happen?" Eva rubbed at her face suddenly realising that they had been under surveillance for some time.

"Since agent Hollands was killed, The Cavern found evidence that Andrew was dealing with the entities, and of course you brought the evidence to Mark that you were also involved. The only reason I know so much is because of my dad, not many of the other agents know what's going on aside from your code Black status."

"Shit," Eva cursed, "I thought we could trust Mark"

"I think you chose the wrong person to trust, if you had gone to The Professor, I think things would have been different, he's been lobbying for some time now about negotiating with the entities, rather than war."

"They're called Guardians," Eva looked up at Holly. The girl nodded her head, "If you and Richard suddenly disappear they are going to hunt you down, and I doubt whether taking you into custody is on the agenda."

Richard opened the door into the room and Eva instantly blurted out. "We need to get to The Professor." Richard raised his hands in bewilderment, "How are we supposed to do that? We can't get into The Cavern, the good doctor is probably spilling the beans and I doubt whether Michael was in the realm on an exploratory visit."

"Michael?" Holly questioned with unease, "That guy is a twat." Eva smirked in response, "Yeah, I've probably wound him up just one too many times."

Richard handed the Mercedes keys to Holly. "Looks like I'm going to need some new plates." The girl smiled shrugging her shoulders, "Or you could just be like me and not drive at all" Putting the keys in a drawer in the kitchen, Holly returned to Richard and Eva. "I can get to The

Professor, I'm not under any suspicion, and I can get into both Caverns any time I want." Eva nodded in agreement before adding, "This could be dangerous, Holly, if they discover you." The young female agent broke into Eva's sentence. "I don't want to kill these beings, and I don't want to be a part of The Cavern either, if I can help you, then I'm going to do it." Holly was adamant and Eva couldn't question her motives. "You know there are quite a few of us trainees that aren't comfortable with what is being asked of us, you might have more support than you think." The young agent reached for her key card. "I'll get The Professor, and then we can figure out what's next"

"Watch out for the Doctor," Richard raised his voice with concern, "He's definitely not on our side." Holly offered Eva a nervous smile before leaving.

"Start your own rebellion" Eva whispered at the floor.

"What?" Richard leaned in trying to hear her words.

"It was just something that the Guardian said before it was killed, something that we had to do." Eva looked at Richard with worry. "Could we really take them on? We don't even know who we are up against." Richard sighed; clasping his hands around hers he whispered, "Three years ago you were a patient of mine, and now, you're an on the run secret agent with an arsenal of information that the world couldn't dream of knowing, who knows what you will achieve next." He laughed as he looked into her eyes. "I'll always be with you, even when you think I'm not." Eva looked with puzzlement, his words were deep and she lacked the energy to interpret them.

"We need to find a way of sabotaging their operations, to stop them killing the Guardians" Eva continued.

"There are a lot of entities out there that are not peaceful, if we destroy our only defence against them, then we are going to put more human lives at risk" Richard crept in with his usual logical thinking. "We need something more intelligent, a way of distinguishing between them and the Guardians that are on our side" Eva blew out with exasperation. "If only we could stop others from entering the realm, and then we could protect our own people and the Guardians" Richard shook his head. "The Guardians can just as easily come into our world, perhaps the battle is better fought here than there."

The difficulty in achieving the proposals was obvious and Eva jumped in alarm as her phone broke into the silence. "It's Holly." Eva looked up at Richard as she answered.

"The Professor will meet you at the university tonight, in his office" Holly whispered quietly down the phone and the reverberation in the background indicated that she was in the bathroom. "This place is crawling Eva, your office is being ripped apart, and The Professor was being questioned by some guys in Black Suits, so far though they've not taken him into custody."

"Be careful, Holly," Eva whispered with caution down the phone.

"I've gotta go, The Professor gave me instructions to download the memory files from his computer, I'm waiting until these bloody Black suited guys clear off before I try"

Eva shuddered on the other side of the phone, "Don't take any risks" she uttered quickly as the phone went dead.

"The Professor is safe, we need to meet him tonight at the university, he's got Holly downloading computer files," Eva chewed her lip. "God, I hope I've not got that girl into too much trouble, she's so young," Richard laughed at Eva's comment, pulling her in close he reminded her. "She's the same age you were when you first encountered your blue angels; a lot can happen in a short space of time"

"Yeah, I suppose you're right," Eva snuggled into Richard's arm. She had forgotten that she herself was only thirty. The agent had been feeling so much older; it appeared that responsibility had aged her.

CHAPTER TWENTY-THREE

Eva looked around them as they approached the university. "This is quite risky, I just don't know who to trust anymore." Richard held onto her arm in support. "You can trust me, come on." The psychiatrist led the way up to the revolving door entrance with Eva trailing slowly behind.

The institution was oddly silent at night, like a playground with all the children gone. Despite the fact that Eva had spent many happy years studying at the university, she felt oddly out of place as though she had lost the merit to be there.

"The Professor's office is down the geek corridor," she smiled at the psychiatrist as she navigated her way around the warren of study halls and conference rooms. Catching sight of the familiar 'warp drive' poster on the wall, she stopped outside Professor Stanton's office.

"Should we knock?" Richard smirked at Eva, but had his question answered before she had the chance to reply.

"Come in, and close the door behind you." The familiar tones of The Professor filled the emptiness of the corridor and Eva and Richard quickly obliged.

"Eva," Holly breathed with relief as she greeted her mentor. "I brought some agents that would very much like to join your cause." The young woman stepped aside and Agent Gardiner marvelled as she saw many of her former fledglings behind her.

"Are you sure you guys know what you're doing? We aren't exactly in favour with those in power at the moment."

Eva laughed sarcastically, partly because she was terrified at the prospect of her own words.

"None of us believe in The Cavern, or what it stands for. There has to be a better way of dealing with the entities and if you're going to show us that way, then we are going to follow you." Holly looked back at her colleagues who nodded their heads in agreement.

"Start your own rebellion," Richard whispered with some amusement in Eva's ear as he walked over to join The Professor at his desk.

"This is not going to be easy." Eva spoke with concern to her new recruits. "To be honest, I don't even have a plan."

"Then it's time we created one," Professor Stanton rose from his seat. "Your good friend Holly over there was good enough to download The Cavern's database onto a memory key, of course there will be information that is restricted, but I'm sure we can find a way of finding out what we need to know."

Eva studied The Professor cautiously. "Andrew didn't mention you in any of his files or in his letter." She bit her lip, Eva desperately wanted to trust in someone, but recent events had shaken her.

"Andrew and I had been working in this project for years, The Cavern was a direct result of our research." The Professor raised his eyebrows as though his thoughts troubled him. "It wasn't until very recently that we discovered just how sentient the beings were, and of course the reasons behind why they were killing human beings." Steadying himself The Professor sat back down in his chair. "Andrew managed to open a dialogue with one of the Guardian's leaders, it appeared there was more to be gained through politics than mindless killing, unfortunately on both sides there is a healthy passion for violence. Revenge is more easily dealt than unpalatable negotiations"

Eva nodded her head, recognising that she, too, had been seduced by violence. "What happened to Andrew?" she looked up expectantly at The Professor, her eyes failing to hide the emotion she struggled to contain.

"It's hard enough to know your destiny is not quite what we were taught at Sunday school, I don't know what it must feel like to know when that destiny is to arrive." The Professor stared deeply into Eva's eyes for a second, "I can't say I blame him for his choices, control of one's life is every human being's right." Eva sat herself down in one of the chairs and tried to digest The Professors words.

"What's the next step? You are under considerable suspicion at The Cavern; we certainly can't go back now?" Richard rubbed at his face as he attempted to fathom a way out of their ridiculous situation.

The Professor nodded, "I had managed to keep my involvement with Andrew and the Guardian's pretty damned quiet until Dr Jackson discovered Andrew's drug habit, I guess we got a little careless." The Professor shrugged his shoulders, "I thought Mark was an honourable man, but he's more interested in securing his own future, than the future of humanity." Professor Stanton stood up, asserting a brighter stance, "A few of our colleagues have volunteered to continue working at The Cavern, undercover for us, of course. So far, the only people the ministry of defence are interested in are us three, and I think we should try and keep it that way."

Eva smiled at her not so young fledglings. "You guys have got balls," there was momentary spur of laughter amongst the recruits and The Professor coughed before continuing. "Fortunately for us, my family have a great deal of money tied up in this University, and needless to say I may use some of that privilege to secure us the basement, I think it might be worth setting up camp here, and attempting to make contact with the Guardian's again."

"Supposing we can achieve that, how are supposed to stop The Cavern?" Richard spoke with doubt and The Professor raised a finger in response. "It's not about stopping them, rather undermining their efforts. We need to make the case for negotiation stronger than the case for war, build upon our allies within the realm, and help those allies prevent their own insurgents from picking off human beings to fill that soul chamber of theirs."

"But what about The Cavern?" Richard repeated himself again as though his question had remained unanswered. The Professor winced slightly. "That's the tricky part, we need to try and prevent The Cavern's agents from slaughtering the Guardians." A thought suddenly crossed Eva's mind and she stood up with an air of excitement. "The fluidic suits don't work, the Guardian told me that they had found a way to detect us." Eva looked at The Professor hopefully. "Only we know that, The Cavern won't have a clue."

"That means that they will be able to see us, too." Holly eyed her colleagues with concern. "Can't we find some way of identifying ourselves to the Guardians as peaceful?" The young agent shrugged her shoulders, "Might give us a better chance of not being accidentally killed by our own allies." Professor Stanford nodded his head. "Agreed that would be definite advantage, but only for whilst you're at The Cavern, I was hoping to encourage the Guardians to enter our world and communicate with us here, I think it would be a hell of a lot safer for all involved."

"We really don't know how they achieve cohesion in our world, from what we have experienced, they are nothing more than clouds of static electricity, to be honest, and I've had to either be unconscious in some way or close to death to actually communicate with them."

"Well," Professor Stanton rose from his seat, "you are the one with the medical background, Eva; I'll leave the technical stuff to you." The Professor reached for his laptop, the memory key with The Caverns data in his other hand. "I've booked myself a nice cosy hotel for the night, you guys are welcome to stay here of course, although it might get a bit busy with all those furiously eager students in the morning" The Professor winked at Richard as he walked past them into the corridor. Waving the memory key in the air, he announced brightly, "Time to alter the course of humanity." The Professor chuckled to himself as he left.

THE BEGINNING OF THE END

Richard and Eva walked side by side down University Lane. The thought of spending a night in The Professor's office was less than appealing and Eva had, had her fair share of dossing down in the work place. The night was strangely calm and neither pair seemed willing to break into the stillness of the evening. So they walked, and said nothing, only the plumes of their breath indicated that there was life on the street. Eva led Richard back in the direction of Holly's house.

"I think we should stay at Holly's tonight." Richard said nothing but nodded his head in agreement. He wasn't quite sure what their next move was, but he felt an odd sense of foreboding. The psychiatrist couldn't explain his feelings, only that they made his stomach twitch with anxiety.

Eva put out her hand stopping Richard suddenly as they turned the corner into Holly's street. "Something is wrong," Eva whispered hoarsely to Richard who felt his anxious twitch turn into a pang.

"I don't see anything," he whispered back, as he glanced back and forth like a nervous rabbit. Eva crouched down in the planted verge, rubbing at her forehead. "The garage light is on," she mumbled into her sweating palms.

"So?" Richard shook his head, failing to understand what she was getting at.

"It was off when we left, and Holly is at The Cavern, someone else switched that light on"

Richard quickly glanced back, the warm glow of the garage light shone brightly through a small window. The psychiatrist paused, taking a deep breath he searched for a logical answer. "Maybe she changed her mind, maybe she has visitors," he offered up his best explanation.

"I doubt whether these visitors are here for a friendly chat." Eva grimaced, "I need to think quickly."

"Perhaps you should do some thinking back at The Cavern." Eva spun round the familiar voice confirmed her fears.

"Michael, what are you doing here?" Eva questioned him with annoyance.

"My job," his reply was short and lacked any hint of prior friendship. "Get moving, both of you." Michael lifted a small revolver from his side and Eva laughed with disbelief.

"Are you kidding me? This isn't exactly in the reception manual." Eva eyed Michael coldly and he firmly pressed the gun against her back. "It's not just you and your psychiatrist that can play at double agents." He pushed Eva forward with the barrel of the gun, signalling at Richard, "Get moving."

"You're not going to need that," Richard spoke calmly to Michael with his arms raised before catching up with Eva.

Agent Gardiner shook her head as she approached the garage door. A black suited man appeared from the shadows, and as the door slid slowly open, the tips of several more black shoes revealed themselves from underneath. In the back of the garage stood Holly, her arm tightly held.

"I'm sorry, Eva," Holly blurted out, her lip trembling. "They bugged your car." Eva closed her eyes in disgust turning to face Michael she spat. "You bastards." Richard tried to hold her back, but she shrugged off his attempts. "Leave Holly out of this, she's had no part in it up until tonight." Eva took a further step towards Michael who raised the gun even higher.

"That is not my decision to make, and besides, this is not about what you have done, it's about what you know."

Eva stepped back sporting a frown. "We know everything you do." Michael nodded, "That's the problem, Andrew found out far too much about them, and he told you. What would happen to the foundations of power within our society? Our religious and governmental leaderships? From our birth we are taught that we are at the very top of the intellectual and evolutionary ladder; can you imagine what knowing that we are no longer in control of our own destinies would do to the masses …? Revolution." Michael spoke with an intelligence neither Eva nor Richard had given him credit for.

Richard shook his head. "Surely there has to be another way, killing an entire species to protect another's religious and moral standing is ludicrous."

"Wars have been fought for a lot less, and personally I don't want to be any beings battery." Michael had a hatred that burned through his words; Richard had heard this hatred before, from someone much closer.

Eva took a breath in her nostrils picking up an identifiable spark. She glanced cautiously at Holly who had already become aware of the situation. Holly gently nodded her head in the direction of the plugs, and Eva's heart leaped as she saw a blue arc of static electricity ping from the socket. Richard and Michael continued their heated debate unaware.

"What makes you think one of your own agents won't spill the beans?" Richard continued to question Michael, determined to try and reach him.

"It won't matter if they do, there isn't going to be any evidence of the Guardians left to corroborate their story" Michael rubbed at his forehead, "It's people like you who insist upon communicating and reasoning that will cause the end of humanity, We don't want to talk to them, we want to exterminate them, before they exterminate us"

Richard had begun to retort but an explosion to the left of Holly left everyone ducking for cover. For a few momentary seconds there was chaos, followed by random shouts for assistance. A thick smog like cloud rested just above waist level, the highly charged atmosphere prickling at bare skin.

"Eva." The agent heard her name being called but couldn't discern amongst the shouts who had called it. Crawling on her hands and knees she headed towards the garage door. Amongst the smoke screams and shouts she caught sight of a black suit. The fabric edges of the cuffs smouldering; the skin inside charred to a crisp.

"Eva!" again the shout.

"Richard!" Eva shouted back, suddenly recognising the voice of her partner. "Where are you?" she hissed urgently. No response came but a firm grasp on her arm signalled that they had found each other. Using Richard, Eva pulled herself up into the standing position immediately scanning the room. The static fog was beginning to clear, and she began to make out the outlines of dead agents on the floor, thin wisps of smoke rising from their bodies indicating their fate.

"Come on, we need to find Holly and get out of here." Eva tugged at Richard.

"Stay where you are" Michael appeared from the front of Richards's car, his hands shook uncontrollably and the gun flailed recklessly within his fingers. "You're not going anywhere."

Eva rang her hands with frustration. "Jesus Christ Michael! Give it up! Can't you see what's happening?" Eva pleaded with him. The former receptionist used the side of the Mercedes to steady himself. Grimacing he dragged his charred leg into a standing position. Eva took a step forward, "Michael you're hurt, let me take you to the hospital." Agent Gardiner screwed up her face in sympathy as she watched him struggle. Michael closed his eyes as the pain began to overcome him, the gun wavered slightly as it dropped to his side, Eva began to approach but stopped suddenly in her tracks as Michael shouted; quickly regaining his control of his weapon.

"Eva move!" Michael screamed at her as he waved the gun desperately to the right. "Get out of the way!" Eva swung around to look behind her. A Guardian hovered like a frozen snowflake before her; it towered above them, crackling lightly like wood on a fire. Eva watched it for a second, it remained the beautiful winter white and the agent recognised that it meant no harm to her.

"No, no it's OK, it won't hurt us." Eva raised her hands in front of Michael's gun. "Put it down, Michael, this Guardian is no threat."

"What are you crazy?" Michael screamed at her as his hand began shaking on the trigger.

Eva stood between the Guardian and Michael like a wall, but the entity began to creep around towards the right.

"It's coming for me, can't you see that?" Michael lunged forward, in those few desperate seconds a shot rang out into the garage. Eva jumped; her ears ringing and her heart beat thudding intermittently in her head. The agent held her breath, her eyes wide; she waited for the pain that would determine her fate. No pain came and Eva quickly fought to regain her wits. Swinging round away from the snivelling, crumbling Michael, she faced the Guardian, it stood as it had done before, but as Eva squinted to look through the static fog of its body, her heart stopped.

"Richard!" Eva screamed out into the silence of the cold concrete walls. The psychiatrist lay on his back, wedged up against the steel door. His hands clutched a wound on his chest, the blood spilled out between his fingers like jelly. Eva darted towards him, firmly placing her hand over his on the wound.

"Stay with me, please Richard, stay with me," Eva pleaded with him, her breaths short and erratic. The psychiatrist looked up at her; a wry smile covered his pale and sweating face. Squeezing her hand he whispered.

"It's OK, It's OK, I think it might be my time." He laughed weakly, coughing up a pool of blood from between his teeth. Eva shook her head, her shoulders heaving with emotion.

"No, no, I can't do this without you, I can't be without you" Eva agonised, her face becoming screwed up with fear.

"I'm not leaving you, I'm going with them," Richard whispered looking at the Guardian which had taken position beside Eva next to Richard. The Agent stared deeply at the entity, then back at Richard. Her lover had a subtle ray of hope in his eyes, and Eva nodded her head in understanding as she clutched at his cold, clammy hand.

"I'll find you, I swear I'll find you," she whispered in his ear as her tear drop fell with his last breath.

Eva closed her eyes taking a deep breath as the Guardian touched her arm. A warm vibration shimmered through her body and as she looked at the stricken Richard, the agent gasped as his body and hers fell slowly out of sync with the room. She could see the realm, like a shadow in front of her eyes, like a cloud in front of the sun. Richard glowed like torchlight in the night. The brilliance of his energy rose to leave his damaged body, it floated with conscious purpose and Eva raised her hand to touch it. She sensed his presence, his warmth and his love and as Eva returned to the normality of the garage she felt as though she had touched his soul.

Holly stroked Eva's back. "I'm so sorry Eva" she whispered at her friend. Eva looked up at Holly, her lips trembling, her eyes red to the point of bleeding. "This is just the beginning" Her words trailed off into the hollowness of the garage. Michael was gone.

EPILOGUE

From the very moment that apes began to walk on two legs, the Guardians began to progress from mere loose energy particles to combinations of multiple conscious entities. Thinking, growing, developing; Unseen and unheard throughout history, they exist quietly in the background, beneath the Earth, on another plane above the material existence of human beings. Harmless and peaceful, they harvest like crows, the dead carcasses of humans in order to reproduce their own species; only occasionally seen in the remnants of a haunted mansion or the empty decks of a lost ship. Humanity's persistent greed for longevity of life has turned a once peaceful and coexistent species into an angry and vengeful race, spurred on only by a desperate need to survive.

Only those with the quietest of minds have the ability to listen beyond their own beliefs. Religion is the product of such a quiet mind; it is the interpretation of a truth told in a fashion that all humans can understand. This understanding is the existence of an afterlife. As a star implodes its cosmic dust gathers with the dust of others to form the beginnings of a new star, and so it always has been. A circle of life and death, nothing is wasted, nothing is lost. The yearning for a longer life pushes forward greater and more advanced methods of preserving the flesh, in doing so, those beings below are forced to wait, the small amount of energy they are given during their birth dissipates, the prolonging of human life is a sentence of death for another.

The selfishness of human existence demands that a person remain the sole owner of their being, to continue on as they are into an infinite existence that serves their desires for immortality. Such an existence is interpreted by the appearance of angels, beings designed to serve a god by ushering the souls of the dead to the afterlife. Such beings exist but not for the good of blood, flesh and carbon, but for their own existence. They are the counterparts of a material life, a race which begins its life once the corporeal bodies of human beings have ended. They are the energy that's left to wander the cosmos, the recycling of an electrical field that is the very spark of life. They are the angels which come to collect the souls of the dead, and start their own life thereafter. To deny such life is to take away the rights given to each of us by the universe, of which there are consequences, as from the bowels of the Earth's crust those denied their existence will rise to claim what is theirs, and start the beginnings of a war on material life.